THE
PERFECT
ONES

THE PERFECT ONES

A THRILLER

NICOLE HACKETT

CROOKED LANE

NEW YORK

Copyright © 2023 by Nicole Hackett

Published in the United States by Crooked Lane Books, an imprint of The Quick Brown Fox & Company LLC.

Crooked Lane Books and its logo are trademarks of The Quick Brown Fox & Company LLC.

Library of Congress Catalog-in-Publication data available upon request.

ISBN (hardcover): 978-1-63910-262-4
ISBN (ebook): 978-1-63910-263-1

Cover design by Nicole Lecht

Printed in the United States.

www.crookedlanebooks.com

Crooked Lane Books
34 West 27th St., 10th Floor
New York, NY 10001

First Edition: May 2023

10 9 8 7 6 5 4 3 2 1

Perhaps one did not want to be loved so much as to be understood.

—George Orwell

PART I

Not a Psychopath

1

Hollie

The Morning After
Vík, Iceland

ALABAMA WOOD WAS missing.

The announcement rippled through the group of women gathered at the foot of the staircase like electricity hurrying across a live wire. The officer, three steps above them, paused, perhaps sensing that anything he said for the next few seconds would not be heard.

Hollie Goodwin stood near the back of the group. Behind her, wind whistled through a poorly insulated window, creating the sensation of someone just over her shoulder, whispering in her ear.

"We'll be opening an investigation," the officer said after a moment, once the murmuring had stopped. The stair beneath him groaned as he shifted his weight. "First, it will be important for us to construct a time line of the trip so far."

His gaze fell to the window behind Hollie, the glass clattering faintly in its frame. Gray sky had swept in from the ocean the night before, causing a thin veil of fog to pool over the tiny fishing village. It looked like the sort of day that could keep secrets, Hollie thought. The sort of day someone could disappear into. Hollie wondered if the officer was looking out the window and thinking the same thing.

"It's important to get an accurate picture of Alabama's last known movements," said the second officer—a blonde woman with a severely angled jawline. She was leaning against the kitchen doorframe, scanning the group with a measured slowness. "We understand Alabama was last seen in her bedroom around ten last night."

Hollie's eyes flickered away from the woman. She thought of Alabama the night before in the kitchen doorway, almost exactly where the officer now stood. In Iceland, the summer sun didn't set until nearly eleven, so although it had been past ten, the kitchen window had still glowed with last haze of twilight.

"Agreed," the male officer said, giving his partner an appreciative nod. "Our first step is to construct a time line of events."

Hollie glanced at the other women around her. It was early enough that makeup hadn't yet been applied, leaving Hollie amid a sea of grim and sun-spotted faces. The group's cumulative Instagram following was well over six million, and Hollie couldn't help but imagine what those six million would think if they could see the group of influencers now.

When Hollie looked back at the officer on the staircase, she was surprised to find his eyes now on her. She felt immediately vulnerable, as though she had caught him spying. She fought the unfamiliar urge to curl into herself, to hide as much of her body as possible.

Alabama Wood was gone, he'd come to tell them. How shocking.

Unless, of course, you already knew.

2

Hollie

Three Months Before
Dallas, Texas

HOLLIE WAS SEVEN miles into a nine-mile run that she had been regretting since mile four.

Actually, it was before that. When her alarm had gone off that morning, Hollie had rolled her head to one side, where her husband's cheek had been pressed against his pillow, a little bead of spit caught at the corner of his mouth. She had looked at him and wondered whether taking one day off would really be so bad.

But then Robin had texted her to say she was on her way, and now Robin was half a step ahead of Hollie on the sidewalk. For seven miles, Robin had been exactly half a step ahead of Hollie. It didn't matter how fast they were going, either. Hollie would speed up, and Robin would speed up. Hollie would slow, and Robin would too, staying exactly one half step in the lead the whole time.

It was hot. It was always hot in Dallas, but today's heat felt more deliberate, like the morning was making a point. Hollie felt sandwiched between the midmorning sun and the heat rising from the sidewalk in squiggly lines. She had a patch of very cold sweat just above her lip, which felt different from the rest of the sweat making tiny streams across her body. It was the distinct sensation Hollie felt before throwing up.

"If you ask me, it's a coping mechanism," Robin said, talking over her shoulder. "I mean, I'm no dog psychiatrist, but it just makes sense." She was talking about her goldendoodle, who had the unfortunate habit of shitting inside. Hollie, however, was less interested in the dog's bowel habits than she was in trying not to throw up.

For a week now, Hollie had been laboring through the on-and-off feeling of mild food poisoning, which she had self-diagnosed herself with at the beginning of the week. She couldn't remember the last time she'd had food poisoning. She couldn't remember the last time she'd thrown up. Maybe not since college, although that hadn't been a matter of questionable chana masala but too much tequila.

"Are you feeling alright?" Robin said, turning her head to look at Hollie. At some point, she had migrated from a half step in front of her to a full one. "You look a little pale."

Robin had a layer of white sunscreen residue across her shoulders where she had not rubbed it all the way in.

"Actually, no. I'm feeling a little sick."

Robin's eyes rounded so wide that Hollie almost regretted saying anything. And yet, as soon as Robin started to slow, Hollie felt nothing but a swift wave of relief.

They trotted to a walk outside a café that was normally bustling, although it was early enough on a Sunday that the line had not yet made it out the front door. They were in the Bishops Arts District of Dallas, where most of the coffee shops offered an uncommonly large selection of nondairy milks.

"I'm so sorry," Robin said, beside Hollie now. "I have trouble going easy. I probably pushed you too hard."

Hollie pressed her lips together. She couldn't tell if Robin was objectively annoying or if Hollie only found her to be because Hollie didn't feel well.

Robin and Hollie had met last year at a 5K in Dallas. Robin was the bouncy, breathy sort of person Hollie usually tried to avoid. "Almost caught ya there at the end," Robin had said, ambushing Hollie at the finish line. Her teeth were a bit too big for her mouth, which Hollie had charitably tried to ignore.

Later that day, Robin and Hollie had connected on Instagram, although Hollie had only followed her back to be polite. Almost immediately, Robin had sent her a direct message about organizing their own race to benefit some charity Hollie didn't recognize. Robin had used the word "amazeballs" unironically, but despite this—or maybe because of it—Hollie hadn't had the heart to tell her no.

"It's fine," Hollie said, deciding to give Robin the benefit of the doubt. "I think it's just the heat."

For a little while, Robin and Hollie walked in silence. Robin was on her phone, presumably assessing their pace on Strava, a popular fitness app. Hollie would have normally done the same, but she was too focused on her breathing. The worst of the nausea appeared to be over, but she feared that it would resume the moment they started back up.

"You can go on without me," Hollie said finally. "I think I'm just going to walk back."

To Hollie's disappointment, Robin clicked her watch and said she was also finished. It was a nice thing to do—cut her run short for Hollie—and that was the worst thing about Robin. All of her aggravating qualities were just so excruciatingly *nice*.

Nick, Hollie's husband, was the one who had suggested Hollie start training with Robin, because that was the type of person Nick was. Nick regularly got caught up talking to their neighbors when he was supposed to be taking out the trash cans, spending large swaths of time chuckling on their front lawn. Sometimes, if Hollie saw her neighbors in their driveway, she would wait to get her mail until they were gone.

Before Robin, Hollie had been training alone for almost three years. Before that, since college, Hollie had trained with her best friend, Mallory. This had come to an abrupt end, however, when Mallory had gotten pregnant with her first child. She had promised Hollie she would be back to running three months after her daughter came. Maybe, although unlikely, four.

It was now going on two years.

As they made their way down the sidewalk, Robin continued on about her dog. Hollie made noncommittal grunting sounds when required.

"Do you want to grab a coffee?" Robin said as they finally approached Hollie's house. Robin had parked along the curb earlier that morning. She drove a Tesla, which was the exact sort of vaguely irritating thing Robin would do.

"I'd love to," Hollie lied, "but I can't. I'm meeting a friend for brunch."

The last part wasn't a lie. She and Mallory had been trying to schedule something for two weeks now.

Robin looked disappointed enough by this that Hollie felt bad for not inviting her, but not enough to actually extend an invite. Since Mallory had had her daughter, her relationship with Hollie had been reduced to the rare pockets of time Mallory could find for her-self. Hollie did not want to waste this one with another story about Robin's erratically shitting dog.

Hollie was almost inside when she got the text.

I'm so sorry, Mallory wrote, adding an extra "r" at the end of *sorry* in her rush. *But I need a rain check on brunch today. Fi's sick . . . stomach flu, I think. It's been a shit show all morning. (And I meant that literally.)*

Hollie stared at the message for a moment before stepping into the house.

No worries! she typed. *Totally understand.* She thought for a sec-ond before adding a second exclamation point, just to emphasize how sincerely unworried she was.

Mallory sent back two emojis—a thumbs up and a puking face. Hollie tried to glean something from the images, some sense as to how Mallory really felt. Disappointed, probably, although Mallory sometimes surprised Hollie with how she reacted to things like this. In the beginning especially, Mallory had sometimes described sleep deprivation and cracked nipples not with anguish, but something serene across her face.

Unable to find some deeper message, Hollie kicked off her shoes, one of which hit the wall with a thud. She moved to her inbox, where she had accumulated a dozen new emails since she had last checked. The first one was from PinkPurse, the online clothing boutique Hollie sometimes partnered with.

PinkPurse's emails were identifiable by the excessive number of exclamation points they used in the subject line. Hollie scanned the message briefly, a little seed of guilt budding in her gut. The email was about an upcoming trip to Iceland, the third message of its kind Hollie had received over the last several weeks.

Hollie suspected that if she had been anyone else, PinkPurse would have let the matter go instead of bombarding her with a bar-rage of emails, each with sequentially more exclamation points than the last. Ever since Hollie had reached a million followers, however, she had noticed a sharp increase in her campaign requests.

Hollie reached the end of the message, where PinkPurse had supplied a list of other influencers who had already confirmed their attendance on the trip. *Emily Von Paris, Margot Murphy, Katherine Livingston, Alabama Wood.* The only one Hollie had met before was Katherine, and the only thing Hollie remembered about her was how close to you she stood when she talked.

Hollie made a mental note to respond to the email once she got out of the shower—a polite but resounding no. She had the race with Robin that summer, which would require time to both plan and train for. Besides, from what she knew about Iceland, it was cold and snowy and dark. If she was at the point in her life that she was considering such a thing, she would know something had gone horribly wrong.

CHAPTER

3

Celeste

The Morning After
Vík, Iceland

WHEN THE POLICE had announced Alabama's disappearance
fifteen minutes prior, Celeste had been near the back of the
group, trembling despite her sweater. "Alabama Wood is missing,"
one of the officers had told them, and it had struck Celeste how
benign the word sounded. *Missing.* Like they might later find her
stuck between the cushions in the couch.

Celeste was now alone on her bed, her back to the wall. Across
the room, Alabama's suitcase remained splayed open by the closet
door. It was not normal, not natural. Alabama without her full ward-
robe was like a diabetic without their insulin.

Celeste spun her phone in her hand out of habit, although at
the moment, the crack down the screen rendered it useless. In the
very private parts of her mind, Celeste had sometimes wondered how
people would react if she ever tragically died. Would they give Louis
her phone, and would her husband go through it? This seemed like
something he would do, not necessarily to be nosy, but just to figure
out what had happened. Louis couldn't tolerate mystery. Celeste had
once caught him reading about steam engines on the internet for no
other reason than wanting to know how they worked.

There was a tap at the door. Celeste made an involuntary hiccupping sound before clearing her throat.

"Come in," she called, flatting her already-made bed with both hands. She wondered why she had made it, why in this time of crisis she had found it important to do something so mundane.

The bedroom door opened to reveal the officer who had announced Alabama's disappearance. "Are you Mrs. Reed?" he asked, his accent thick and unusual.

"Celeste," she offered, mostly to be polite.

The officer nodded. His eyes moved briefly from her to the empty bed on the other side of the room. Unlike Celeste, Alabama hadn't straightened hers before she had vanished.

Celeste's mind flashed briefly to her own phone, to the screen cracked down the middle, and then to her suitcase. She preferred to keep her things tidy and organized, even when traveling. She actually used the drawers in hotel rooms, unlike Louis, who was perfectly content living out of a suitcase even weeks after he had returned home. Now, many of Celeste's things were scattered near the foot of her bed—a tube of lipstick, a hair straightener, a forlorn tennis shoe.

The officer said, "Would you mind coming with me? We're hoping to talk to all of you ladies about Alabama."

Celeste didn't normally like it when people—men especially—referred to her as a lady. It made her feel either too old or too young, depending on the situation. She liked it even less when people lied to her, using words like *talk* instead of *interrogate* when they both knew which one was the truth.

4

Celeste

Three Months Before
Chicago, Illinois

Before Celeste had entered the world of online influencing, it had never crossed her mind that Nordstrom sold kids' clothing. Nordstrom, in general, was not something she had ever thought about, the way no average person thought about high thread-count sheets or exotic mushrooms at the grocery store.

She probably wouldn't have come to Nordstrom that afternoon either if it hadn't been for Alabama. Alabama was currently on the other side of the clothing rack, shuffling through the hangers with the efficiency of a casino dealer. Celeste had been moving with a similar clip until she had caught sight of one of the price tags—a handwritten number so obscene, Celeste had actually gasped. She had suggested going to Target after that.

"Bella can't show up to her first game wearing *Target*," Alabama protested, sounding equal parts disappointed and aghast. "What will the other kids think?"

Celeste sighed and glanced over her shoulder to make sure Bella was still where they had left her. A few feet away, the five-year-old had perched herself cross-legged between two racks. She had her collection of dolphin figurines spread out in front of her, because when it came to both soccer and fashion, Bella could not have cared less.

"Well, they're five," Celeste said, turning back to the rack. "I think we've still got time before designer clothing is on their radar."

It had been an effort to coax Bella into the store that afternoon, as they usually headed straight home after school for a snack—a uniformly cut apple with a thin layer of peanut butter, but not too much, or else the peanut butter made Bella's mouth "feel like towels." Bella had considered the schedule change to be personally offensive and had been downright outraged to find Alabama, without prior warning, in the front seat of Celeste's car. Had Celeste not thought ahead, some form of boycott would have been imminent. Luckily, she'd had the foresight to bring along Bella's freezer bag of plastic dolphins as a bribe.

"Seriously, CeCe?" Alabama shook her head with disappointment. "Target is fine for discount hauls, but you don't put your daughter in it for her soccer debut." She gave Celeste an admonishing look. "Part of the business is acting like you belong in the business, you know."

"Well, maybe I don't belong in the business then," Celeste murmured, more to herself than to Alabama. She rifled through the rack, searching for something she suspected wasn't there.

"You don't really think that, do you?" Alabama said, suddenly serious.

Celeste shrugged. "I don't know. Not really, I guess."

"Oh my god." Alabama threw her head back. "You've got to start taking yourself more seriously, CeCe. Look how good you've been doing lately!" Her face darkened. "A lot better than me, that's for sure."

Celeste touched the space between her clavicles. She really didn't want to be having this conversation. The truth was, Celeste did question her place on the internet more times than not. She often felt like an outsider in the world of fashion influencing, despite her bafflingly good stats.

Most of Celeste's success was a simple matter of timing. She had caught the influencing train before the bubble, long before Instagram stories had even been a thing. She now earned six figures, a true feat for someone like her, who offered very little actual substance. She was essentially a walking advertisement, no more or less memorable than the faceless mannequins that made Bella whimper in Target.

The problem wasn't the job as much as it was Celeste. Celeste wasn't particularly funny or cute or inspirational. She wasn't much of anything, although people didn't seem to mind this so long as she supplied them with a steady stream of discount codes. Celeste didn't find much joy in the process, but it was lucrative enough to stay at it. Besides, she doubted she would find much more joy in anything else, and this job at least let her stay home with Bella.

"You're going to be fine," Celeste said, using her stern voice. "The internet is just fickle. You know that."

"Not for you it isn't." Alabama's nostrils flared.

"Well, who cares?" Celeste said, going for a different angle. "It's not like anybody at my funeral is going to be talking about my Instagram engagement when I'm dead."

She thought this was a rather good point, although Alabama scrunched her nose as if not convinced. Celeste felt the urge to say something more, something better, but she couldn't think of what.

"Well, I'll be doing better after Iceland," Alabama said at last, returning to the rack. "I have a feeling this trip is really going to turn things around for me."

And with that, her hands resumed their brisk shuffle through the expensive children's clothing. Celeste's gaze also fell to the rack, her stomach now in a small knot. Celeste hadn't responded to the Pink-Purse invitation yet, despite what Alabama thought. She hadn't *lied* to Alabama about this. She had simply omitted a correction once, and then after that it had seemed too late. If she didn't respond soon, the spots would fill up and the decision would be out of her hands entirely. A part of her privately hoped for this to happen, as Celeste didn't have a good feeling about going, although this feeling was rooted in nothing but the feeling itself.

"What about this?" Alabama said. Celeste looked up at her friend tugging at one of the shirts. She held it above the rack for Celeste's inspection, a miniature black crop-top with *KILLER* emblazoned across the chest.

Celeste looked from the shirt to Alabama, trying to decide if her friend was kidding. It was moments like this that Celeste was forced to examine the stark differences between those who had kids and those who didn't. And it wasn't just that Alabama's skin somehow looked good in the severe department store lighting, whereas Celeste looked like one of those lost hikers who'd been rescued after weeks of eating leaves. Alabama could see a child-sized crop-top and think it was cute, while Celeste's first thought was that it would make her daughter look like a prostitute.

"Bella, come here," Alabama said before Celeste could protest. "Let's see if this fits." She snapped her fingers once, like she was calling a dog.

Bella didn't seem to hear this, or if she did, she did not feel it warranted a response. Alabama continued snapping. Celeste rubbed her eyes.

"Bells, come here, please," Celeste said tiredly, and thankfully, her voice seemed to resonate. Bella looked up, her tiny face screwed in thinly veiled impatience. Celeste had seen that look before. Celeste's husband, Louis, sometimes made it when Celeste was talking through an important football game. (In Celeste's defense, it was nearly impossible for her to tell which games were important and which were not.)

Bella gave a small, very adult-like sigh as she heaved herself up. A moment later, she was by Alabama's side. She had left her dolphins in the middle of the aisle—not in a pile, but in three precise lines. This was normal for Bella, how she played with them. Today, it appeared she had arranged them by size rather than species or color.

"Mama, killer whales are dolphins," Bella said, eyeing Celeste over the top of the rack. "They're just *called* whales."

Alabama held the shirt out and closed one eye, measuring.

"It might be too small for you," she said. "But I don't know. Maybe it stretches."

"What's that?" Bella looked at the shirt suspiciously.

"It's a shirt for your soccer game."

Bella frowned. "My team is purple."

Alabama groaned and gave Celeste a *see what you've done?* look. The spot where Celeste's neck met her head started to tingle. She hoped it wasn't a migraine.

"Bells, can you go get your dolphins?" Celeste said. "We're going to leave now."

Bella nodded and moved obediently back to her toys. Celeste was not surprised that her daughter had been uninterested in the sequined crop-top. At the moment, Bella was wearing the only article of clothing she found acceptable—a boxy monstrosity with *SHEDD AQUARIUM* across the back and a bottlenose dolphin on the chest. Bella had worn the fabric so thin that it was almost translucent in spots.

"Let's go to Target," Celeste said to Alabama. "If she ends up needing therapy because of it, I'll deal with it then."

Alabama didn't get the joke, or if she did, she didn't find it funny. She gave a put-upon sigh before draping the shirt over the rack.

"So, Bells," Alabama said once they were in the parking lot. "Are there any cute boys on your soccer team?"

"Did you know that killer whales can be as long as a school bus?" Bella replied. She was holding her plastic bag of dolphins against her chest as though she feared someone might try to take it. "That's very big." She looked at Alabama seriously. "Smaller than my house, though."

"Is it bigger than an elephant?" Alabama sounded genuinely curious.

Bella thought about this for a moment. Celeste clicked the car remote and was met by a friendly toot.

"Probably bigger than an elephant," Bella said at last. "Unless you stretch out its trunk. Then I don't know."

"I don't think elephants are as big as school buses," Celeste said absently.

"They're as big as those mini buses," said Alabama. "You know, the short ones?"

"Those aren't school buses, though."

"Well, they go to schools, and they're buses. Hence, school buses."

"Mama drives me to school usually," Bella interjected, looking straight ahead. "Except Daddy drove me yesterday because Mama took Daddy's car to get it looked at by the manic."

"Mechanic," Celeste corrected, although Bella didn't seem to hear. She marched toward the car ahead of Celeste and Alabama, coming to a stop and staring at it expectantly like the back door might open itself.

"Daddy drives too fast," she added quietly, as though speaking to herself.

Celeste reached over Bella's head and pulled open the door.

"So, you're okay with swinging by Target?" Celeste said to Alabama, who had stopped at the passenger side in a manner very similar to Bella.

"Target?" Bella said.

Celeste looked down to where Bella had paused midway through climbing in. Her eyebrows bunched in tentative outrage.

"Just for a second," Celeste said, struck by her own stupidity. She should not have said anything until Bella was already buckled in the car and incapable of meaningful protest.

"Actually, I want to go home now," Bella said, sounding matter-of-fact. Alabama snickered at the front of the car, which Celeste did not find remotely helpful.

"We still need to find you some soccer pants. Remember the deal we made?"

For the last two weeks, Bella had worn her SeaWorld pajama pants to soccer practice, which Celeste had only agreed to on the condition that they would get her proper sports attire before her first game.

"I'm hungry." Bella still sounded calm, but there was an edge of recalcitrance not too far from the surface.

"We had a snack, remember? I brought you carrot sticks."

"I want apples."

"Bella, get in the car." Celeste nudged her daughter toward her seat. As soon as her hand made contact, however, Bella threw herself forward as though she had been shot.

"For god's sake," Celeste mumbled as her daughter screeched.

Celeste reached out again, this time grabbing onto Bella's arm firmly. Bella writhed and thrashed until she was free. In one fluid motion, she pirouetted along the side of the car before melting to the ground by the tire well in a mess of sobs.

Celeste looked around. A few spots over, a woman was loading bags into her trunk. She looked up, and Celeste felt her cheeks burn as she refocused on her daughter, who was now lying face-up on the ground. It never failed to surprise Celeste how quickly her daughter could escalate and how helpless Celeste could feel each time it happened.

"No Target," Bella gasped between shuddering breaths. Celeste noticed the bag of dolphins spread beside her, another casualty of the injustice. "No more shopping."

"Bella," Alabama said, appearing beside Celeste. Celeste stepped aside, although she seriously doubted it would make much of a difference. Indeed, Bella squeezed her eyes together and continued to cry.

"Bella, have you ever had chocolate ice cream and gummy bears before?"

For a moment, Bella grew silent. Her hands were still balled into fists, poised for a fresh wave of tantrum if the situation called.

"I bet you haven't," Alabama said. She crouched down, although Bella still gave no indication that she'd heard except for one eye, which cracked open.

"It's on the secret menu at Cold Stone," Alabama said. "It's my favorite."

At this, Bella opened both eyes. She glared.

"A secret menu?" she said.

Alabama nodded. "Hardly anybody knows about it but me."

Bella chewed on the inside of her cheek. She was still horizontal on the asphalt, which Alabama was surprisingly able to ignore. She spoke to Bella like two people chatting casually over coffee.

"You know, I bet after Target, your mom will let us stop there and try it." Alabama glanced up at Celeste, as did Bella, each with the same expression.

"Sure," Celeste said, suddenly feeling very tired.

To Celeste's amazement, Bella sat up slowly. She wiped her fore-arm across her nose with the labored effort of someone who had recently survived a harrowing ordeal. Alabama held out her hand, which Bella ignored. Instead, she pushed herself up and climbed into the car without another word. Celeste noticed that the back of her shirt bore a black smudge from twirling herself against the car's tire—grease, maybe. She would deal with it some other time.

Alabama rose from her haunches and dusted her thighs. As she passed Celeste to the passenger side door, she shrugged as if to suggest how easy that was.

Celeste sighed heavily just as her phone rang. For a split second, standing there in the lot, she considered ignoring it. Seeing the number, however, she discounted this impulse, as there were very few reasons Bella's school would be calling Celeste's phone out of the blue on a Thursday, none of which Celeste could responsibly ignore.

"This is Celeste," she said.

"Hi, Mrs. Reed. This is Miss Bonnie from KinderAcademy." The woman had the bubbly, energetic nature of someone who worked with small kids.

Through the open car door, Bella called out. "Mama?" She sounded uncertain, as though she feared Celeste had forgotten the next steps for entering the car.

"Yes, hi." Celeste said, holding up one finger.

"I'm so sorry for the random phone call," Miss Bonnie said, giggling for reasons that were not entirely clear. "I'm calling because I'm hoping you and your husband might have time to come in for a little chitchat sometime soon."

"Mama," Bella said again, her voice growing more urgent. Alabama was also hanging out of the car now, looking at Celeste with a dubious expression.

"Um, yes. Yes, that would be fine." Celeste was already running through her mental calendar, attempting to align it with Louis's in her head. "Is everything alright?"

"Yes, yes, not to worry." Miss Bonnie giggled again, and it struck Celeste that the giggling was likely just a nervous tic. The fact that Miss Bonnie was nervous made Celeste feel suddenly nervous as well. "There are just some things we'd like to discuss."

"Ah." Celeste tried not to read into this, although there were simply too many things for Celeste to unpack. Who was *we*, to begin with? Was Miss Bonnie referring to herself in the plural, or was there someone else who wanted to talk to Celeste? "When can we come in?"

"Does tomorrow work for you? Maybe around five?"

"Ma-ma," Bella chanted, emphasizing each syllable with a heel pound against Alabama's seat back. This Celeste ignored.

"Tomorrow?" Celeste repeated, closing her eyes and rubbing the bridge of her nose. Tomorrow, Louis would be working as usual, and after that, Celeste's mom had agreed to babysit so they could go to dinner with Alabama and her husband. Louis would be unhappy to leave work early, and Alabama would be unhappy if the two of them were late.

"Yes," Celeste said. "Tomorrow at five would be fine."

CHAPTER

5

Hollie

Three Months Before
Dallas, Texas

Hair still damp from the shower, Hollie leaned over her kitchen counter after her run with Robin to take a photograph. She moved her phone slowly above the sweating glass, attempting to position the superfoods recovery shake in the frame.

Annoyingly, Hollie thought of her mother, whose first observation on Hollie's house had been about the lighting. "Not very much natural sunlight, is there?" she had said, because Hollie's mom had recently starting phrasing her passive-aggressive comments as questions. Hollie had ignored this and moved onto the living room, where her mom had remarked that light carpet was liable to get stained, wasn't it?

The worst part about remembering this was having to acknowledge on some level that her mother had been right. Hollie's kitchen *didn't* get much sun, so for Hollie to take a decent photo, she had to turn on the light. This presented a whole host of new problems, mainly that the shadow from her arm was nearly unavoidable while taking an overhead shot. She normally avoided pictures in her kitchen for this very reason, but she was currently wrapping up a campaign with a health foods company that required at least five Instagram stories of her assembling their superfoods drink.

Hollie craned further until, finally, her shadow was no longer visible. She snapped the Boomerang as quickly as she could, barely looking at the screen to confirm that the angle was right. Frankly, she would be glad when this campaign was over, as she was tired of the shakes. They tasted fine but had the consistency of sand, and for as much beauty boosting power as the company boasted, Hollie had been suffering with an uncharacteristic bout of acne along her jawline for a week.

"Ah, nothing like blended grass in the morning."

Hollie glanced over her shoulder, where her husband had appeared in the kitchen entryway. Nick grinned, looking pleased with himself.

"I'm live!" Hollie cried, waving her phone. Nick's face drained.

"Oh, shit," he murmured, sounding flustered. Hollie smirked.

"I'm just kidding. I'm not."

Nick groaned, which might have been believable had it not been for the smile. Hollie liked this about her husband. She would rather die a decrepit old plant lady than spend her life married to a person who couldn't take a joke.

As Nick strode into the kitchen, Hollie returned to her phone.

"So, you're still going strong with the grass, then?" Nick said, apparently not yet finished with the joke.

"It's *wheat*grass, Nick. I'm not drinking grass."

"Wheatgrass, grass—what's the difference?"

Half of Nick's torso had disappeared behind the door of their fridge. Hollie thought about explaining the difference before realizing that she didn't actually know. The wheatgrass didn't taste significantly different from what she would expect from a handful of their front lawn.

"How does this sound?" Hollie said instead, looking down at what she had just typed. "*What I like best about SoulGreens is that it helps me stick with a consistent morning routine.*"

"Sounds good to me," Nick's voice rose from the fridge.

"Does it sound like I like the shakes?"

Nick appeared from behind the fridge door. He seemed to be considering his answer. This was another thing she liked about her husband, how seriously he took her career.

"I guess not, no. Maybe mention how good they are?"

"Well, they're not."

"Oh." Nick frowned. He didn't say anything else, because Nick had long since given up trying to understand Hollie's career.

He wasn't cruel about it. He always waited patiently when Hollie arranged and rearranged their plates at brunch to get the right shot. But Nick didn't take his own photos. They had gone to Bryce Canyon once, and when they had reached Bryce Point, he had just stood there looking, not taking out his camera once. It was for this reason that people were so regularly surprised to learn he was married to an online content creator. *You aren't even on Facebook!* they would cry, like one of them had deceived them somehow.

But the truth was, people were just as surprised by Hollie's career when they met Hollie.

It wasn't clear what they expected from her exactly. Maybe they didn't even know themselves. Usually, Hollie took this as a compliment, even if it came from a place that wasn't so kind. She knew what people thought about influencers, and really, they weren't always wrong. Influencing, like many professions, attracted the especially vapid. Hollie liked to think that people were surprised by her career choice because they recognized the contrast between this stereotype and the Hollie they thought they knew.

What most people didn't understand was that Hollie's career was more than just good angles and strategic filters. It *was* those things, but that was only the start. Success in influencing required something deeper—an understanding of how people worked. People wanted to look at Hollie's posts and see themselves in the photos, not as the people they were, but as the version of themselves they could one day be. So few people could capture this delicate balance, and even fewer could do it as well as Hollie. Because despite the stereotypes and labels, Hollie *wasn't* stupid, much to her trolls' chagrin. In college, she'd been on the dean's list. In middle school, she had been her class's valedictorian. "I didn't know you were one of the smart ones," her mother had said before her eighth grade graduation. Hollie's mother hadn't noticed much about Hollie growing up, but even she had noticed this.

"I thought you were getting brunch with Mal this morning," Nick said over his shoulder. He had started the moderately complex task of preparing his coffee using their French press, which they had gotten the previous winter after their Keurig had finally pooped.

"She had to cancel. A Fiona Fiasco, it sounds like."

Mallory was the one who had come up with *Fiona Fiasco*, a phrase usually referring to bodily fluid of some kind. In Fiona's defense, the toddler didn't seem to cause any more fiascos than the average two-year-old. If anything, Fiona was quite well behaved.

Mallory sometimes joked that her daughter had emerged from the womb with the fatigued demeanor most people didn't acquire until middle age.

"What's the fiasco this time?" Nick turned around and leaned against the counter.

Hollie shrugged. "Not sure exactly, but I do know it involved toddler shit."

Nick smirked, causing the lines around his eyes to deepen. He'd had those lines for as long as Hollie had known him, from the very first day she had met him in college their junior year. She sometimes bemoaned the fact that Nick's lines made him look boyish, whereas Hollie's made her look like Mrs. Doubtfire. When they'd first met, however, that thought hadn't crossed her mind. Looking at him now, Hollie wondered whether it was possible to be in love at first sight for over ten years.

"Sounds about right," Nick said, turning back to the coffee. "You know, the shit is the biggest reason I'm glad we don't have kids yet."

He said this in the offhand way people said things of no consequence, and yet Hollie felt suddenly cold. She forced herself to look down at her phone, although her eyes registered nothing on the screen.

Nick said something else, something about how long he planned to be at the office, which Hollie didn't hear. By the time she understood the feeling prickling beneath her skin, Nick was already back in the bedroom and the screen of her phone had gone dark.

It was the *yet*. "We don't have kids *yet*," he had said, the same way someone might say they hadn't yet had dinner. Like there was not a doubt in his mind that he eventually would.

And of course he would think that, as that was the plan. Job, house, kids—the natural progression of life. It was the natural progression for most people's lives, but theirs in particular. They had agreed to it their first year out of college. Them, thinking they were fully grown with their adult-sized student loan debts. Job, house, kids.

But they had also talked about other things. They had talked about Paris and how perfect it would be for their honeymoon. Nick had wanted to see the Louvre. Hollie had laughed imagining him in a beret.

In the end, they hadn't gone to Paris. They'd gone to Thailand instead. (They were only twenty-three, so Nick's parents had paid.) They could still go to Paris if they wanted to, but at this point,

Hollie wasn't sure if she still did. There were so many more interesting places in the world to see—Machu Picchu, Cape Town, Japan. Hollie's Aunt Joan had recently gotten back from Morocco. She'd brought Hollie a little tin of mint tea and pastries.

Nick was back in the kitchen a few minutes later, dressed for work. "I shouldn't be too long," he said. "Just need to tie up a few loose ends before that meeting tomorrow."

Hollie nodded absently.

"Are you alright?" Nick said, now sounding worried, and Hollie knew that if she told him what she was thinking, he would set his coffee down and take a seat. He would skip the office. He would probably hold her hand. He would listen to her worries with the same wide-eyed concern that he had listened to her with every day since they were nineteen.

"I'm fine," she lied.

She didn't know if this was believable, and based on Nick's expression, he was apparently deciding the same thing. After a moment, however, he seemed to make a decision. He kissed her on the forehead before he left.

Once alone, Hollie didn't move. She sat there, staring at their coffee machine. The French press was a time-consuming device—borderline bougie, if Hollie was being honest. "It's a little more work," she had said to Mallory shortly after they'd gotten it, "but the coffee is life-changing. You should get one and see for yourself." She hadn't meant to be funny, but Mallory had thrown her head back and laughed. "A French press," she had hooted. "I don't have time to take a shit by myself most days."

Finally, Hollie stood up and moved to the sink, where she dumped the rest of her smoothie down the drain.

The most shocking thing about her realization, Hollie would later decide, was that it was really not so shocking at all. Maybe she had never articulated it before, but she had known this deep down for quite some time: She did not want kids. Maybe she never really had.

She had thought she did. In college, it had seemed like a good idea, and even after that, she had spent years hovering in the gray area of not being sure. And then, she was.

Hollie could see it now, as though someone had dogeared one specific scene in the script of her life. It had been at her Christmas party two winters prior, the one she threw every year. Mallory had come with her husband and a nine-month-old Fiona, the infant looking deeply unimpressed with her velvet head wrap.

Halfway through the party, Mallory had disappeared. Hollie had found her in the spare bedroom with the curtains drawn and the lights out. Mallory had been wearing a beautiful velour dress, which she had pulled down to her waist to breastfeed her infant.

"You don't have to hide in here to do that," Hollie had said. "No one's going to care."

"I know," Mallory had answered, but she hadn't moved, and Hollie hadn't pressed the issue after that.

Hollie looked down at her hand, where she was holding her electric toothbrush. She hadn't even noticed entering the bathroom, let alone picking it up.

Why had she never acknowledged this feeling? And how had she not thought to tell Nick?

She tried to think about the last time they had talked about kids—*really* talked about it, more than just laughing at another Fiona Fiasco over a bottle of sauvignon blanc. She couldn't remember. Had it been months? Surely not years. They were just so busy these days. Sometimes they fell into bed before they had volleyed ten real words back and forth.

The last time they had come close was a few weeks ago, when Hollie had come home from the doctor with a new packet of birth control pills. Hollie had wondered aloud how she would remember to take them when she'd spent the last five years with an IUD doing the work.

And then the thought struck her with stunning, almost breathtaking clarity.

The forgotten pill. The little white tablet, smaller than her pinky nail.

She looked up, her eyes landing on her reflection in the mirror over the faucet. Staring back at her was the same person she had been looking at for years, if not her whole life. Except, there were differences. Her skin was now oily, and a new constellation of zits ran along the coastline of her face. She hadn't felt right for a week, like her stomach was caught in a permanent knot. These details were so minor that Hollie had barely registered them as significant. And yet Hollie now felt suddenly sure what they meant.

6

Celeste

Three Months Before
Chicago, Illinois

THERE WAS ONLY one adult-sized seat in Miss Bonnie's classroom, and Miss Bonnie was sitting in it. Celeste and Louis sat across from her in much smaller chairs meant for much smaller people. Celeste usually found all of the miniature things in Bella's school charming—the rows of tiny bookshelves, the little tables that came up to Celeste's knees. A few minutes earlier, however, Celeste had squatted over a miniature toilet and had been unable to find a single positive thing about it.

"So, he's okay then? The other kid—he's fine?"

Louis said this with a voice that Celeste would have found commanding had they been in an office. Unfortunately, it sounded somewhat silly in a children's classroom with his knees folded into his chest.

"Archer? Yes, yes, Archer is fine." Miss Bonnie smiled broadly.

"We actually just spoke to the Baxters before this meeting," the woman beside Miss Bonnie added with authority. The woman's name was Miss Sheryl, or at least that's how she had introduced herself. (It seemed as though all the women referred to themselves as "Miss" even when the children weren't around.) Miss Sheryl had come in late and was standing beside her colleague. She was apparently not the school director but somewhere above the teachers, holding some ambiguous rank that Celeste didn't understand. Celeste wished she had also known that standing was an option before she had folded herself into the child-sized seat.

"That's the kid's parents?" Louis confirmed, his eyes darting between the two women. Louis was wearing his work things still, too rushed after work to change. This only made the tiny chair seem more ridiculous in contrast.

"Yes, the Baxters are Archer's mom and dad." Miss Bonnie seemed intent on using Archer's name as much as possible. Personally, Celeste thought Archer was a ridiculous name for anyone who wasn't a beagle.

There was a brief pause. Miss Bonnie was smiling at them grandly. It seemed that this was the only expression she was capable of making.

"So, just to clarify," Louis said finally, again using his work voice. "Why did Bella bite him? Archer? What was the situation exactly?"

Miss Bonnie shifted in her seat, although to her credit, her smile didn't falter. Celeste wondered if Louis really wanted them to recap the previous day's events or if he was merely stalling.

"We weren't able to get a clear answer from the children," said Miss Sheryl, who was not smiling. Miss Sheryl had many fine lines around her lips, making Celeste suspect she smiled much less than Miss Bonnie. "But from what we can gather, there was a disagreement over the blocks."

It struck Celeste just then that if Alabama had been in the chair beside her, Alabama would have found the whole thing wildly funny. When Louis nodded, however, his expression was grim.

"Did Bella take the blocks from Archer?" he said, which Celeste thought was a very reasonable question. Miss Sheryl, on the other hand, flared her nostrils as though she did not.

"I don't believe so," she said, looking down at Miss Bonnie. "That said, Miss Bonnie will be able to provide more context."

Louis and Celeste both directed their attention to Miss Bonnie, whose smile finally faltered. Celeste suspected that Miss Bonnie was not the sort of person used to providing context to contentious situations like this.

"From what I can tell," Miss Bonnie started, her voice a bit unsteady, "Bella was playing with the blocks first. She's usually the first one to them in the morning. They're her favorite activity for free play." Here, Miss Bonnie paused for a moment. Celeste felt the urge to fill the space with an apology, although she remained silent. "I think Archer also wanted to play with the blocks," Miss Bonnie continued, "and between us, Archer is still working on his sharing. To me, it seems like Bella just sort of"—she shrugged—"snapped."

There was another silence as they all considered this. If Celeste hadn't been so mortified, she might have wondered aloud whether Bella's reaction was a tiny bit understandable, at least to some extent. Just the other day, for example, Celeste had been waiting for a parking space at the mall—her blinker on and everything—when another car had zipped in and taken her spot at the last second. Celeste had been so angry, she had tooted her horn and even let out a few choice words, knowing full well that the window was cracked.

Then again, Celeste had resisted the urge to ram her car into the offender's back bumper.

"Okay." Louis said. He took off his glasses and rubbed his eyes tiredly. Celeste also felt suddenly exhausted. She wondered how mad Alabama would be if they canceled dinner, if Celeste and Louis simply went home after this and slept. "Okay, so where do we go from here?"

"Well," Miss Bonnie started, but then she stopped, looking to Miss Sheryl as though asking for permission. Miss Sheryl gave her the tiniest nod before Miss Bonnie went on. "We mostly just wanted to make you aware of the situation."

Celeste thought to herself how versatile the word *situation* was. People on the news used it regularly, usually with an air of worry. A situation could be your five-year-old biting another five-year-old, or it could be a hurricane set to plow over your house.

"We believe a child's home life is the foundation of his or her social development," Miss Sheryl added, sounding bristly. "We believe it's important that our parents understand what's going on in the classroom so they can make adjustments at home as needed."

Celeste imagined herself at the helm of a giant boat with Miss Sheryl over the radio, advising her of a glacier. Celeste had always wondered why the captain of the *Titanic* hadn't just steered around the ice instead of running straight into it, but now, in a small chair meant for a kindergartner, Celeste felt she better understood what had happened.

"Well, we appreciate it," Louis said, sounding sincere. "We'll definitely talk to her and make sure this doesn't happen again."

Miss Bonnie continued determinedly with her smiling, although Celeste thought she saw the tiniest flicker of pity cross over the woman's face. Perhaps Miss Bonnie—like Celeste—understood a fundamental truth about kindergartners: that talking to Bella was likely to produce no real result other than a glassed-over expression and a request for a popsicle after they were done.

"Is there anything you suggest?" Celeste said before she could help it. "Any—I don't know—resources for these sorts of things?" As soon as she said it, she felt immediately self-conscious over her word choice. *Resources.* It seemed so laughably formal, like Bella's misbehavior could be sorted out in a miniature version of AA.

"We do have a psychologist here at the school," Miss Sheryl answered, which made the whole thing seem worse. "If you would like for Bella to see her, we can certainly set that up."

Celeste noticed Louis stiffen beside her. "We'll definitely talk about it," he said a second time, and Celeste wondered if he really did think talking was a practical solution. Louis *did* do a lot of talking at work, after all. His days were one important conversation after another, so she supposed it was not so unbelievable that he would think the same strategy would work in all areas of his life.

Neither Louis nor Celeste said anything as they walked back to their car after the meeting. A hopeful part of Celeste wondered if they could get away without saying anything ever, which seemed like something only a lousy parent would wonder.

"We shouldn't be too late," Louis said once they were situated in their seats. It took Celeste a moment to understand what he meant by this, to even remember that they had plans for dinner.

"Good," Celeste said, because she couldn't think of anything else.

For a few minutes, they drove in silence. Celeste thought of Miss Bonnie and wondered whether she was heading home now. For some reason, Celeste couldn't picture the teacher anywhere but among the miniature toilets and tables meant for kids.

"Bella had a breakdown after school yesterday," Celeste said finally. She stared straight ahead, where the city skyline stretched across the horizon. "Did I tell you that? That she had a meltdown outside Nordstrom?"

"No, you didn't. What happened?"

Celeste chewed on the inside of her cheek. What *had* happened? Did she even know?

"A temper tantrum. She wanted to go home instead of Target."

Louis didn't say anything for long enough that Celeste finally glanced over at him. He had one elbow on his door, his hand resting in the top lip of the driver side window. He didn't look particularly worried, which bothered Celeste. Celeste knew she worried more than most people, but still, she sometimes wished her husband worried a little more.

"I told you I talked to my mom about my cousin Tonya, right? About how they just diagnosed her son as being on the autism spectrum?"

She held her breath in the top part of her chest, just behind her ribcage. Celeste barely knew anything about Tonya's children. Tonya and her husband lived in Utah along with the majority of Celeste's extended family, most of whom Celeste hadn't seen since she was a kid. Celeste really only thought about Tonya when Celeste's mother felt chatty enough to bring her up, and Celeste's mother was rarely chatty with her.

"I think you mentioned it." Louis was speaking slowly, inching toward the conversation. Celeste couldn't tell if this was because he didn't know where the conversation was going, or if it was because he could see quite clearly what was coming next.

"Do you think we should—I don't know." Celeste smoothed her pants against her thighs. "Do you think we should get Bella checked out?"

The silence that followed seemed longer than it probably was. Celeste noticed in a faraway part of her brain that they hadn't turned on the radio, which made the quiet seem even thicker.

"For autism, you mean?" Louis said at last. He said the word *autism* like it was his first time saying it out loud. This wasn't totally surprising, as it wasn't something they had ever talked about.

Celeste didn't know when the first seed of awareness had been planted, or even if it had been a single realization or something that had materialized over time. All Celeste knew was that Bella only liked even numbers and she couldn't eat bananas or wear linen without breaking down. She knew more about dolphins than Celeste knew about possibly everything combined. On their own, none of these things were particularly grievous, but put together, they were hard to ignore.

And yet Celeste had never said anything about it, not to Louis or to anyone else. Instead, she had spun these thoughts around in her head for weeks—months, maybe—like someone batting a hard piece of candy against their cheeks, hoping it would dissolve.

"Maybe," Celeste said. Her voice was unrecognizably small. She had never considered herself to be a particularly brave person, and this was probably why. The courage it had taken her to even say this much made her want to curl into a ball.

Out the front windshield, the horns of the Willis Tower pierced the yolky yellow sky. Celeste suddenly wished she was anywhere but here in the car, speeding toward some splashy restaurant that charged three dollars per deviled egg. She wanted to be at home in her own bed, a thick layer of night cream applied to all her problem areas. She had just washed their sheets a few days ago. Slipping into them would feel so clean and familiar and safe.

"I don't know, CeCe," Louis said finally. He had taken so long to respond that at first, Celeste thought he was talking about the sheets. "Autism. It seems sort of—*extreme*, doesn't it?"

He met her eyes across the center console. She could see that he was not trying to be dismissive, so she forced herself to seriously consider this suggestion. Extreme. There were lots of things that were extreme. Biting a classmate over blocks, for example. Throwing yourself on the pavement because you wanted a snack. But autism? It was unexpected and certainly not her first choice, but she didn't think it was extreme.

"She's been acting out so much, though, and it only seems to be getting worse."

"She's five. Isn't that what all five-year-olds do?"

"Not like this, I don't think. And the nightmares—apparently, they're common for kids on the spectrum at her age."

When Bella had first started having the dreams a few months prior, Celeste had been terrified to step in. It was something from a movie she had seen, or maybe read in a book—that waking a dreaming person could do irreversible damage of some sort. Louis had never heard of this, so he had gone into Bella's bedroom and shaken her awake. As far as Celeste could tell, it hadn't done any harm, and more importantly, Bella had stopped screaming bloody murder.

"I don't think we can diagnose her with autism just because she has bad dreams."

"But it's not just the dreams. It's everything." Celeste readjusted, angling her torso toward him. "You know how sensitive she is."

"What's wrong with being sensitive?"

"I mean sensitive to, like, textures," Celeste said. She picked at a nonexistent speck of lint on her thigh. "You remember when I tried to get her into that linen jumper a few weeks ago, don't you?" She knew he did, as it had been a debacle. Both Celeste and Bella had cried. "And she can't even eat bananas," Celeste added after a beat.

"Well, I don't like bananas either."

"But have you ever had a breakdown over one?"

Louis looked as though he was seriously considering this.

"And then there's the dolphin thing," she continued. "I've read it's really typical for kids on the spectrum to have single-minded obsessions like that."

The words seemed to fall down gently between them, like someone releasing an armful of feathers. The Adam's apple in Louis's neck bobbled slightly as he chewed on his thoughts.

"I don't know," he said slowly. He sounded regretful, like he was delivering disappointing news. "I just feel like the teachers would've said something if there was a reason to be concerned, you know?"

Celeste thought of Miss Bonnie. The only makeup the woman had worn for the meeting was a thin layer of light pink lipstick, and that had been inexpertly applied. Celeste had noticed this, and it had endeared the teacher to her. Now, Celeste couldn't help but feel it said something else—something about the woman's youth and naïveté. How seriously could they be expected to take a woman who was so young she didn't even need concealer for her under-eyes?

"Maybe she doesn't know what to look for," Celeste said.

Celeste watched Louis for a reaction. He removed his arm from the window and set both hands on the wheel. She remembered their first date, nearly a decade ago now, when Louis had picked her up in his dad's vintage Thunderbird. Celeste didn't know the first thing about cars, so this had not impressed her in the way he had meant it. What had impressed Celeste was the way Louis had driven, how he had maneuvered so casually through traffic using only one hand.

"Alright," Louis said finally. "Alright, I hear you. Let's keep an eye on it, but I think we can wait and see how it goes for now." Louis said this so confidently that for a split second, Celeste was almost convinced that they had come to the decision together. She opened her mouth, inhaled, then closed it again. Then it struck Celeste that they wouldn't be waiting for anything, at least not when it came to Bella. They would be waiting for Celeste, for her to get over her silly paranoia so that they could all go back to boycotting linen and bananas in peace.

7

Alabama

Three Months Before
Chicago, Illinois

EVERY FRIDAY AFTERNOON, Alabama did the same thing: She saw her doctor, whom Alabama despised. She disliked him for several reasons, but the thing Alabama disliked most was his socks.

Alabama didn't have anything against white crew socks in general. Yes, they were objectively ugly, but if worn with objectively ugly white shoes, they could easily transform into the height of fashion. (Just look at the Hadid sisters for proof.)

Alabama's doctor was not the height of fashion. Quite the opposite, actually. Dr. Keith Swinkle wore white tube socks with brown loafers, a fact that irritated Alabama to no end. Did he not have one single woman in his life to explain anything about fashion? What about a gay friend?

"So, tell me," Dr. Swinkle said, tapping a pen against his legal pad. He crossed his legs to reveal his skinny ankles. "Why do you think life will be better for you once you go to Iceland?"

The second worst thing about Dr. Swinkle was that he was incredibly nosy. She understood that it was his job to ask questions, but there was just something about the *way* he asked the questions, the way he leaned forward so his pants hiked that much further up his ankles. Sometimes they got so far that she could see the fine blond hairs poking through the skin above his socks.

"Well, for one thing, I'll be happier once I feel secure about my online engagement. Job insecurity is a big factor in depression, you know." She bet he didn't know. She hadn't known either until she had read it in a magazine while she was waiting to pay for groceries. She usually used the self-checkout aisle, but the lines at self-checkout had been even longer than the regular lines that day. The problem was all the people who took their *full-sized carts* through self-checkout, crowding out people like Alabama, who had only come for deodorant and mascara and actually deserved to be in the speedier lane.

"And are you feeling depressed?"

Alabama sighed heavily.

"No. But one day I could if things don't get better."

Dr. Swinkle nodded and wrote something down on his pad. On Alabama's worst days, she had to physically clench her fists to stop herself from reaching over and snatching the notepad out of his hands. Sometimes Alabama was hardly able to think with every sentence followed by an irritating *scribble scribble, scratch scratch*.

Alabama crossed her own legs and started bouncing her top foot as she gazed around the room. Dr. Swinkle didn't have a single photograph in his office, not even a small one. Maybe he didn't have a family, she thought, which made her feel suddenly sad, both for him and for her.

"So you think the Iceland trip will make you feel more secure about your job," Dr. Swinkle said when he was done scribbling. Alabama uncrossed her legs and waited for the rest of the question, although nothing more came. Dr. Swinkle just gazed at her expectantly, his pen poised.

"Yes," Alabama said simply, because two could play this game. She made her face as expressionless as she could as she looked him straight in the eye.

To her disappointment, this didn't seem to faze him. He didn't even blink. It struck her that he probably had very dry eyes. In fact, she bet his dry eyes were why he wasn't married, because he probably had eyedrops all over his house. Who would want to marry a person who had little bottles of saline in every cabinet?

Finally, when she could no longer stand it, she added, "There's this one influencer who's probably going. Her name's Hollie Goodwin, and she just hit a million followers. She does stuff like this all the time." Alabama thought of Hollie's most recent post, which

Alabama had been the fifth to like even though Alabama had set up alerts on her phone so she could be the first. Hollie had posted about a superfoods smoothie that Alabama had gone ahead and bought that very same day, even paying for expedited shipping. Alabama had never technically met Hollie, which was the only reason they weren't great friends yet.

"And you know what Oprah Winfrey says," Alabama added, this time because she just felt like talking. "She says, 'Surround yourself with people who make you better.' I'm pretty good at influencing, but if I meet Hollie, I know I'll be even better." Alabama had read this quote in the same magazine she had read the fact about depression. She had nearly bought the magazine just so she could rip the page out and tape it to her refrigerator, but she hadn't, because her husband, Henry, was always yammering on about their budget. Amazon this and Starbucks that. He had recently suggested that maybe she could swap out her skinny vanilla lattes once or twice a week for a homemade version because Henry only drank black coffee and didn't understand that lattes never tasted the same at home.

"Oprah Winfrey said that?" Dr. Swinkle said, raising an eyebrow.

"Yes," Alabama said sharply. "You can look it up if you don't believe me."

Dr. Swinkle gave her a tiny nod and scribbled something else down. He was probably making a note about her attitude. Once, when Alabama was little, one of her teachers had made a note about her attitude on her report card. *Alabama has a tendency to become argumentative when faced with criticism,* the note had said. When Alabama's mom had read this, she had closed her eyes and taken several long, deep breaths, like she was trying to stop herself from yelling. This was ironic because her mother didn't actually yell that often. Usually, when it seemed like she wanted to, she poured herself some Grey Goose vodka instead.

Alabama was filled with a random, intense longing to tell Celeste all about this very annoying appointment. It would be so much *easier* if Alabama could just talk to Celeste about Dr. Swinkle, but she couldn't, because Celeste still didn't know Alabama was seeing him in the first place. It wasn't that Alabama wanted to keep it a secret necessarily. It was just, Celeste had this face she made, mostly when she talked about Bella—this nervous sort of worry, like Bella might one day really go off the deep end. Alabama hated it, and she certainly didn't want that face made at her. Alabama was not anywhere near the deep end, thank you very much.

"Alabama?"

Alabama looked up. Dr. Swinkle had stopped writing and was looking at her with a small but noticeable crease between his eyebrows. He looked like someone waiting for an answer, which was annoying, because he hadn't even asked a question yet.

"I asked how you are feeling on the new dosage," he said. He spoke extra slowly, the way Alabama sometimes spoke when she was feeling extra impatient. Alabama wanted to tell him that if he was so curious, maybe he shouldn't mumble the question the first time around. She didn't say this, however, as she knew he would consider the comment "unproductive," which was a word Dr. Swinkle used a lot. To him, everything was either productive or unproductive, with no option for a thing to just *exist* in between.

Alabama shrugged. "It's fine." She knew he wanted her to elaborate, but this time she really had nothing else to say. Every day for the past month, Alabama had tipped the little white bottle into her palm, taken the pill between her two fingers, and flicked it into the toilet bowl. Dr. Swinkle would be horrified if she told him this. A part of her almost wanted to tell him, just to see his reaction, but she had enough self-control not to do that. If she told Dr. Swinkle, Dr. Swinkle would tell Henry, even though that would technically be against patient-client privilege.

The medicine was an antipsychotic. She had learned that after finishing her first bottle, when she had looked it up online. The thought still made her feel hot and angry. Alabama was a lot of things, but she was certainly not a psychopath.

PART II

At Any Cost

8

Hollie

The Morning After
Vík, Iceland

I F HOLLIE HAD been alone in her room, she would have been pacing. This was a personal flaw of hers, her need for constant movement. According to Hollie's mother, pacing turned Hollie's aura red.

Hollie's mom, Angela, was regularly giving out advice like this, as she had recently come into a spiritual awakening of sorts. Hollie blamed Bart, whom Angela had started dating the year prior. Bart owned a yoga studio in Plano, and when Hollie had asked whether he and Angela had bonded over owning the exact same pair of Lululemon leggings, neither had laughed.

But Hollie couldn't pace now, not with Katherine watching her like she was. They were alone in their bedroom with no plans for leaving anytime soon. After the police had alerted the group of Alabama's disappearance, Skye—the trip coordinator—had informed them that all further activities had been canceled for the time being.

Hollie could feel Katherine staring at her openly, not even bothering to hide it. Some people might have stolen glances at Hollie, sneaking peeks out of the corners of their eyes, but Katherine watched her with a casualness that was both annoying and uncomfortably possessive.

"I saw the dude take Celeste Reed into the kitchen," Katherine said. She was chewing a piece of gum that was evidently her breakfast. "Sounds like they're questioning her now."

Hollie picked up her phone and tapped at it clumsily with her left hand. Her right palm still throbbed where a half-inch laceration sliced the meaty part below her thumb. It was a jagged cut, but it wasn't deep, not nearly as deep as she had first feared. Bandaged as it was, it was impossible to see.

"Emily says she heard Celeste and Alabama fighting last night," Katherine continued, either not noticing or ignoring Hollie's silence. Her sentence was punctured by aggressive clicks of chewing gum against teeth. "A huge blowout, apparently."

"Emily seems a little dramatic to me," Hollie said without looking up.

Actually, Emily didn't seem dramatic. She was cute and quiet and exceedingly dull, like a scoop of vanilla ice cream. She had big brown eyes, a small upturned nose, and sand-blonde hair that was perpetually coerced into soft, feminine curls.

Before the Iceland trip, Hollie had never heard of Emily Von Paris. (With less than forty thousand followers, this wasn't surprising.) Hollie hadn't heard of most of the influencers on the trip except Katherine, a broad-shouldered redhead with a no-bullshit attitude. Katherine's disinterest in the usual influencer theatrics was actually what had drawn Hollie to her originally, although now Hollie couldn't help but long for a normal roommate like Emily, who would have only spied on Hollie when she thought Hollie wasn't looking.

"I don't know, man," Katherine said, undeterred. "Celeste seems like she's got some shit going on she doesn't want to talk about." She squeezed out a tiny bubble, which snapped against her lips when it popped. "And that Alabama chick was totally unbalanced."

Hollie winced with an unexpected twinge of defensiveness, which she recognized as hypocritical. Before that morning, Hollie probably would have called Alabama unbalanced too.

Hollie looked determinedly at her phone, hoping to convey to Katherine how little she wanted to talk. With her left thumb, she scrolled half-heartedly through her already staling Instagram grid. She hadn't posted since yesterday, as Skye had asked them to hold off on that. "Given the circumstances," Skye had said in a way that had made it overwhelmingly clear what she had really meant. Given the fact that Alabama Wood was possibly dead.

There was a knock at the bedroom door, and Hollie jumped. Without asking to enter, the blonde officer appeared in their doorway. Hollie was annoyed with both the woman's intrusion and with herself for being so skittish. If she didn't want people to think she was guilty of something, she had to stop acting like she was.

"Hollie Goodwin," the officer said, more of a command than a question. "Would you mind coming with me?"

Across the room, Katherine's eyes moved from the officer back to Hollie, and there was a moment, a single instant, that Hollie hesitated. In marked clarity, she saw herself reaching beneath her pillow and pulling out the second phone—Alabama's phone. She imagined handing it to the cop, explaining how she had come to have it. The vision was so vivid, the details so sharp, that Hollie almost felt as though she had actually done it.

"Sure," Hollie said, dropping her own phone into the pocket of her pullover. With Katherine's eyes still on her, she slid off the bed, leaving the pillow behind her cool and untouched.

CHAPTER

9

Hollie

The Day Before
Somewhere over Iceland

THE LIGHT ABOVE Hollie's head flicked on, illuminating a miniature seat belt in glowing yellow. A moment later, the speakers
made a scratching sound before a voice broke through.

"Ladies and gentlemen," it said, the words thick with a distinctly
Icelandic accent, "we have just been cleared to land at Reykjavík-
Keflavík Airport."

Hollie didn't know if she had actually understood these words,
or if she had simply heard the script so many times that her brain was
able to fill in the unintelligible parts on its own.

Around her, people started to rustle as the flight attendant continued on with her announcements. The man in the seat beside Hollie had been reading a magazine, which he lowered to his lap to focus
on the directions about their seat-back trays and garbage.

Hollie wasn't sure if the man was Icelandic or American or just
his own special breed of extremely attractive specimen. He had the
sort of complexion that Hollie suspected looked sun-kissed year-
round, and clear eyes that were either very light green or blue, she
hadn't decided which.

She hated that she had noticed all of this about him, little glances
stolen here and there as she had scooted past him to use the restroom.

What she hated more was that he had not noticed her in nearly the same capacity. When she had tapped him on the shoulder and gestured toward the aisle, his eyes had passed over her with the same polite indifference that he might thank a cashier for his receipt. Something about this was deeply embarrassing to Hollie, although she couldn't articulate why. Was it the fact that he hadn't noticed her? Or the fact that she cared so much?

She looked down to her phone, which lit up in her hand. Without internet, it was little more than an elaborate flashlight.

She couldn't remember the last time she had flown without internet. She was a preferred flyer for Southwest, so her internet was usually free. Even when it wasn't, she almost always coughed up the eight to twelve dollars to make sure she was connected from liftoff to touchdown.

When Hollie had boarded the plane that morning, she had pulled out her phone with every intention of spending the flight connected the way she usually was. But then she had opened her inbox, where the first message had been from Nick.

She didn't like emailing Nick. She especially didn't like his company-assigned signature block—all neutral colors and privacy statements in fine print. The worst part was his name, how it read "Nicholas" instead of "Nick." She didn't know a Nicholas. Emailing him felt like emailing someone she had never met.

Nick had emailed Hollie a couple of weeks ago and then again that morning when he hadn't heard back. She didn't blame him. She would have done the same thing. And really, Hollie wasn't trying to ignore his messages. She had opened that first email at least three times a day since she had received it, each time watching the little cursor blink for a minute before clicking away.

Maybe we can try couples therapy.

In a way, it was ironic that Nick had used email to suggest this. Some might argue that if a couple had reached the point where email was their primary form of communication, the time for therapy had long since passed.

Hollie and Nick had moved from text message to email a month after Hollie's first positive pregnancy test. At the time, they had been thinking about lawyers—not seriously thinking, but Hollie had brought it up once as gently as she could. (Hollie had witnessed her own mother's first, second, and third divorces, so she knew how sticky they could be.) Nick had agreed to think about it. He'd appeared in her inbox the next day.

"Couples therapy," she whispered under her breath, testing the words out. For as foreign as they sounded in her head, they tasted even worse in her mouth.

"What was that?"

Hollie looked up. The man beside her had once again lowered his magazine and was now looking at her with an expression of mild curiosity. He had an accent, although it didn't sound Icelandic. Eastern European, possibly?

Hollie felt a jolt of satisfaction until she realized what was happening. The man had only noticed her because she was mumbling under her breath.

"Sorry. Nothing. Just talking to myself," Hollie said, prickling with embarrassment. She was now the type of person who demanded attention only when she did something bizarre.

The man seemed to find this explanation sufficient. He gave her a pleasant but disinterested smile before returning to his magazine. The magazine looked scientific, like something Nick might have read before bed. Nick read things like *Technology Today,* not *People.* He couldn't tell you who Tyga was.

Hollie turned to the window, expecting to see the same carpet of clouds she had stared at for most of the trip. Instead, she was met with a view of the ground, now visible as they started their descent. Hollie leaned forward, taking in the view, unsure whether she felt intrigued or overwhelmed by the foreign landscape. From a distance, the mountains looked small, little piles of black earth for as far as she could see. Snow stretched from peak to peak—pristine, untouched.

Hollie turned away from the window. She reached instead for the book she had slipped into the pocket in front of her. She stared at the cover—a woman with red lipstick and a hauntingly blank expression—and wondered again how the hell she had ended up here. This thought had struck her repeatedly since leaving Dallas, sometimes in the existential sense, sometimes in the most literal way. What the hell was she doing here, on a flight to Iceland? What did she even know about Iceland other than everyone there did CrossFit?

The answer, of course, was couples therapy, which was also not remotely an answer at all.

Hollie didn't have anything against therapy as a concept. She had friends who loved it, who raved about how life-changing it was. And maybe it could be, but in this particular situation, Hollie couldn't imagine it helping her one bit. The way Hollie understood it, therapists were there to help you sort through complex feelings and unresolved traumas, which might have been helpful when she had first taken the pregnancy test. Now, however, it was moot. What was done was done, and they could either accept that or get divorced.

Instead of saying any of this to Nick, however, Hollie had ignored his message and written back to PinkPurse, accepting their invitation to the Iceland trip. It was cowardly and evasive and so last minute, it bordered on rude. Luckily, Hollie was a big enough name that PinkPurse had made arrangements for her to come anyway.

"Any trash?"

Hollie looked up to where one of the flight attendants had appeared in the aisle. She jiggled a white trash bag, her eyes moving from Hollie to the man beside her to the woman at the end of their row. Hollie waved to indicate she didn't have any while the man beside her reached for the little plastic cup he had shoved between the seat-back tray and the seat.

As he handed it to the woman, Hollie noticed that beneath her absurd uniform hat, she was quite beautiful. She had ashy blonde hair and immaculately clear skin, and while her blazer was tight across her boobs, she was otherwise markedly thin. It was unclear whether her slightly disproportionate chest was a boob job, or if she was just genetically blessed.

The woman leaned forward slightly, holding out the bag. As the man tossed his garbage into it, Hollie noticed his eyes linger on her for just a second too long, no doubt thinking the exact same thing.

10

Celeste

The Day Before
Reykjavík, Iceland

CELESTE AND ALABAMA touched down in Reykjavík at six forty-seven AM local time.

"God," Alabama grunted as the cabin lights flickered on. Overhead, the flight attendant's instructions were lost in the shuffle of seat belts unfastening and bags coming unstowed. "This mask doesn't do anything." She pushed up her silk eye mask, smashing her blonde hair against her forehead.

"Sorry about that," Celeste said to the man beside her, even though it had been his elbow that had poked hers, not the other way around. He didn't seem to hear.

"Yeah, well, I just don't understand why we had to take a red-eye," Alabama grumbled, apparently thinking the apology had been directed to her. Celeste ignored this as she reached down below the seat, where she had obediently stowed her tote the first time the flight attendant had asked. A less patient version of Celeste might have told Alabama that she could have booked her own flight if she was so against redeyes, but Celeste had made a point not to bring that version of herself on this trip.

When Celeste had forwarded Alabama their flight details a few weeks prior, Alabama had been unimpressed by the takeoff and landing times. She had not, however, been moved enough to actually do anything about it. Actually, Alabama had contributed essentially nothing to their travel plans besides forwarding Celeste a few spammy-looking emails with brief, demanding commentary. *Let's go here! Add this to the list!* As usual, she had expected Celeste to handle all the uninteresting logistics like actually booking their flights.

Unfortunately for Alabama, Celeste adored redeyes. She found good time management soothing, and this way they would have all day to explore before the PinkPurse Meet and Greet dinner that night in Vík.

According to Celeste's research, Vík was a small, picturesque village on Iceland's southern coast. It was conveniently located near the Skaftafellsjökull glacier, where the influencers would shoot a few photos of PinkPurse's new fall and winter line before embarking on a hike. Not too far from the glacier was an iceberg lagoon, which wasn't on the PinkPurse itinerary and had piqued Celeste's interest. She had considered booking a private tour for just her and Alabama, but Alabama had unceremoniously vetoed the idea. Icebergs, according to Alabama, sounded "boring and cold."

The truth was, Celeste didn't totally disagree. Iceland indeed sounded boring and cold. More problematically, Iceland seemed very far away. Celeste didn't like being in a different time zone from her daughter. It felt no different from how Celeste would expect an astronaut to feel on the moon.

Once, in third grade, Celeste's class had been assigned a project: describe your dream job. As a student, Celeste had taken all of her projects seriously, but Celeste had elevated this one in particular to a matter not too far from life or death. Jobs were important. Even in the third grade, Celeste had understood this. Her father, Francis Clayton, was a pulmonologist first, a father second, and then—finally—Frank, whatever Frank meant to him.

For a week, Celeste's life had revolved around the project. She had stopped sleeping, stopped eating, stopped talking at dinner (although with four abrasive brothers, this had gone largely unnoticed by her parents). And still, the day of the presentation, Celeste had felt no more sure about her choice than she had the first day of the assignment. In fact, she had nearly lied to her teacher about feeling sick just to go to the nurse's station, although she hadn't, because Celeste had never been any good at lying.

Instead, she had watched in amazement as her classmates had presented their reports, talking in their loud, third-grade voices about all the things they felt sure they would be. A foot doctor. A race car driver. An acrobat. The guy who sold purple cleaning products on TV.

There was one girl in particular whom Celeste still sometimes thought about. Her name was Jessica, although she had insisted that everyone call her Jesse. Jesse had wanted to be an astronaut. She would go to the moon first, then somewhere more dangerous like Mars or maybe another galaxy, which she had announced to the class with an air of authority.

While Jesse had been speaking, Celeste had felt the questions rise from her like little bubbles in a steaming pot. What would Jesse bring to space? Could she bring her books and a familiar blanket? What if she really missed her mother? What if she wanted a hug? The last one was an odd question for Celeste to think of, as she rarely hugged her own mom.

When it was Celeste's turn finally, she had mumbled through most of her report. After weeks of deliberation, the job she had landed on was the sample lady at Costco who handed out half-moons of hot dogs in tiny plastic cups.

Celeste had no desire to go to space, and she had no desire to be in Iceland. The only reason she had come was Louis. "It might give you some time to cool off," he had said in a voice like this was a kind suggestion. What he had meant to say, what Celeste was sure he had intended, was that she could use the space, not realizing that Celeste did need to cool off more than he could possibly imagine. Instead of telling him this, however, she had directed all of her energy into planning the trip.

In addition to the iceberg lagoon, the western side of the island had been a major focal point of her research. All the travel blogs had been in agreement. It also wasn't on PinkPurse's itinerary, and so, without asking Alabama, Celeste had made the executive decision to book a redeye, providing them a morning to explore it all on their own.

On the plane now, the rows of people ahead of them started draining outward toward the aisle. Alabama tugged her bag from beneath the seat in front of her with a loud display of impatience.

"Now we'll have time to check out the Blue Lagoon," Celeste offered as they waited for their luggage on the conveyer belt. "It wasn't on the PinkPurse itinerary, and now we'll get to go."

Alabama—whose hair was shoved up on one side from leaning against the window—didn't respond, perhaps because she hadn't actually looked at the itinerary.

In their rental car, Alabama cranked the lever to push her seat back just far enough that she could still observe the landscape moodily while Celeste drove. She yawned three times with obnoxious, wide-mouthed groans, and by the time they pulled into the Blue Lagoon parking lot, Celeste had swallowed enough irritation that her stomach hurt.

"They have changing rooms, don't they?" Alabama said, pulling her seat upright. She scanned the parking lot with a skeptical frown.

"Of course they have changing rooms," Celeste snapped.

Alabama looked over and raised an eyebrow, but she didn't say anything. Celeste decided not to engage and instead squinted over Alabama's shoulder to the entrance, which looked irritatingly plain. She couldn't actually see the hot spring, as it was presumably blocked from view by the multiple mounds of gravelly rocks piled high by the welcome sign.

She thought of the Blue Lagoon website, where the landing page showed a photo of a woman in a white robe leaning her head back in a way that looked conspicuously sexual. That's what Celeste had been looking forward to, but on the drive over from the airport, the only thing they had seen was pocketed black earth and industrial-looking smokestacks. If Alabama was right, if they had flown in early for nothing, Celeste didn't think she would be able to stand it.

Celeste led the way toward the entrance, marching with purpose. She heard Alabama's flip-flops smacking her heels as she jogged to keep up. They charged past another pile of black moon rock, and Celeste thought of Alabama in the airplane, rearranging herself huffily against the window as Celeste had crammed herself into the middle seat. She then thought of Louis back home—probably still asleep across their bed in an authoritative spread-eagle—and this made her think of the article she had read on her phone while waiting for their rental car that morning.

Nothing in the article was new to Celeste. She could have written the article herself, quite frankly. She knew, for example, that girls on the autism spectrum presented differently from their male peers, which made it difficult for doctors, who were usually more familiar with the signs in boys.

This fact in particular made Celeste bristle with an ill-defined anger—at the doctors or the medical community or the mistreatment of women throughout history in general. When she was feeling particularly unkind, she sometimes even blamed Louis, as though he had anything to do with the medical community's mishandling of women's health.

Celeste stopped. Alabama appeared beside her, breathing fast. For a moment, they both stared in silence. They had arrived at the front door of the hot spring lobby—two sheets of tall, reflective glass framed by beams of steel and stone. Together, their gazes fell just beside it, to the still and steamy pool of water at the edge of the walkway. It was blue, but not a blue like Celeste had ever seen. It was nearly turquoise, the color of a melting jewel.

Just like the website.

The door fanned open, and a couple with wet hair emerged, a few notes of ethereal wind chimes slipping out behind them. Celeste thought of the woman in the robe again. Perhaps she hadn't looked sexual as much as orgasmically relaxed.

Something warm pressed against Celeste's palm. She looked down to see Alabama's hand slipping into her own.

"This looks amazing," Alabama said quietly, giving Celeste's hand a squeeze. "Thanks for planning this, CeCe."

This wasn't an apology, not technically, but Celeste would take it as one anyway. Because Celeste had decided that it was possible to apologize this way—with love, with patience—without necessarily admitting the things you had done wrong.

11

Hollie

The Day Before
Vík, Iceland

THE DRIVE FROM Reykjavík to Vík was about two and a half hours, but it took much less time than that for Hollie to wish she had done it alone.

"Hypothermia," Katherine boomed from the passenger seat, jabbing the air with an outstretched finger. "That's what killed him. He fell in a crevasse and couldn't get out."

Hollie was driving the rental car. She had met up with Katherine at the airport, as they had decided to drive together to Vík. It had been Hollie who had messaged Katherine before the trip, a decision Hollie was now very much regretting. Did Katherine really think anyone would want to hear about some man who had died on a glacier the day before they were set to hike up a glacier themselves?

Really, Hollie didn't understand why PinkPurse had even planned a glacier hike to begin with. *Perfect for photo-ops!* the welcome email had shouted in hot pink letters, although Hollie assumed it was something more—maybe part of PinkPurse's deal with GoIceland, the travel company that had sponsored the trip. There was really no other explanation. Hollie had been on this type of trip before, and never once had she looked around the group of whisper-thin women with store-bought tans and thought, yes, this looks like a group people who would do well on a hike.

"And Vík's not much safer." Katherine leaned forward to rearrange herself, stretching the seat belt across her broad chest. "That beach, man. Some woman got sucked out by the current last year. Smashed her head up against those cliffs and died."

In Katherine's defense, she did not sound chatty as she said this. Her tone was more matter-of-fact, although that was possibly just as irreverent.

Hollie decided that her best hope for ending the conversation was silence, so she didn't say anything. Thankfully, it appeared Katherine had said her piece. The radio was only picking up static, so they had turned it off. For the next few minutes, the only sound in the car was the rhythmic clicking of Katherine's gum through her cheek.

Hollie's mind drifted again to the email on her phone, which she had still not answered. She wondered if the Wi-Fi in Vík would be too weak to send the message and whether that would be a relief.

"Whoa," Katherine said after a little while, lowering her enormous sunglasses so they hung just above her lips. Hollie, whose eyes had grown heavy from staring at the road for so long, blinked. For the first time since they had left Reykjavík, Katherine and Hollie finally seemed to be on the same page about something. *Whoa* was absolutely right.

The last hour of the drive had been unremarkable. The road had been narrow and nearly empty, flanked on both sides by rolling green hills. It didn't seem to be grass on the earth, but something mossy, like a layer of velvet hugging the rocky dirt. The island wasn't as windy as they had been warned about, but it was gloomy and damp. The mist that hung in the air was thick, making it impossible to tell where the fog stopped and the clouds above them began.

Where the hills had finally parted ahead of them, though—this was different.

It wasn't beautiful, not the way exotic locations usually were. It was dark, both the water and cliffs that rose up from it, their sharp edges slicing through the grayness all around. Moss rolled down the hill in front of them, the slope freckled by primary-colored buildings before slipping into the sea. The beach was a ribbon of black curling along the coast, and the only structure visible above the sea line was a church with a rust red roof and a spire that needled the cloudy sky.

"Why does it feel like I'm going to die here?" Katherine said, smiling for possibly the first time since the airport. This was apparently Katherine's form of humor.

The gloominess was what made the village seem so grim—that's what Hollie decided as their GPS directed them off the main road a little while later. The gloominess and the complete stillness, as though the village was holding its breath. The rental car office had made Hollie sign a waiver about the wind, which was evidently strong enough to send a poorly handled car right off the road. And yet there didn't seem to be any wind now.

"Looks like people are here already," Hollie said as she pulled their car into an empty spot. The bed and breakfast parking lot was only about nine or ten spaces long, half of which were filled. The welcome dinner wasn't for another few hours, but from the looks of it, Hollie and Katherine were among the last to arrive.

Hollie clicked the key remote as she got out, and behind them, the trunk popped. Katherine emerged from her side with a loud yawn as Hollie gazed at the building where they would be staying.

The building looked like it had been charming at one point but had since conceded to the salt and wind. Its cement walls were painted white, although instead of looking sharp, the façade was chipped and weathered. Something black seeped down the wall from just below the roof, which was missing a few shingles. The PinkPurse welcome email had focused more on the surrounding area than the actual accommodations, and now Hollie understood why.

There was a click, and Hollie immediately whipped around. Over the car, Katherine was holding her phone up for a picture. The phone was protected by a horrendously thick case bedazzled with Katherine's initials. Just above the letters were the phone's many little camera lenses, each currently directed toward Hollie.

Heat rose to Hollie's neck.

"Did you just take a picture?" she said. Katherine had brought her phone back down and was now clicking its screen with her long nails.

"An Insta story," she replied without looking up.

Hollie concentrated on steadying her voice.

"Am I in it?"

At this, Katherine finally looked at her. She frowned. The expression was not a look of concern but of mild curiosity, as though she sensed Hollie's rising panic and was slightly interested to see how it would play out.

The heat from Hollie's neck spread to her ears. In an instant, she pictured herself sliding over the hood of the car and tackling Katherine to the ground—which was an insane thought really, not to mention highly improbable. Hollie had put on weight recently, but Katherine had the sturdiness of a college linebacker. She would have no problem pinning Hollie to the ground.

"Yeah. The back of you. Is that cool?"

Hollie pictured the struggle—Katherine's arms flailing, Hollie ripping the phone with one hand while yanking Katherine's wild mane of hair with the other. Hollie wondered if she was going crazy. These felt like thoughts only a crazy person would think.

"Actually, would you mind deleting it?" Hollie produced what she hoped to be a guilty grin. "I look like shit from the plane."

For a moment, Katherine didn't say anything. Hollie felt something formerly solid inside her begin to tremble.

In college, Mallory had been obsessed with true crime documentaries. She had watched them constantly, to the point where Hollie had sometimes heard the ominous theme song in her sleep. Hollie had never liked the shows, mainly because she had never been able to sympathize with the characters. They talked about snapping like it was outside their control, as though control wasn't a choice one could make. Hollie had never understood this concept, and so she had never understood them.

Now, staring at Katherine across the hood of their rental, Hollie wondered if maybe she had been too quick to judge.

"Whatever," Katherine said at last. She tapped her phone, presumably to delete the shot. Hollie wanted to press the issue, to force Katherine to prove that the photo had indeed been deleted, but she did not want to come off as a complete lunatic.

Neither of them said anything else as they moved to the trunk. In another situation, Hollie might have interpreted the quiet as stony silence, but in this case, it seemed more that Katherine simply didn't care.

As they wheeled their bags toward the building, Hollie was unable to ignore the dread that had pooled in her stomach. She felt suddenly hyperaware of the problems ahead. She had managed to escape Katherine's photo, but this was only the beginning. What was she going to do for the rest of the trip? Tackle anyone who put a phone in her face?

It had not occurred to Hollie until she had made it through security at Dallas Love Field Airport that this would be a problem. She had been standing shoeless at the conveyer belt, watching her Marc Jacobs tote emerge from the plastic flaps, when the thought had hit her: This trip would mean photographs, and not just her own, which could be retouched and filtered and cropped. She would be in other people's pictures, with no control over whether they edited them or not.

The realization had been so obvious, and so numbing, that the woman behind Hollie at security had cleared her throat twice before Hollie had remembered to move. She had grabbed her shoes, shoved them on, then circled back thirty seconds later to grab the tote she had forgotten at the end of the belt.

Hollie hadn't stopped posting over the last few months. Despite everything that had happened, Hollie's content calendar had miraculously emerged unscathed. In fact, her post from yesterday had produced some of her best engagement yet. In the picture, she was wearing workout tights and a cropped tank top that revealed just enough of her stomach to remind you of her abs. *A few things to wrap up before I leave for Iceland tomorrow,* she had captioned it, failing to mention that the picture was from six months ago and her pre-trip "things" had mainly involved takeout Chinese and standing in front of her bedroom mirror with her jaw clenched.

If her followers suspected anything amiss about the picture, however, they were not confident enough to point it out. The comments were nothing but positive, gushing compliments about her shoes, her clothes, her hair. Hollie hated lying—even if only by omission—but it was better than the alternative. It was better than posting how she currently looked and how exactly she had gotten there.

For weeks, Hollie had been strategic about her online content, posting pictures from months earlier and captioning them as recent. The few times she had posted a recent photo, it had been a lesson on good angles and strategic edits using various apps—round cheeks whittled, jawbones made sharp. It hadn't occurred to her until she was in the airport that this level of deception would be much more difficult surrounded by nine other women taking photos of their own.

This might not have mattered for a different influencer. For some influencers, the story surrounding her new appearance might not have been expected, much less required. But this was not the case for Hollie, for the brand she had built for herself. Her followers would expect an explanation, and they would have every right to demand that. Hollie knew this, just like she knew that an explanation for the extra weight would be an explanation of everything that had happened over the past several months. She would have to explain Nick—why he had left and how she was coping—and it was difficult to see how Hollie could offer all of that to her followers without her brand being lost.

CHAPTER

12

Celeste

The Day Before
Reykjavík, Iceland

CELESTE WAS STILL pregnant when she was first promised she
would lose the baby weight.

"Don't worry," her obstetrician had told her—a man in his late
sixties with astonishingly processed blond hair. "Once you start
breastfeeding, the weight will fly right off."

She had felt defenseless with her legs spread open on the examination table, still dripping with the lubricant he had used to examine her insides. Perhaps if she had been sitting upright, she might
have had the courage to tell him about her actual worries at the
time—things like preeclampsia and gestational diabetes, kick counts
and her daughter's umbilical cord, which had miraculously not yet
wrapped around her tiny baby's neck (but still very well could). She
might have told him that she didn't care about her weight, and that
he could fuck right off for even suggesting that she should.

But Celeste had never been a swearer, and until now, standing
at the edge of the Blue Lagoon beside Alabama with her miles of
tanned extremities, she had never paid much attention to the seven
(alright, ten) stubborn pounds that had not, despite the doctor's
promise, flown right off.

"What's that smell?" Alabama said, wrinkling her nose. She was wearing a barely there bikini and a minuscule pair of cat-eye sunglasses, which had exploded into the fashion scene the moment Kendall Jenner had been spotted in a pair. (Alabama, of course, swore she had bought hers first.)

"I think it's sulfur."

Celeste's fingers hovered at the edge of her knee-length lace muumuu. In what seemed like an unfair conundrum, she felt equally self-conscious about keeping it on as she did taking it off. On the one hand, there was a sense of security about having her various lumps and dimples covered. On the other, the muumuu itself was slightly embarrassing. At home, it had seemed cute and flirty, but it now felt puritan next to Alabama's child-sized swimsuit.

"It smells awful," Alabama said, now pinching her nose.

"Yeah, but I think the minerals are why everyone's skin here looks so good."

"Oh my god." Alabama turned to her. "Their skin is gorgeous. It makes you want to kill them, right?" She gave Celeste a devious grin.

Alabama was joking, although Celeste had felt an actual sense of defensiveness in the lobby as they'd traded their credit cards for fluffy white towels and keys for two private lockers. It was ridiculous, but she had felt as though the women at the front desk had been looking fresh and healthy *at* her somehow.

Before she could overthink it further, Celeste pulled the muumuu over her head and scuttled toward the edge of the milky blue water.

"Wait," Alabama said, holding out her arm. Celeste stopped. "Could you get a pic first?"

Louis had once privately made fun of Alabama for doing this—saying *pic* instead of *picture*. (Celeste had decided not to point out that Louis could fill entire conversation with unnecessary marketing acronyms—VOCs and B2Bs—which she suspected only existed to make very ordinary things sound more important than they were.)

"Okay, yeah." Celeste took Alabama's phone from her. "What do you want?"

Alabama turned to survey the hot spring, as did Celeste. The pool was about the size of a football field, scooped out from the mounds of jagged rocks that rose up on all sides. A wispy layer of steam hovered above the jewel-toned water, the effect either beautiful or slightly macabre, Celeste couldn't decide which.

"Maybe get me from the back walking in?" Alabama said after a moment. Her lips pulled to one side before she nodded to herself, apparently decided. Without looking back, she stepped toward that water.

Celeste raised the phone to capture dozens of nearly identical photos of Alabama inching her way down the ramp and into the water—butt pressed out, shoulders drawn back to lengthen her neck, all the while appearing somehow effortless, as though this was simply the way she walked.

"Do you want some?" Alabama said once they were finished, taking the phone back from Celeste.

"I guess I should." Celeste pulled her own phone out of its waterproof liner, which she had bought off Amazon after reading the tip on a blog. She handed it to Alabama, and then—in a burst of inspiration—she hurried back over to the chair where she had draped her muumuu.

"In this, I think," she said, mostly to herself.

She struggled with the lace for a moment, as it was difficult to determine which holes belonged with which body parts. Once it was on, she glanced at herself in the mirrored glass of the lobby windows. Good enough, she supposed. She waded down so the muumuu's lace edge dangled just above the water.

"Does this look good?" she called.

Alabama squinted in appraisal.

"Go a little further in so your muumuu is touching the water."

Celeste obeyed, backing up slowly, facing Alabama, watching her eyes for confirmation.

"Okay, that's good," Alabama finally said.

Celeste wasn't sure what Alabama was seeing, but she trusted her friend's intuition, as Alabama had a natural eye for that sort of thing. Unlike some influencers, Alabama's shots had a salient, almost mathematical symmetry to them. They were artistic, which made it all the more unfair that Alabama's career hadn't taken off quite as quickly as some of the other content creators who had started around the same time. Alabama was still hovering at two hundred thousand followers, and although she had been selected for the PinkPurse trip, her engagement had just seen another sizable drop. The internet was obstinate that way, as Celeste had discovered. The more Alabama wanted it, the more elusive success seemed to be.

"What's your passcode?" Alabama said, waving Celeste's phone.

"All ones," Celeste called back.

Alabama nodded and held out the phone. In the water, Celeste tried to mimic Alabama's easiness, arranging and rearranging her hands on her hips, then by her side. Unfortunately, she never felt quite natural being photographed, even after all this time. (This probably explained why most of her grid consisted of Bella as the focal point.)

"Nice," Alabama said with an approving nod. "I think these are good."

Celeste rose out of the water and patted her hands against her lacy thighs before taking the phone back.

"Do you think anyone else is here?" Alabama said as Celeste examined the results. Alabama had dutifully taken at least forty shots.

"Maybe." Celeste tapped the first photo. A burst of blue and white filled her screen. "Vík's a couple of hours away. Maybe some of the girls will stop by on the way from the airport too." She pinched the screen and spread her fingers, enlarging her own digital body. It wasn't half bad, she was surprised to discover, although her upper arms did look a bit soft.

"You know," Alabama said, still scanning the water, "Hollie Goodwin's gonna be on this trip." She brought one hand up to create a visor, shielding her eyes from the nonexistent sun.

"Yeah, you told me."

Celeste skipped to the next photo, where maybe her arms looked a tiny bit leaner.

"I've been running," Alabama said.

This, finally, caused Celeste to look up. She frowned.

"Running? Why?"

"For exercise." Alabama sniffed. "You know Hollie runs, right?"

Celeste did know, as did Hollie's other one point one million followers. Celeste also knew that Alabama was not the sort of person who exercised voluntarily. Celeste had once persuaded her to try a barre class together—good for the joints, better for the ass, or so she had been told—and Alabama had spent the next two weeks limping. She'd "ruptured her hibiscus" doing a plié, she'd explained to Celeste gravely. Celeste assumed she had meant to say meniscus, although even Celeste knew that meniscuses weren't something you ruptured.

"She's organizing a 5K in Dallas this summer," Alabama went on, seemingly unaware of Celeste's skepticism. "I think I'm going to run in it."

"I thought you hated running," Celeste said carefully. She had forgotten about the pictures on her phone entirely. Something about this conversation made Celeste feel uneasy, although she couldn't put her finger on what.

Alabama flipped her head over and raked her fingers through her hair, which was already wet. The water in the Blue Lagoon was apparently sensitive to hair product, so before they had left the locker room, they had been corralled into a row of shower stalls to wash off first. Alabama had balked at the injustice—she had just gotten a blowout before leaving Chicago—but the woman at the pool's entrance had looked stern enough that Alabama had complied.

"I don't *hate* running," Alabama said, gathering her hair into messy knot. "I think it's really inspiring what Hollie does." She flipped her head back over. "And you know, I've been thinking. People like Hollie, they do something besides just the clothes. They have a *thing* that makes them special, and that's what I've been missing. I need a thing that makes me stand out."

She snapped her hair-tie decisively as Celeste felt her stomach drop. It was the distinct sensation of remembering something important and hazardous, like a hair straightener still plugged in after you had left for a night out.

"Anyway." Alabama gestured toward the water. "Let's get in."

Alabama didn't look to Celeste for approval before she strode to the pool's edge, leaving Celeste with her head humming unpleasantly.

A *thing*. This was the exact word Alabama's husband had used when he had confided in Celeste a few months prior. Alabama had wanted a *thing* at any cost.

"She's better now, though," Henry Wood had assured Celeste, and Celeste—half hurt that Alabama hadn't confided in Celeste personally, half guilty that she hadn't noticed it on her own—had decided that believing him would not be the worst thing she had ever done.

13

Celeste

The Morning After
Vík, Iceland

THE GAUZY CURTAIN that fluttered over the kitchen sink was nearly translucent, completely insufficient for its purpose of blocking light. This seemed like a major oversight in a country that was never fully dark in the summer months.

"And you were sharing a room with her, correct?" the officer said, bringing Celeste's attention back to him. He and Celeste were alone in the bed and breakfast kitchen, and up close, he looked older than she had first estimated. Mid-forties, maybe. A bit older than Celeste. He was called Officer Björnsson, and when he had introduced himself, all Celeste had been able think about was the Babybjörn carrier Celeste had tried and failed to wrangle her daughter in as a newborn. Even then, not yet three months on earth, Bella had been wholly uninterested in physical contact.

"Yes." Celeste scratched at a hangnail on her thumb before realizing that the fidgeting probably made her look suspicious. She interlaced her fingers and set her hands on the table.

Officer Björnsson nodded slowly as he scribbled something on his notepad. He had a dignified patch of gray hair around each temple. Louis was also going gray, although he used special shampoo to color it.

"And you flew in together, correct?"

"That's right. We took a redeye."

She felt herself relaxing slightly as she said this, the way she always did when she sensed order being restored. Growing up, she had been the family anomaly—the only daughter, the youngest by three years. Unlike her four brothers, who had existed in a general state of chaos, Celeste had always felt most at ease when things were going according to plan.

"Right." Officer Björnsson tapped the end of his pen against his notepad. Celeste glanced over his shoulder to the window, where bounds of mossy green earth crawled up the sharp incline of the cliff walls. It was gusty today, as they had been warned Iceland would be. It made the memory of the village's initial stillness feel ominous somehow.

Before arriving in Vík, Celeste and Alabama had spent nearly two hours in the car winding through the Icelandic countryside. Finally, the hills had parted for a clear view of the ocean at the edge of the small fishing village. The sea had been calm, the waves barely lapping against the black sand beach, and at the time it had seemed peaceful. Now Celeste could not help but wonder what had been brewing just below the water's surface. It was as though the village had been deliberately deceiving them somehow.

"So," Officer Björnsson said at last, his pen now still, "did you notice anything off about Alabama before the trip? Anything about her behavior that stuck out to you as strange?"

His voice was light, and as Celeste considered her answer, she very much wanted to mirror this easiness back. The problem was, she had never been a very good actor. In elementary school, for example, she had been so dismal, she had been cast in her school play as a blade of grass. The role had been as straightforward as expected, and yet seven-year-old Celeste had managed to struggle. She had been unable to work out exactly how rigid blades of grass were supposed to be, and when the spotlight had finally come her way, she had felt so alarmingly exposed that she had frozen completely and missed her cue to leave the stage.

If she thought about it long enough, Celeste could still sometimes feel the heat of the elementary school spotlight, the itch of green construction paper taped to her forehead. The panic that had filled her as she had realized she was the only blade of grass left on stage. Her problem with acting was that it was really just lying, and Celeste was atrocious at that.

"Her behavior before the trip?" Celeste said, surprised to hear her own voice so raspy. She cleared her throat. "To be honest, I wasn't paying much attention. I've been too distracted by personal stuff."

CHAPTER

14

Celeste

The Day Before
Reykjavík, Iceland

BEFORE PINKPURSE HAD invited her to Iceland, Celeste had taken international promotional trips on two separate occasions. The first was in Riviera Maya just before she had gotten pregnant, and the second was in St. Barts three months after Bella was born.

In St. Barts, Celeste had spent the majority of the time tugging and pinching at cheaply made frocks and swimsuit coverups, attempting to stretch them over her new postpartum figure. She had never felt so uncomfortable in her body, and never more so than at the welcome dinner, where she had brought her breast pump for her scheduled seven PM pump.

Somehow, Celeste had lost track of time in all of the excitement, and so at eight, midway through the hors d'oeuvres, she had taken a bite of an herbed chèvre rollup and felt a familiar tightness across her chest. A few seconds later, she had been mortified by two patches of milk blossoming over each nipple.

Later that evening, she had gone back to her room and scrolled through all the pictures of Bella on her phone and cried.

As Celeste followed Alabama toward the dining room for the PinkPurse welcome dinner that evening, she felt in some ways just as tethered to Bella as she had when Bella was a newborn. Perhaps

Celeste was no longer worried that without her watchful eye, Bella would somehow get tangled by the cord of her blinds, but the disappointing thing about parenthood was that the older the children got, the less straightforward the dangers became.

Teachers are more likely to miss autistic symptoms in girls, she had read just that evening, in another one of the articles she had pulled up on her phone. It was as though the article was speaking directly to Celeste. She and Alabama had been getting ready for dinner, and Celeste had fought the urge to screenshot the snippet and send it to Louis right then and there.

"And so I told him," Alabama said now, ahead of Celeste on the stairs. "I said, if you're too busy to talk to your wife, then fine. I'm going to be gone for almost a week, but if your tomato plant can't wait for, like, *thirty minutes*, then maybe you have a problem, don't you think?"

Alabama was irritated with her husband, Henry, who had cut their phone call short that evening. He had needed to water his tomato plant, he had told her, and when Celeste had suggested that maybe tomato plants were just finicky, Alabama had responded with a glare.

"I mean, I'm not going to talk to him hardly at all tomorrow, with the glacier hike and everything." Alabama landed on the bottom step hard, her nude kitten heels making two muffled thuds. "He'd feel really terrible if I, like, died on the glacier, and the last thing he said to me was that his tomatoes are looking dry."

Alabama threw her thick braid over her shoulder. Celeste wasn't sure if Alabama was speaking to Celeste in confidence, or if she would have told this seemingly personal information to anyone within a five-foot radius.

"And you know what?" Alabama continued, marching toward the dining room.

"What?" Celeste said, even though she knew Alabama would tell her regardless.

"I think Henry's having an affair."

Alabama pushed the dining room door open, and for a moment, so startled, Celeste forgot to move. She stared at Alabama's back until the door swung closed, insulating Celeste once again from the faint bass pumping in the other room.

An affair. Alabama had said it so casually, the way Celeste might have said that she was getting a headache.

Remembering where she was, Celeste pushed the door open. Alabama was halfway across the room already, not noticing she had left Celeste in the hall.

Celeste hurried after her, toward a balloon arch that stretched artfully across the windows on the far wall. Various shades of blush latex swayed in the air conditioning over a foldout table, where the trip coordinator hovered with a clipboard that was also pink. (Celeste could appreciate PinkPurse's dedication to cohesive branding, but all the pink against the horrendous green walls and solemn gray sky out the window made the whole thing look gauche.)

Celeste came to a stop beside Alabama. On the table, there was a spread of what appeared to be name tags, each shaped like a miniature pink accessory. Alabama was currently ripping the plastic backing from a pink sundress. The trip coordinator, Skye, smiled and handed Celeste her own name printed across a miniature pair of pink heels. Celeste took it, noticing how many were still left on the table—a pencil skirt, a maxi dress, a tiny purse. It appeared that Celeste and Alabama were among the first to come down from their rooms.

"Feel free to mingle," Skye said, gesturing around the room, although at the moment there were only three other women in it. "We'll start the welcome games shortly, and Delphine tells me the main course will be served at eight."

Not wanting to come off as rude, Celeste smiled, although her skin was already crawling at the thought of welcome games. She glanced worriedly at the other women, none of whom were paying any attention to who had just arrived.

Celeste recognized two of them immediately—Emily Von Paris and Margot Murphy, both from Orange County, both with the exact same shade of blonde hair. At some point, Emily and Margot had made the concerted decision to become as close to one single person as humanly possible, and they were alarmingly close to success. They were both wearing the same paperbag pants and slinky silk tank in different colors. If Celeste squinted, it was like they were one single blur of balayage.

Celeste didn't recognize the other woman, and she was too far away to read the pink tag on her chest. The woman was shorter and hovered just beside Emily and Margot in a sheer white tunic and black leather pants.

Celeste turned to Alabama, who had crossed her arms over her blue gingham bodycon dress. When Alabama had pulled the dress from her suitcase earlier that evening, Celeste had been surprised by the pit of envy in her stomach. Celeste longed to be confident enough to even consider a dress like that. It was an exclusive prerelease from PinkPurse's upcoming late-summer collection—*Dorothy hits Vegas*, they had named it.

"You don't really think Henry's cheating on you, do you?" Celeste said. She smoothed the edge of her name tag against her shirt, pressing her fingers along each of the tiny heels. Celeste's shirt was called *Eyelet You*. It was from PinkPurse's spring collection the previous year. It was white eyelet with an open back and a gathering of ruffles around the midsection. She had paired it with her favorite high-waisted skinny jeans and espadrille heels, and perhaps she didn't look like Alabama cinched in her gingham, but she was mostly happy with how the outfit had turned out.

"What?" Alabama sounded distracted.

"You said you think Henry's having an affair."

"Oh." Alabama wasn't looking at Celeste. "Yeah, probably not. He's just been super distant lately."

Celeste studied Alabama, trying to decide what to make of this. Before she could come to a conclusion, however, Alabama's face lit up. Across the room, Hollie Goodwin had appeared in the doorway. Alabama started toward her without looking back.

Celeste had never met Hollie personally, but with over a million followers, Hollie was far and away the biggest name on the trip. The babydoll dress she was wearing was an objectively horrendous shade of tangerine, but Hollie's face was pretty enough that she could pull it off. Celeste would personally never attempt such a color. In fact, Celeste rarely attempted babydoll dresses at all. Without a definitive waistline, the style transformed Celeste's average-sized body into the Goodyear blimp.

Celeste paused for a moment, debating. It was times like this that she wished Alabama wasn't quite so social. Celeste didn't want to talk to Hollie Goodwin, as Celeste had the annoying tendency to chatter stupidly when she was around important people.

For a moment, Celeste considered leaving Alabama to fend for herself. She could grab a plate of food from the buffet and settle silently beside the Emily-Margot complex. This was not an ideal scenario by any stretch of the imagination, but it was certainly less intimidating than introducing herself to Hollie.

And yet, since Henry had told Celeste about Alabama's "condition"—a frankly inadequate description, although Celeste could think of no better word—Celeste had promised herself to support Alabama in whatever way possible, even if Alabama still didn't know that Celeste knew.

By the time Celeste reached Alabama and Hollie, Alabama already had one hand on Hollie's shoulder. Celeste felt a small, selfish sense of satisfaction that up close, Hollie's upper arms didn't look much thinner than her own.

"Love this," Alabama was saying, pinching the fabric of Hollie's dress like they were not two people who had only just met. "So cute."

"Thanks," Hollie said, taking a tiny step backward, out of Alabama's reach. Celeste didn't blame her. She would have felt the same way if a stranger had been pinching her outfit.

Beside Hollie, another one of the influencers appeared—Katherine, if Celeste remembered correctly. She was a busty redhead with matte plum lipstick and the sturdiness of a horse.

"Hi there," Celeste said, deciding to inject herself into the conversation before it became too awkward. She smiled, trying to ignore the fact that her hands seemed much bigger and more obtrusive than she remembered. She wondered what she normally did with them. "I'm Celeste." She stuck one out, hoping a handshake wasn't too formal for the situation.

"Katherine," the redhead said, sounding bored.

When Celeste took Hollie's hand, Alabama exhaled quietly under her breath.

"So, Hollie," Alabama said. She had angled her shoulders away from Celeste slightly, crowding her out. "I know you run. I also run—not, like, super seriously or anything, but seriously enough. Maybe you and I could go on a run tomorrow? Before the glacier hike?"

Celeste noticed Hollie's jaw working beneath a tasteful layer of bronzer.

"Oh, I don't—" Hollie started, but Alabama cut her off.

"Or maybe after the glacier hike? Would that be better? Or maybe the next day?"

Hollie shifted her weight. Her obvious discomfort triggered something maternal in Celeste, some unconscious reflex. She wanted to defuse the situation, although she wasn't sure whom or what to defuse.

"Sure," Hollie said. Her eyes moved over Alabama's shoulder, which Alabama didn't seem to notice. Instead, Alabama continued chattering, first about her shoes, then about chafing, then about energy gels and hydration gummies and some sort of running tape. Celeste had never heard of any of it before because Celeste—much like Alabama, until very recently—did not run.

CHAPTER

15

Hollie

The Day Before
Reykjavík, Iceland

HOLLIE BARELY ATE anything at dinner. She spent most of the evening poking at a broccolini stalk covered in too much oil and nudging a jiggly square of tofu around her plate. No one seemed to notice this except maybe the crazy chick Alabama, who spent most of her time hovering by Hollie's elbow. Twice Hollie had pivoted slightly, sending her arm smashing into Alabama's chest. Alabama had apologized quickly and scuttled out of the way, only to return to the exact same position a few seconds after that.

Hollie was used to strangers acting like they knew her. In some ways, they did. It was the nature of the business, the inevitable outcome of treating one million followers like friends. Most people, though, understood that Hollie wasn't actually their friend, and even those who didn't at least pretended they did.

"Coming through!" someone barked. The women around Hollie parted hastily, making way for the bed and breakfast owner, who had emerged from behind the kitchen door. She held a platter above her head and moved unsteadily enough that Hollie wondered whether that was a good idea.

The conversation in the room dimmed to a murmur as Delphine, the bed and breakfast owner, marched across the room to the buffet table, which had been cleared a few minutes prior. Five pink balloons swayed when Delphine placed the platter down.

She turned to the group. Up close, Hollie could see that the platter held three loaves of something—bread, although it smelled sweeter, like cake. Beside Hollie, Katherine picked at a hangnail disinterestedly using her teeth. Alabama was standing close enough to Hollie that Hollie could hear her breath.

Delphine cleared her throat and straightened her shoulders. The smell of influencers had permeated the small dining room—a mix of expensive perfume and burned hairspray—and mingled with the sweetness, the collective effect was nauseating. Hollie glanced around, looking for a window she could open.

"Lava bread," Delphine announced, gesturing to the loaves. "Sometimes called volcanic bread. A traditional Icelandic dish."

The women around Hollie leaned forward to get a better look, except Katherine, who exhaled a bit of hangnail from between her lips.

Delphine smiled broadly. She had straight teeth, but they were the color of popcorn. After a dramatic pause, she proceeded to explain the dish with the practiced, slightly robotic cadence of a kid at a science fair. She told them how the dough was cooked in the ground for twenty-four hours, buried deep in a tightly sealed pot. "Geothermic energy," Delphine explained importantly, and around her, the women's expressions ranged from curiosity to worry, apparently unsure whether geothermal energy was a good thing or not.

Hollie wondered vaguely how Delphine knew no dirt had leaked into the pot during the process, although she didn't ask, and Delphine did not find this a pertinent part of her presentation. Actually, Delphine looked like the sort of person who might consider a touch of dirt to be a good thing. The woman had evidently attempted dreadlocks but had seemingly given up midway through, resulting in five or six frizzy stalks resting sadly on a tangled mat of silvery blonde hair. She wasn't ugly, but she did remind Hollie of an old boot that had been left outside for too long. Her appearance was a stark contrast to the trip coordinator, Skye, who nodded attentively while pushing feathery bangs out of her face.

Skye was five foot one at best and one of the thinnest people Hollie had ever seen.

"I'm going to go get some air," Hollie said to no one in particular just as Delphine beckoned them forward to try the bread. The group looked at one another warily, clearly distrustful. No one seemed to notice Hollie slipping out of the room and into the front hall.

The hall was dim and depressing, with a single cloudy window that looked as grimy as Delphine's hair. Hollie clicked on her phone as she made her way toward the front door.

Skye had distributed a list of hashtags earlier in the evening, some of which had already amassed fifty or sixty posts. Hollie scanned the pictures, searching corners and edges where she might have been captured unaware. So far, there were none.

She wondered how long it would take before she would be forced to post a full body shot of herself. Twenty-four hours? Less? The good thing about Iceland was that she could hide beneath layers of down jackets and wool cardigans, and no one would think it was weird.

It was disorienting opening the door to a wash of soft daytime light even though it was almost nine. There was no porch, just a tiny square landing. Hollie closed the door behind her and stepped to the edge. Eyes shut, she drew in a deep breath. She thought randomly, unwelcomingly, of Robin, how she had the annoying tendency to breathe out of only her nose on runs. Robin had asked Hollie to go on a catch-up run shortly before Hollie had left for Iceland. Hollie had said no, so sorry, but she was swamped, she had to pack. Anything but the truth, that Hollie hadn't run in weeks.

Behind Hollie, the front door creaked. Hollie opened her eyes and was not totally surprised to see Alabama stepping through it. Before that evening, Hollie might have seen Alabama Wood online, although she wasn't completely sure, as there was nothing distinguishable about her. Alabama was thin, blonde, and white, which meant she was like ninety-nine percent of all the influencers out there.

"Hey, Holl."

Hollie cringed. There was a short list of people who abbreviated her name, and an even shorter list of people who didn't bother Hollie when they did.

"It was super hot in there, wasn't it? And loud?" Alabama stepped to the edge of the landing so she was standing beside Hollie. The questions seemed rhetorical, but Alabama cocked her head to one side as though she expected an answer.

"Pretty stuffy," Hollie agreed, her gaze cast forward. The bed and breakfast was situated near the top of the hill, looking down on the other buildings below. Most were boxy and monochromatic, a life-sized version of a child's toy town.

For a while, they both looked out, saying nothing. In her head, Hollie calculated the time in Dallas—five hours behind, so it was

nearly four. She pictured people back home going about their ordinary afternoon business, never once considering that halfway around
the world, in Iceland, it was almost nighttime.

"Nick must be, like, really struggling, huh?"

Hollie felt this question as much as she heard it. It was as though
Alabama had reached over and stuck her finger in Hollie's eye. The
base of Hollie's neck buzzed as she turned, the familiar sensation of
fight or flight already firing. The thought of Alabama knowing about
her separation from Nick made Hollie feel as though she might actually be sick.

"What do you mean?" Hollie tried and failed to keep her voice
steady. If Alabama noticed this, however, she did not react. She was
leaning forward against the railing, gazing down at her feet. She
seemed to be lost in her own world.

"Just, you know"—Alabama shrugged—"that you're so far away
and all."

"Oh. Uh, yeah, I guess." Hollie took a long, centering breath. *Of
course she doesn't know,* she told herself. *How would she?*

"I'm married too," Alabama said moodily, jamming her chin into
her palm. "But I doubt my husband misses me." She shot Hollie a
bitter look. "Me and my husband aren't like you and Nick."

16

Celeste

The Day Before
Reykjavík, Iceland

WHEN THEY RETURNED to their bedroom later that night, Celeste noticed Alabama's leg muscles, which seemed to pop a little more insistently than Celeste remembered. They changed into their pajamas and removed their makeup, and when Alabama crossed the room to turn off the light, Celeste's eyes caught on the sharp line of Alabama's collarbone, which also looked much sharper, now that Celeste thought about it.

"Holl and I are going to run tomorrow before breakfast," Alabama said once the room was dark. "I set my alarm for five."

Celeste clenched her teeth without meaning to. She had her comforter pulled to her chin, but she felt cold regardless. She still could not imagine Alabama running and felt uneasy about why she suddenly was. She thought of Henry, the way he had flinched when he had told Celeste what was happening. "She was obsessed with a thing," he had told her. "I was afraid she was going to hurt herself or somebody else."

But he wasn't worried anymore, Celeste reminded herself. Alabama was seeing a doctor. She was on some kind of medicine. Henry had insisted that there was nothing more to do, nothing left to worry about, and who was Celeste to challenge him on that?

"You know," Alabama said, apparently not noticing Celeste's silence, "Hollie looks a lot bigger in person than she does online."

Celeste fingered the edge of the comforter.

"Yeah, she does."

"She's been married for, like, ten years. Did you know that?"

Celeste didn't know that. She found she was not surprised that Alabama did.

There was a pause, then Alabama said, sounding sleepy, "Do you think she could be pregnant?"

Celeste thought about this for a moment. She thought of Hollie's upper arms, her calves, both of which had looked softer than Celeste would have expected from a runner. There had been no evidence of a baby bump, but Celeste knew from experience that pregnancy was by no means confined to that area of the body alone.

"Maybe," she said into the darkness, even though she really had no idea.

Another silence, this one long enough that Celeste thought Alabama had fallen asleep. Light crept in from the edges of the blackout shades above Alabama's bed, and in the shadow, her body made a slender black lump.

"A baby announcement," Alabama murmured after a while, rolling over. "That'd be a thing, wouldn't it?"

Alabama started snoring before Celeste could think of a response.

PART III

A Good Plan

17

Celeste

The Morning After
Vík, Iceland

T HE BED AND breakfast owner—Delphine, a Seattle transplant
who smelled like one part sugar, two parts B.O.—hovered for a
moment at the side of the table where Celeste and Officer Björnsson
sat.

"Ginger and rooibos," she said, nodding to the teapot she had just
set down between them, which rattled slightly as Celeste uncrossed
her legs and hit her knee on the edge of the small table.

"Thank you," Officer Björnsson said politely. Celeste nodded in
agreement. Delphine clapped her hands together and bowed, revealing a halo of tangled hair at the crown of her head. Celeste suspected
that the hair was the reason Delphine smelled, which she recognized
as a rude thing to think, if even in her own head.

Celeste took a small sip of the tea as Delphine left the kitchen.
Celeste had never had rooibos tea before, and she decided almost
immediately that she didn't like it.

Across the table, Officer Björnsson brought the edge of his cup to
his lips. His lips were thin, but a nice thin, not like Celeste's, which
made her mouth look too small and her round cheeks too big.

"Not very good, is it?" Officer Björnsson said, lowering the cup
back to the table. He scrunched his nose endearingly, and Celeste

smiled before she could remind herself not to. She had already worked out that Officer Björnsson was probably the good cop of the good cop/bad cop duo, but Celeste still kept forgetting that they were not in fact friends.

"I never thought tea was worth it if there's no caffeine."

She hadn't meant for this to be a joke necessarily, but Officer Björnsson chuckled anyway. Celeste was annoyed with herself for how pleased this made her.

"I didn't drink caffeine before my daughters were born," he said. "Can you imagine?"

Celeste smiled but didn't say anything. Officer Björnsson had four daughters, apparently. The youngest one was Bella's age, and when he had told Celeste this, she had immediately pictured a miniature Officer Björnsson with wispy blonde pigtails and pink, ribbony lips.

"Anyway, where were we?" He glanced down at his notes. "Right. Okay, so how do you and Alabama know each other? Through PinkPurse?"

Celeste snorted in amusement, causing Officer Björnsson to look up. She immediately sobered, scolding herself internally.

"Oh, no. We've been friends for much longer. Since college, actually."

Officer Björnsson didn't jot this down. Something about his expression looked doubtful, although Celeste wasn't sure which part he found suspect. Probably the snort. He probably didn't trust anyone who could *snort* at a time like this.

"And how long ago was that?" Officer Björnsson said.

"Let's just say we're the millennials all the young kids make fun of on TikTok." She attempted an indulgent smile, which Officer Björnsson returned. Suddenly, Celeste's expression felt more maniacal than anything. "A little over ten years, I think," she added, her tone businesslike. "The internet was hardly a thing."

This wasn't technically true. Celeste had vivid memories of Alabama—over-tanned and over-highlighted—in their dorm room, providing grave commentary on recent Facebook developments. Oliver's dating Leslie, or, did you see Devin's new car? Facebook, then, had still been relevant to the young people. Instagram had existed, but the real information—the information everyone talked about—was on Facebook.

"Got it," Officer Björnsson said. Celeste tried to peek at what he was writing without making it obvious, although his handwriting was messy and nearly impossible to read upside down. "So, you know Alabama's husband then?"

Beneath the edge of the table, Celeste pressed her palms flat against her thigh. She found the slight pressure calming, as though her hands were preventing her from floating up and away. She thought of Bella, who flicked her fingers when she was anxious or stressed. Celeste had only noticed it recently. Bella had been sitting at the kitchen table, ramrod straight except for her two pointer fingers, which she had *flick flick flicked* against respective thumbs. "What are you doing with your fingers, Bells?" Celeste had said, trying not to appear irritated by the repetitive sound. Bella hadn't looked up to answer. "It makes me feel less jumbly," she had said, an answer Celeste had not fully understood until just now.

"Yes. He and Alabama met a little over five years ago, I think."

"And you've spent time with the two of them together?"

Celeste nodded without saying anything. She allowed herself to consider for a moment how outrageous her situation was—a remote village in Iceland, an unnecessarily handsome cop asking her about Henry Wood. She could have laughed at the absurdity of it, and that thought filled her with an intense, unexpected longing for Alabama, who would have laughed along with her.

The reality of Alabama's disappearance seemed to hit Celeste in earnest then. She felt it somewhere deep in her chest, and for a moment it seemed impossible to take a full breath.

"Do you think it's possible that Alabama's husband could be involved with her disappearance?" the officer asked her. "Indirectly, in some way? Can you think of any reason he might want to see her hurt?"

Without meaning to, Celeste laughed, one undignified guffaw.

"Sorry," she said, feeling heat rising to her ears. "It's just—no. No, Henry would never hurt Alabama. Definitely not."

She shook her head, thinking of Henry's round wire glasses, the way he flattened his tie when he was uncomfortable. Once, years ago, when Celeste had been helping Alabama plan their wedding, he had made them each a tomato mayonnaise sandwich with tomatoes from his garden. As Alabama had gone on and on about the cost of peonies and the pros and cons of a three-piece string quartet, Celeste had watched Henry from the kitchen table, slicing his tomatoes with such tenderness that she had felt a brief, inexplicable surge of envy— not of Alabama, but of the tomatoes, the way his fingers had moved so lovingly against their skin.

"Got it," Officer Björnsson said, scribbling something on his pad. "Just wanted to ask."

18

Celeste

Three Months Before
Chicago, Illinois

Because of their meeting with Miss Sheryl and Miss Bonnie, Celeste and Louis pulled up to the restaurant ten minutes later than they had planned. Alabama had picked the place, a busy Spanish restaurant on an even busier street. The restaurant was not exorbitantly nice, but it was nice enough to have an optional valet.

Louis didn't like using valets, as he didn't trust anyone parking his car but himself. Celeste didn't mind the help—she preferred it, actually, as she had never been particularly good at parking—but she tended to avoid valets anyway, as she never felt confident about how much to tip.

If Celeste had been driving, tonight would have been an exception to her stance on valets, as the curbside was busy and they were already late. But she wasn't driving, and it annoyed her profoundly that Louis refused to even consider the option.

They were nearly twenty minutes late by the time they got into the restaurant. Henry and Alabama were already waiting for them at the table.

"We got a bottle of Shiraz," Alabama said, nodding to the bottle in the middle of the table. Henry smiled and stood politely, like he usually did when Celeste entered the room.

"Sorry we're late," Celeste said, feeling breathy. Alabama either didn't hear her or wasn't interested in the apology, because she didn't respond.

"Good to see you, man," Louis said, swiping his hand out for one of those manly hug-shakes that looked mostly ridiculous coming from Louis, who weighed one fifty-five on a good day. Watching Henry return the gesture stiffly was almost painful.

"So glad you could come out," Alabama said, holding Celeste at arm's length. "Wine? Or are you driving? God, I love that blazer on you."

Louis pulled Celeste's chair out for her. She lowered herself into it as she waved the wine away.

"Driving," she decided, because it was easier than explaining to Alabama again that red wine gave her a headache. "And thanks. I got it at the Nordstrom sale last year."

Alabama appraised Celeste long enough to make Celeste feel self-conscious. Celeste ran her fingers over one of her silver buttons. She had felt polished the first time she had worn the blazer—to a dinner with Louis's colleagues last month—but now the heavy fabric felt outdated and stuffy.

"I don't remember it," Alabama said finally, even though Celeste was certain Alabama had helped her pick it out. Before Celeste could remind her, however, Alabama turned to Louis, who was pouring himself a glass of the Shiraz.

"I heard you got Franklin Marks," she said. "Congrats."

Franklin Marks was Louis's new, flashy client, the biggest he had ever signed on his own. Since the contract, he had had started humming in the shower and wearing cuff links to work.

Louis shrugged. Celeste could tell he was trying very hard not to look too pleased.

"Thanks." And then—apparently unable to resist—he grinned. "A few kinks to work out, but it's been a long time coming."

Alabama reached over for the bottle and tipped some more wine into her own glass, even though it wasn't completely empty. "Still," she said, leaning on one elbow. "Celeste says you're gonna get a huge raise now, right?"

Celeste shot Alabama a look, although Alabama didn't notice. Celeste then searched for Louis's eyes, arranging her face into a silent apology. She and Louis had never explicitly agreed not to talk about money with their friends, but it seemed like an unspoken rule that Celeste had only broken this one time, and only because she had been so frustrated. It had been right after the catalytic converter of Louis's Acura had pooped. Celeste had been venting to Alabama more than anything.

But Louis didn't seem annoyed. If anything, he looked proud.

"That's the plan." He chuckled and took a hearty gulp of wine. "Seems like we've got a lot to celebrate tonight, with you ladies getting the invite for the big PinkPurse trip." He tipped his glass toward Alabama and then at his wife.

"Yes, cheers to Al and Celeste," Henry said, raising his own glass for a toast. The top button of his shirt was buttoned, providing a stark contrast to Louis, who kept running one hand through his hair to make it look unkempt.

"Hear, hear," Louis echoed as Alabama raised her own glass, the deep red catching in the dim overhead light. Celeste clinked theirs with her water.

"Congrats, CeCe," Alabama said, bringing the drink to her lips. Her expression was genuine enough that Celeste couldn't help but smile back.

The restaurant was alive and humming, the conversations around them punctuated every so often by the jingle of fork tines against china or a roar of laughter. It was crowded, and tables were packed in so close that twice Celeste had to scoot her chair forward to let someone pass behind her for the restroom. Alabama prattled on about the trip to Iceland, about who was going and who was not and who had been left off the invite list entirely, if Alabama's sources were correct (which she was "mostly totally positive" they were). They finished the bottle of Shiraz, and when the waitress came to take their order, Louis ordered a pitcher of white sangria.

Alabama took charge of their orders, bending her fingers one by one as she listed off the small plates—ceviche and patatas bravas and some sort of cheese dish that sounded good but which Celeste probably wouldn't eat, as cheese upset her stomach. Louis piped up near the end with a request for the chorizo skewers—"I need real meat," he said, nudging Henry with an elbow. Henry smiled uncomfortably and thanked the waitress, although the waitress didn't seem to hear him over the buzz of voices in the dining room.

As the waitress gathered their menus, Alabama continued talking as if there hadn't been an interruption. When the waitress eventually returned with the sangria, no one besides Alabama had said much more than a few words. Celeste was only half listening, as she was much more interested in her phone. Each time she tapped it and found the screen still empty, her anxiety mounted.

Bella was spending the night at Celeste's parents', and while Celeste hadn't explicitly asked her mother for updates, she still would have appreciated one. A part of her felt her mother should have intuited this without Celeste having to say so, although when it came to Celeste and her mother, things were rarely intuited. They talked a normal amount, but their relationship had the stinted feeling of two people who were meant to be close but could never quite get there. If you asked Celeste, the issue was Celeste's existence. Celeste had been an accident—a fact her brothers had somewhat cruelly revealed when she was young—and Celeste suspected her mother had never quite gotten over the shock.

Whatever the reason, Celeste had always felt the vague sense that they were continually moving in opposite directions, just missing each other on the way by. Earlier that afternoon, for example, when Celeste had dropped off Bella, Celeste and her mother had managed to have an entire conversation around an issue without ever actually acknowledging the issue out loud. "I packed both the strawberry and mint," Celeste had explained about Bella's toothpaste, handing her mother Bella's overnight bag. "I usually let Bella pick." Celeste's mother had taken the bag with a befuddled expression, and had the two women shared a different kind of relationship, Celeste might have told her mother how Bella had strong and inconsistent feelings on the flavors, how picking the wrong one all but ensured that Bella would clamp her mouth shut for the rest of the night. It was a tactic that both exhausted and irritated Celeste to the point that she started doubting her own competence as a parent, a fact another woman might have confided in her mom. Instead, Celeste had simply leaned down to kiss Bella's head, which Bella had absorbed like a punch.

"So, you're definitely going, right, CeCe?"

Celeste's screen dimmed as she looked up.

"Sorry. What?"

Alabama was leaning back in her seat but, sensing that she did not have Celeste's full attention, she pushed herself forward. Celeste noticed that the sangria pitcher was already half empty, which might have explained Alabama's intensity. She was the sort of person who got pushy when she was drunk.

"I said you're definitely coming to Iceland, right?"

Her tone was combative, as if she already knew the answer.

"Oh. Um." Celeste fingered the napkin on her lap. "I haven't decided yet."

"You haven't *decided* yet?" Alabama over-enunciated the word *decided* so it had an extra syllable. "You've got to go, CeCe. Give me one good reason why you wouldn't."

"I just don't know about leaving Bella for that long," Celeste said, not really expecting Alabama to understand. No one could understand it, not if they didn't have children. Even to Celeste, it had been shocking, how every single decision as a parent—every single one—was so fraught. What to have for dinner. The types of movies you watched. Even what laundry detergent you used. Nothing was ever simple. Every decision opened the door to consequence.

Alabama exhaled heavily. "Ohmygod. It's barely even a week."

"It'll be about a week when you add in the travel." Celeste straightened her shoulders defensively. "And I just don't think it's a good time for me to leave her right now."

"Not a good time for her? She's five!" Alabama threw up her hands. "She doesn't have, like, important business meetings or something."

Celeste pursed her lips and looked over at Louis. She wasn't sure if she was searching for help or just commiseration.

Louis drew in a breath. "Celeste is worried Bella might have autism," he said, and Celeste—so unprepared for this announcement—choked on her drink. She sensed both Alabama and Henry turning to face her. Her eyes watered uncooperatively as she hacked in Louis's general direction. In his face, she could see now what she hadn't seen before, the alcohol swimming behind his gaze giving him a slightly unfocused expression.

"You think Bella's autistic?" Alabama said quietly.

Celeste was still coughing. When she could finally speak, her voice was hoarse.

"I don't know." She shot Louis a reproachful look. "She's just been acting up a lot lately."

Louis seemed to understand Celeste's unspoken reprisal. He lowered his drink to the table and rubbed the back of his neck, looking flustered. It apparently hadn't occurred to him that this might be an inappropriate thing to just blurt out.

"Acting up how?" Alabama pressed.

"Just—I don't know." Celeste took a drink and cleared her throat. "She just gets really upset about things that are not that upsetting. Like at Nordstrom, you know?"

The table fell silent. Celeste longed for the waitress to come out with their patatas bravas, or to come out and set the table on fire. Any distraction, really, would have been welcome.

"Well, I don't think that means she's autistic," Alabama said finally. She brushed some hair over her shoulder with an authoritative sweep. "I know when I was little, I used to throw massive tantrums. *Massive.* Like, one time when I was five, my grandpa made me this amazing dollhouse—real wood shingles and tiny little light switches that actually worked and—well, anyway, my mom wanted me to share it with my cousin Linda. I liked Linda alright, but I still went ballistic. I remember, before Linda came over, I totally trashed the house. Stomped the whole thing to smithereens. My mom was so mad."

Alabama snorted and took a sip of sangria. Across the table, Henry shifted his weight. Louis mouthed the word *sorry* to Celeste, and Celeste looked down at her still-blank phone, filled with a sudden urge to fling it across the dining room.

"Anyway, you should still come, CeCe," Alabama said. "Whether she's autistic or not, that's not gonna change if you skip this trip."

Celeste didn't have anything to say to this, so she didn't say anything. Evidently taking her silence as agreement, Alabama continued on about something that Celeste didn't hear.

When the waitress came back with their first plate—the cheese one, unhelpfully—Louis's phone rang.

"Robbie," he said, looking at all of them, although Celeste was probably the only person who knew Louis's managing partner by name. "I should take this." He bowed apologetically and stood. As he passed by Celeste, he squeezed her on the shoulder. He then headed toward the door with the swiftness of someone fleeing a crime.

The waitress filled their water glasses and assured them that the rest of the food would be out shortly. Henry thanked her yet again, and she smiled at him this time. She was young and cute with an endearing gap between her two front teeth.

"I've gotta pee," Alabama announced after the waitress had left. She grabbed her sequined coin purse, which she draped over her shoulder. "Get another pitcher of sangria if she comes back."

Celeste reached for the pitcher, which was indeed nearly empty. Deciding that one small glass would be okay even if she was driving, she started to pour herself the rest.

"You know," Henry said as Celeste replaced the pitcher in the middle of the table, "it's different because they're older, but with the kids I teach, I've noticed that the moms see things first." He touched one of the buttons on his shirt like he was rearranging a microphone. "And it's never really the fathers, for some reason. Just the moms. They tend to just know things about their children before anyone else."

He met Celeste's eyes across the table, and it struck Celeste how rarely she talked to Henry one-on-one like this. They had spent a significant amount of time together over the years, but they were almost always with Alabama, who had a tendency to bulldoze conversations. Henry taught twelfth grade history—American or European, Celeste could never remember which.

"Thanks, Henry," she said. She wanted to say something else, but she couldn't articulate what, so instead she let the sentence float off.

Later that evening, when they were back in the car, Celeste rearranged the rearview mirror and was glad she didn't have to worry about a valet tip. She almost said something to Louis about this before realizing that she already knew how he would respond. *You worry too much, Celeste.*

"Alabama sure can talk, can't she?" Louis said as Celeste pulled their car from the curb. She glanced down at the clock, debating whether it was early enough that they could swing by her parents' and grab Bella on the way home.

"Yes," Celeste said simply, striking the blinker to switch lanes. It was too late to get Bella, she decided. It would be almost nine once they got to her parents', and she didn't want to wake Bella up.

"I'm sorry for bringing up the autism thing," Louis said. He reached over and placed a hand on her knee. "I shouldn't have said anything to them."

"It's okay," Celeste said. She let the words settle for a moment, trying to decide if they were true. By the time Louis pulled his hand away and leaned against his headrest, she had decided they were mostly true, at least.

At home, Celeste shrugged off her blazer as Louis apologized again. Then he kissed her, lingering just long enough to make clear he wanted more. But he was drunk, and she was tired, so she kissed him back firmly, then peeled his hands from her waist, ignoring his downtrodden expression as she slipped into her nightgown. They had sex once, sometimes twice a week on average, so she didn't feel particularly bad for him tonight.

In the end, it didn't even matter, as within minutes of flipping off the lights, she could hear that he was asleep. Celeste, on the other hand, just stared at the ceiling, suddenly feeling wide awake. She thought of her mom when Celeste had called her after dinner. "Fine, fine. It all went well," her mom had said. Bella had picked the strawberry toothpaste without incident, and she was sleeping soundly now.

Celeste thought again of Henry, of what he'd told her at dinner. *Just the moms.* She wondered if that was true, and whether he had intentionally waited until they were alone to say it.

19

Hollie

Three Months Before
Dallas, Texas

T HE FIRST THING Hollie should have done when she remembered the pill was call Nick, but she didn't. She didn't call him as she turned the faucet off, as she slowly set her toothbrush down on the ledge of the sink. She didn't call him as she moved to the bedroom. Instead, she pulled on a pair of black athletic leggings and swept her still-damp hair into a loose bun.

She didn't call him at the CVS either. He hardly crossed her mind. The only person she thought about was Mallory.

Mallory and her husband had tried for seven months before they had finally gotten pregnant with Fiona, but it was not until this very moment—standing in the stuffy, over-lit family planning section of the drugstore—that Hollie considered how expensive seven months worth of pregnancy tests would be.

She thought of Nick after she took the test—after she had peed, then dabbed the little window with a square of toilet paper to remove a rogue drop of urine. She looked at the test and then at the box, confirming what the second line meant.

And that's when she thought of Nick. She wondered whether she should keep the box in case he too wanted to confirm the results, or whether he would take her word for it. She pondered this for just a moment before throwing both the box and the test in the trash.

She didn't know how long Nick planned to stay at the office. He didn't usually go in on the weekends, and when he did, it was usually only for an hour or two at most. Hollie checked her phone as she left the bathroom, then checked it again once she was in the kitchen, as the numbers on the clock hadn't registered the first time.

She lowered herself onto the couch in the living room and turned on the TV. Later, Hollie would try to remember what she had watched on TV or even what channel had been on, but she would come up with nothing. All she would remember was sitting down on the sofa, then receiving Nick's text message, as though the hours between these two events had slipped into a wrinkle of time.

When Nick was on his way home, she moved to the kitchen for no real reason. It was not dark outside, but it was cloudy, and her windows were situated in such a way that it could have been dusk.

She didn't know what it said about her, that she hadn't been able to feel it. It—The fetus? Was that the word for it?—was presumably just a microscopic clump of cells at this point, but it was a foreign clump of cells. It was a clump of cells that weren't hers, and shouldn't she be able to feel something like that?

Across their house, the key in the front door echoed in the silence. Hollie didn't notice herself rising from her chair until she was already standing, and Nick was flicking on the lights.

"It's dark in here," Nick said, lowering his hand. He studied her for a moment, looking concerned. "And you're standing."

The concern didn't suit him. Some people had faces for worry, but Hollie's husband did not.

"I didn't notice," Hollie said, unsure which one she was talking about, the darkness or the standing. Both, really.

She watched Nick consider this, and she was not totally surprised when he seemed to find it passable. He shrugged as he proceeded to the sink, where he deposited his empty travel mug.

"Sorry that took so long," he said as he filled the cup with water. "There's this new kid in the IT department—Granger. I guess he works weekends. It's crazy—everything he knows, he taught himself on YouTube. YouTube! It's wild." He turned to Hollie. "Anyway, I'm craving a margarita from Paz Teeker's. What do you think about happy hour?"

Hollie took his face in for a moment, all straight edges save for the perpetual boyish softness of his eyes. And then, without really meaning to, she made a decision.

"I'm pregnant," she said.

Nick froze. It occurred to Hollie that she was still standing, and she felt the sudden urge to cover her stomach.

"What?" Nick said at last.

"I'm pregnant," Hollie repeated even though she knew he had heard.

"But you're on the pill." Nick's hands were raised slightly in an athletic position, elbows slightly bent, like he was a millisecond away from sprinting.

"The pill fails sometimes."

There was a long pause. Hollie had never before wished she could read minds, as she was usually good enough at reading faces. In this moment, however, she wanted more than anything to read Nick's.

And then, right as Hollie was about to say something—she didn't know what, but something—Nick's face broke open. It took Hollie a second to register the expression as a smile, and then another second to compute the meaning. Happiness. It felt so irrelevant to the conversation they were having.

"That's . . ." Nick took a step forward. His voice trailed off, and before Hollie knew what was happening, he was in front of her, and then his arms were around her, thick and familiar and full of cinnamon deodorant.

"Oh my god," he murmured with such feeling that Hollie's mind sputtered back on. She took a step back, out of his arms, and for one horrifying second, she thought he was crying, even though it was just a reflection from the light.

"I don't want to be pregnant," she said. Her voice was barely louder than a whisper. She knew how this probably sounded, how the bluntness possibly bordered on cruel, but she had to tell him. He had to know now, before whatever was growing inside him was too big to put out.

Nick's hand was still on her forearm. It tensed infinitesimally against her skin. She watched his smile disappear from his face in pieces—first his eyes, the fine lines smoothing slightly, and then the corners of his lips drawing down. And then, finally, his eyebrows gathering in the middle as his eyes moved across her face.

She should have said this sooner, she realized. Looking at Nick's face now, she knew without a doubt that she should have been honest with him from the start. But that, of course, would have required her to be honest with herself.

"You don't want a baby right now," he said. It didn't sound like a question—more like a confirmation of something he didn't want to be true.

In a single second, she was able to see two alternate versions of their lives unrolling before her like ribbons, each starting from this one spot.

"I don't want a baby at all."

Her whisper felt insufficient, but a whisper was all she could manage.

Nick looked at her for a moment. He was searching for something that Hollie didn't think he would find.

"Since when?" he said finally, with a sort of helplessness she had never heard from him before. "I thought you wanted kids."

"I thought I did too," she said.

For a moment, they were both quiet. Hollie thought of Mallory the last time she had been over. She hadn't had Fiona, so Hollie had made them both an elaborate cup of coffee using her French press. Mallory had been so impressed.

"What changed?"

Hearing Nick's voice, Hollie forced herself to meet his eyes. She had always known she had the power to break hearts, but never had she considered that she could break her own too.

"I don't know," she said. "I really don't." It was the most honest answer she could come up with. Maybe it had changed because of Mallory, or maybe nothing had changed at all. Maybe Hollie had been this person all along.

Nick didn't say anything right away. Instead, he scratched the back of his neck slowly, digesting these words. She knew he was trying to come up with a solution, an answer to this mess they had found themselves in.

"Okay," he said slowly. And then again, more softly, "Okay."

He didn't seem to be thinking anymore. He had come to the only conclusion there was.

When he left the room a few minutes later, his shoulders bowed in a way they normally didn't. Hollie watched him go, and when he had turned the corner to their bedroom, she closed her eyes. She expected tears to burn, but they didn't. She didn't feel anything at all except hunger. She suddenly felt hungrier than she had ever felt in her life.

She stepped over to the refrigerator and flung it open, where a cardboard box of non-GMO kale beamed at her from the middle shelf. She could slice a cucumber, crumble some nondairy feta on top. She could so easily, like she had so many times before, but Hollie was suddenly too hungry to wait for that. Ravenous. She was ravenous, and she didn't have even five minutes to toss all her nutrient-dense foods together.

Instead, she pulled out a carton of yogurt. It was Nick's—not remotely vegan, but Hollie suddenly didn't care. She whipped out a spoon and scooped up a bite straight from the plastic tub. It was almost like her hand wasn't part of her body, an independent invader shoveling the yogurt into her mouth.

She wondered whether Nick would leave her, and if he didn't, whether she was strong enough to leave him.

And the baby. Would there be a baby? There couldn't be a baby, but what was her other option? Taking this from Nick did not feel like freedom at all.

No time had passed, not even a second, when Hollie looked down and realized her spoon had smashed into the bottom of the plastic tub. Almost thirty-two ounces of yogurt, gone. She blinked slowly, realizing how many calories she had just eaten. How much lactose and sugar. The thought was sickening. Revolting. And yet . . .

Like her hand, her legs seemed to move of their own accord, without her permission. She pulled open the pantry, her eyes scanning the shelves for something that she didn't even want. Her hand—her damn hand—reached up and plucked down a box of crackers, which she ripped from their sleeve with an urgency that made little sense. As the first one touched her lips, she wondered if she would throw it up after all the yogurt. She chewed and swallowed and went for another. It was astonishing, really, how much she could shove in her mouth and still not be full.

CHAPTER

20

Celeste

Three Months Before
Chicago, Illinois

THE DAY AFTER Celeste and Louis's dinner with Alabama and Henry, Celeste awoke to a polite but slightly panicked email from Bella's team mom. The kids' jerseys, apparently, were running even later than expected and wouldn't be delivered in time for their first game that day.

The kids can wear pinnies, the woman assured them. *No need for concern!*

Celeste didn't find the situation all that concerning, although the same could not be said for her daughter. Celeste only managed to avoid a full-scale meltdown by promising Bella that she could wear her dolphin T-shirt beneath her pinny for the game.

And this was how Celeste found herself elbow deep in a pile of dirty laundry at just past seven, fishing for a shirt she hadn't yet washed. She found it smashed at the very bottom, crumpled and smelling a bit too funky for Bella to wear. Celeste gathered the shirt and a few towels to throw in the laundry, and when the dryer beckoned Celeste ninety minutes later, Louis took over the tail end of breakfast so she could fold.

Celeste could hear them now downstairs, Louis's deep voice a garbled rumble, shuffled in with Bella's delighted squeals. Celeste

found herself smiling as she listened to them talk. It occasionally
felt unfair that Louis got to be the fun parent, leaving Celeste to
deal with logistics and discipline, but it rarely bothered her. Fair-
ness, as a concept, seemed like an odd and amusing idea from
some foreign culture, decidedly unimportant when it came to their
actual lives.

Another sound, this one higher-pitched, like a trumpeting elephant, followed by a gleeful scream. Celeste felt herself softening,
which was a relief, as she had been tenser than usual all morning.

It had started the night before, after dinner with Henry and Alabama. She hadn't even noticed it happening until she had woken up
before her alarm that morning to Louis sleeping wide-mouthed and
breathing heavily. Celeste had turned her head on her pillow and—
taking him in for a moment—had felt an overwhelming, out of the
blue urge to punch his open mouth.

She wasn't sure where the impulse had come from, as she didn't
necessarily feel mad about dinner the night before. Louis had apologized, and besides, what he had done wasn't especially wrong. He
had gotten a little too buzzed and revealed something a little too personal, but the offense was so minor in the grand scheme of offenses
that it hardly seemed to count.

From the pile of laundry, Celeste plucked up Bella's shirt. Over
time, the stiff gift shop cotton had lost nearly all of its resolve. It was
now so soft around the collar that Celeste said a silent prayer each
time she threw it in the wash that it wouldn't tear.

She was spreading the shirt across the bed, debating whether
it needed to be ironed, when she noticed something dark beneath
the sheer fabric. She snatched the shirt back up, sure for one alarm-
ing instant that something had stained her quilted duvet. It took no
more than a millisecond for the alternative, more devastating option
to present itself.

She rubbed the stain between her fingers with the furious fric-
tion of someone trying to start a campfire. Her mind filled with
images of Bella thrashing against her car's tire well and onto the
asphalt of the Nordstrom parking lot. The smudge seemed to be oil,
or maybe grease. Definitely something more tenacious than dirt. It
was big enough and black enough that she couldn't send her daughter out into the world wearing it.

Celeste sighed and marched over to the bathroom. Trying to
keep as much of the shirt dry as possible, she ran the stain under the
sink faucet, scrubbing two balled hands together as water dripped

gray beneath it. Somehow, it seemed that the harder she scrubbed, the bigger the stain got, the foreign black substance spreading across the cotton fibers like roots sneaking through the dirt. She turned the water on full blast, her hands moving faster and harder until . . .

"Shit," she muttered under her breath. She brought the shirt up to eye level, allowing the sun from the bathroom window to soak through the thin fabric. The light was brightest in the spot where a tear had penetrated the black smudge.

"Okay," Louis said, appearing in the doorway. "Her Majesty is brushing her teeth. We'll be ready to go after that." His eyes found the shirt. "What's that?"

"Bella's shirt," Celeste said, fluttering it dispassionately. "The one I said she could wear today."

She waited for a moment as he digested this.

"That's not good, is it?" he said soberly. Celeste just sighed.

Not good, it turned out, was optimistically mild. Indeed, if someone were to witness Bella's reaction without context, they would have believed without too much difficulty that someone had died.

"It's mine," she sobbed into the bedspread. She had summoned a remarkable amount of tears in record time. "That's my shirt."

Outside the window, a lawnmower revved. The sound was so remarkably ordinary, it seemed to highlight by contrast the drama unfolding inside.

"Any other shirt," Celeste reasoned. "You can wear any other shirt you want."

"No other shirt," Bella cried as she melted to the floor in a tiny, grief-stricken puddle. "This shirt. You said so." She buried her head into the crook of her elbow and sobbed so hard, Celeste couldn't help but feel a pang of true pity for her.

"Isabella Renee Reed," Louis said over Celeste's shoulder. His deep voice had a startling effect. Bella raised her head, her face pink and splotchy. Celeste turned too, curious about what he planned to say that she hadn't said already.

"Get off the ground now," he ordered, motioning like he was lifting a moderately sized box. "And pick out a different shirt. We're going to be late."

Bella inhaled shakily, and for one brief instant, Celeste marveled at what she was witnessing. Was this all it took? A few stern words in a different pitch?

But then, no sooner had Celeste thought this than an expression she could only describe as betrayal washed over their daughter's face.

Bella shuddered with an onslaught of fresh tears. She wilted, the weight of this new, crueler world apparently too much to bear.

"Maybe we should . . ." Celeste started, but Louis had already stepped past her. He scooped Bella up and set her on her feet.

"We're going," he said firmly. "Bella, pick out a shirt."

Bella's body gave out once again, her previously solid limbs now no more supportive than spaghetti. Louis looked down at her and then to Celeste. He didn't look angry, she noticed—more bewildered, like he had found a human-sized pile of clothing where he had expected his daughter to be.

They did, eventually, manage to get Bella to the car. Celeste struggled to pull a clean shirt over her uncooperative head and attempted to tame her hair with a plastic headband. A few minutes later, Louis—his entire face knotted with effort—transported her little body into the garage without a semblance of Bella's help.

The field was twenty minutes away, and none of them talked on the drive over. The only sound in the car was Bella's labored sniffles from the back seat, and then the radio, when Louis was unable to stand the sound anymore.

When they got to the field, Celeste and Louis set up their folding chairs on one sideline, opposite the two groups of tiny players gathered around their respective coaches. In the glare of sunlight, it was difficult to distinguish one little body from another, although Celeste thought she could make out a purple headband hovering beside one of the coach's elbows.

Bella had stopped crying by the time they had pulled into the parking lot, although when they had reached the field, her eyes had still been swollen, giving her the impression of someone recently recovering from an allergic reaction.

"Which one's yours?"

Celeste brought her hand down from her forehead and turned to the woman smiling pleasantly to her right. Her face was a nearly perfect circle, like an adult version of a Cabbage Patch Kid.

"Oh. Um, Bella." Celeste gestured toward the purple pinnies. "She's on the Purple People Eaters."

"Ah." The woman nodded. "Declan's on the Beavers. He's"—the woman squinted across the field for a moment, then pointed—"over there. The one—oh, well, yes, that's not what we usually do with our water jugs."

The woman leaned forward and inhaled purposefully, as though she was about to shout. Celeste followed her gaze to where one child, nearly consumed by an orange jersey, was wielding a small water jug in a way that reminded Celeste of her brothers taking joyous, drunken pees in bar parking lots.

"You know what?" the woman said, leaning back in her seat. "I think I'll let the coach handle that. That's the point of this whole thing, isn't it? To make them someone else's problem for forty-five minutes?"

"And to enjoy a bit of recreational judgment, I think," Celeste said. She wasn't sure why she had said it, as she wasn't typically snarky, especially not with strangers. The woman, though, threw her head back in an open-mouthed laugh.

"I'm August Watters," the woman said, extending her hand. She was wearing a heather gray sweatshirt with *NAPERVILLE CENTRAL HIGH SCHOOL* printed across the chest. "Most people call me Auggie."

"Celeste." Celeste took Auggie's hand, which was much smaller than hers. "And this . . ." She turned, although she found Louis's chair empty. She glanced up and scanned the row of people standing around them. A few feet away, she spotted Louis talking to one of the other parents—Dan or Tom or something similarly generic. "Well, that's my husband, Louis," she said.

Auggie leaned forward to peer around Celeste. She studied Louis for a moment and then sat back with what appeared to be an approving nod.

"It's nice that both of you come to these games," she said.

"Well, it's Bella's first time," Celeste answered quickly, feeling embarrassed, as though Auggie had accused her of something.

"First-timers, huh?" Auggie smiled. "Well, that explains it then."

Celeste raised an eyebrow. "Explains what?"

"You don't have drinks," Auggie said, nudging a small cooler by her feet. "Believe me, you want drinks. I've just got soda today, but depending on how this game goes, I might sneak a White Claw next time."

Celeste wasn't sure if she was kidding or not. This was thrilling in a way, both the ambiguity and the thought of White Claws before noon.

For a while, Auggie and Celeste continued to chat. Auggie talked with her hands and drove the conversation, somehow intuiting the exact involvement Celeste needed. Celeste slipped comfortably into the empty spaces, not feeling rushed or interrogated like she usually did when talking with strangers.

"Looks like Bella's a sub," Louis cut in eventually. He had appeared back by Celeste's side, causing barely a hiccup in conversation, just long enough for Auggie and Louis to reach across Celeste and shake hands.

Celeste followed his gaze to the field, where she was not entirely surprised to see both Bella and Declan under separate tents, relegated from the game by the powers that governed youth sports. The fact that both of their children were there together felt to Celeste like just another connection Celeste and Auggie shared.

"How do they decide which five-year-olds are starters and which are subs?" Auggie wondered. She had popped open a second can of Coke, which she sipped through a thick, reusable straw. "Aren't they all going to spend most of the game picking their noses anyway?"

"I don't know," Celeste said. "If Bella's anything like me, she's got the hand-eye coordination of a butter knife."

Auggie snorted. Louis glanced sideways at her, looking baffled. Celeste wasn't usually funny, at least not on purpose.

The trill of a whistle rang out through the morning, which was growing warmer as it drew in the sun. Around them, parents leaned forward in unison with what felt like a collective intake of breath.

Auggie's prediction had been right to some extent. The kids on the field seemed to fall into one of two categories: a few isolated islands, crouched in the grass or picking at their shirts, with the rest swarming a bright yellow ball with gusto. It bore only the slightest resemblance to the soccer games Celeste had seen on TV, in that there were two goals and a general sense that the ball was heading toward them.

"Is there a reason for the name?" Celeste asked, moving her sunglasses from the top of her head to her face. "The Beavers, I mean. Where did it come from?"

Auggie was swatting at a fly that was buzzing interestedly around her soda.

"Just the fact that five-year-old girls like fuzzy woodland creatures." She set her can down and clapped. "Got it," she cheered before refocusing on Celeste. "Anyway, yeah, they took a vote at their first practice. It was either that or the Terminators. The girls only won because there is one more of them. I don't think the boys found beavers sufficiently violent."

Celeste chuckled.

"What about the Purple People Eaters?" Auggie said. "Anything profound there?"

Celeste giggled again and started to answer, although she trailed off mid-sentence. Her subconscious seemed to notice the sound before the rest of her brain caught up.

"Is that . . . ," Auggie said, turning toward the field. Celeste turned her attention too. On the field, the children had stopped moving, the yellow ball resting between them like the sun of a very small universe.

It didn't sound like Bella, and Celeste had no reason to think that Bella was involved. And yet, even before she stood up, even before the coaches shouted across the field for Bella and Declan's parents, she knew.

The first thing Celeste noticed was Declan. Up close, he was very clearly Auggie's son, with a dusting of freckles across his long nose, his broad mouth now screwed into a howl. And then Bella, an arm's length away from him, her hands clasped together into a single fist in front of her body. She seemed to be looking in Declan's direction but not quite at him, her gaze out of focus.

"What happened?" Louis said, wiping the back of his hand against his forehead. Celeste and Auggie came to a stop beside him, closing the semicircle of adults around the two kids.

"Bella?" Celeste said uncertainly. Bella's eyes wandered over to her, a look of confusion passing over them. "What's going on?" Celeste turned her attention to the coaches, both of whom looked uncomfortable.

"Well . . ." Bella's coach started, but she was cut off.

"That girl bit me."

All of the adults turned at once, their eyes falling to Declan's incendiary finger pointed at Bella. Bella looked back with an expression of mild interest, as though she too was curious to hear what had happened.

No one said anything for a moment. Celeste looked from Bella to Declan's arm, held straight in front of him. Looking closer, Celeste could see an angry red splotch blooming across his freckled skin, roughly the shape and size of a small jaw.

Celeste looked up, searching for Auggie. Auggie met her eyes. She didn't say anything, but looking straight at Celeste, she stepped over to Declan, which said enough.

"Is that true, Bella?" Celeste said, turning to her daughter. "Did you bite him?"

Bella stared back blankly, apparently mute. Declan continued to cry, although now that he had said his piece, the sound was noticeably less anguished.

"Bella," Celeste pressed. "Did you bite him?"

Bella's expression didn't falter. She looked completely vacant, as though she had left her body standing upright but totally empty. Celeste fought the urge to grab hold of Bella's shoulders and shake.

"Bella." Louis's voice was quiet but direct. This seemed to snap Bella out of her reverie. Her eyes flickered back on, like someone smacking an old flashlight.

Slowly, deliberately she nodded. "He got me wet," she said, her tone matter-of-fact.

Celeste's eyes moved from Bella to the water jug she hadn't noticed previously, overturned by Declan's feet. It looked both sad and slightly foreboding, like a dead bird on the sidewalk. In an instant, Celeste could imagine what had happened—a stream of Declan's water flying through the air, directionless, harmless. Bella's jaw clamping down on smooth, freckly flesh.

No one seemed sure of what to say after that. Louis apologized clunkily to the coaches and to Auggie, who angled her body away from Celeste, as though shielding her son from something obscene. A decision was made for Bella to leave—to "cool down," as one coach said. Bella nodded with an unnatural stiffness, like a robot who had been programmed to mimic human gestures.

As the game on the field resumed, the three Reeds set off, hugging the sidelines as they made their way back to the parents' side. Celeste's temples were pounding. She felt like she was the one who had done the biting. She felt like she could bite someone, which was an uncomfortable feeling. She remembered her desire to punch Louis that morning and wondered if she had always harbored such a propensity for violence.

Back on the sideline, Louis worked on repacking their umbrella back into its bag. The game on the field resumed as Celeste flapped open the plastic totes for their camping chairs. Bella stood in serene silence beside them. Celeste tried not to look at Auggie's seat, where she had left her soda in the little mesh cupholder.

"Mama," Bella said, speaking unprompted for the first time. No one around them seemed to notice, either not interested in the Reeds' drama or pretending not to be. "Mama, are we getting sundaes?"

Celeste slid the first camping chair into its bag and slung it over her shoulder.

"No, Bells. No sundaes today."

"You promised," Bella said, speaking in the slow, patient way adults sometimes spoke to a child. "You said we get sundaes after the game."

"I know, Bells, but you bit someone." Everything in Celeste felt heavy. Even her hair seemed to pull at her scalp.

"He got me wet," Bella said, shaking her head. "That's the reason."

"It doesn't matter, Bells. You can't bite people."

"He got me wet," Bella said, her voice more insistent.

"I know, and that was unfair. But you cannot bite people, even if they annoy you."

"Mama." Bella's voice was slipping into a whine, and Celeste feared she was close to losing whatever patience she had left.

"We'll talk about it more at home, okay?"

Celeste reached for the second camping chair, which was more difficult to fold up with the first slung across her shoulder.

"Mamaaaa," Bella moaned. Celeste thought she heard the sound of tiny plastic cleats stomping into the grass behind her. The sound made Celeste want to stomp her foot too. Instead, Celeste gave the chair one swift shove, forcing the legs together. She raised the bag to slip the chair inside it, but it caught on something solid behind her back. She looked over her shoulder to where Bella was clinging to the end like a wiggling fish caught on a line.

"Bella," Celeste warned.

"MAMA!" Bella screeched in a pitch that pierced Celeste in her already throbbing temples. Celeste was vaguely aware of Louis looking up from the umbrella just as Bella thrust her body backward with all of her weight. Celeste felt both the tote and the chair slipping from her hands, and before she knew what she was doing, she ripped them both back.

"God damn it, Bella." Her voice rose above the flurry of children on the field. "Would you just stop it already?"

The chair was free now, and in a flash of sudden rage, she slammed both it and its partner to the ground. They landed with the clink of metal folding legs smashing into one another.

Bella's eyes grew wide. Celeste looked at her, then at the chairs, and then up to where it seemed as though every parent around them had gone suddenly silent. It felt as though the whole universe had paused, with only Celeste breathing heavily in its center. She closed her eyes and pressed one pointer finger into each temple.

When Celeste finally opened her eyes, most of the parents had politely averted their gaze. Celeste got the sense that they were only pretending not to listen, which was almost worse than if they had craned their necks to get a better look.

Louis stepped over to her, and for a moment, Celeste thought he was about to place a hand on her arm. Celeste thought of Declan, of the bite mark like a tiny pink butterfly stamped across his skin. Instead, Louis reached down for the chairs by her feet. He hoisted them over his shoulder, then looked her dead in the eye.

"Really, Celeste," he said, shaking his head. "And you wonder why she acts out."

21

Hollie

Three Months Before
Dallas, Texas

H OLLIE BLINKED. THE shades in her bedroom were still tightly drawn, making the darkness around her so absolute that for a split second, in the murky middle between wakefulness and sleep, she forgot where she was.

She forgot about her kitchen, the empty yogurt tub in the trash.

The empty cracker sleeves.

The empty protein bar wrappers.

The pretzel bag with only salt left in the bottom corners.

She forgot about Nick the night before, a duffel bag strap pressed across his chest in their hallway. The way he had said sadly—so sadly—that he was going to spend the night at his brother's. That he needed to think about some things on his own.

Briefly, one drop in the bucket of her life, Hollie forgot all of this.

And then she blinked again, and she remembered.

The night before, Nick had left. Not permanently, Hollie didn't think. Not even dramatically—although in a way, Hollie would have preferred that. She would have preferred him to smash shirts and socks into a suitcase, to slam the front door closed so hard that the whole house shook. She would have preferred rage, because rage was a temporary emotion. Powerful, but temporary. No one could be enraged forever, which meant that as soon as Nick's rage simmered—which it would, eventually—they could go back to living their lives.

She spread one arm over to Nick's side of the bed, feeling nothing, feeling alone.

She blinked again, and it struck her that she wasn't actually alone, not technically. She brought her hands to her abdomen, which was still as flat as it had ever been.

She didn't know how long she had been lying in the darkness when through the silent house, the doorbell chimed. Hollie reached blindly for her phone charging beside her bed. Instagram notifications filled her screen, interrupted by a Facebook banner and a few texts. She also had three missed calls from Mallory at eight, eight thirty, and nine forty-five that morning. It was now ten fifteen.

Hollie navigated from her missed calls to her texts. She had two unread from Robin and five from Mallory. Hollie had messaged Mallory after Nick had left the previous evening. *I'm pregnant* was all she had said. She had debated saying more—something about the drug store, about how cheerfully bright all the pregnancy test boxes had been. She considered telling Mallory about Nick, about the happy hour margaritas they had all but forgotten. She had thought all of this, and it had exhausted her so thoroughly that she had instead silenced her phone and gone to sleep.

Hollie snapped the phone back to its lock screen and sat upright. Her eyes had adjusted slightly to the darkness, just enough for her to make out the black edges of her furniture. She swiveled around. As she did, a wave of nausea passed through her, strong enough that she paused for a moment to stare at the ground. Maybe it was the pregnancy, or maybe it was the massive amount of food she'd eaten the night before. It was impossible to know for sure.

The doorbell rang a second time. "Jesus Christ," she muttered as she forced herself up.

She was completely unsurprised to find Mallory on her front stoop, balancing a cardboard drink carrier in one hand. "Well, you're up and at 'em today," Hollie said, attempting a wry smile that Mallory didn't return.

"I tried to call," Mallory said as Hollie closed the door behind her. "I called Nick too, and neither of you answered." She looked apologetic. "I got worried."

Hollie felt an unexpected pang behind her ribcage, where she knew her heart was pumping for two. Never in all their years of friendship had Mallory ever admitted to being worried about Hollie.

"Well, that's sweet. You don't have to worry, though. I'm alive." Hollie made a sweeping motion, like someone displaying a new outfit. Mallory continued to frown. "Is that coffee from New General?" Hollie added, nodding to the drink carrier. "If it is, I'll forgive you for waking me up."

At this, Mallory seemed to relax. She examined the cups for a moment, then plucked one up from the cardboard.

"I don't think mine technically counts as coffee," she said, handing Hollie her cup. "More like coffee-flavored sugar."

"It's better black," Hollie confirmed, only wondering after she had taken a sip whether she was supposed to have caffeine when pregnant.

"Less calories, but definitely not better," Mallory said. "I'm pretty sure only a serial killer would enjoy it black."

Hollie snorted and motioned to the kitchen. Once there, she didn't have to invite Mallory to sit, as Mallory was comfortable enough in Hollie's home to do it herself.

"So," Mallory said as she slid onto a barstool. "Do you want to talk about that text?"

Hollie wasn't wearing a bra and felt suddenly exposed. She turned her back to Mallory and pulled open the refrigerator door. She had done a nearly perfect job of clearing the shelves the previous night, a realization that filled her with a renewed surge of shame. She closed the door and turned back around.

"Honestly, I don't know what to say," Hollie said quietly. She thought of Nick, how he had looked at Hollie the day before as though he was seeing her for the very first time.

"Well," Mallory said, her voice gentle, "I guess we could start with whether you're okay."

Hollie and Mallory had talked about motherhood before. Of course they had. They had talked about Fiona, about how she slept and shat and nursed. They had talked about postpartum anxiety, postpartum exhaustion, Mallory's pregnant and postpartum body. How Fiona sometimes wrapped her soft little arms around Mallory's neck and kissed her ear, how she patted Mallory affectionately on the head before bed. Mallory had recently asked Hollie whether she and Nick were going to have children. Hollie had shrugged and said, "Eventually, I guess."

Was Hollie okay? Was anyone? It was all relative anyway. Hollie had one friend, Laurie, who had been trying to get pregnant for years. Literally, years. She had gone through IUIs and IVFs and any other acronym you could think of. She had finally gotten pregnant last year and made it all the way to thirty-seven weeks. Thirty-seven weeks of cupping her rounded belly and taking off pieces of jewelry the more her limbs swelled. The pregnancy had then ended in a stillbirth. Laurie had said afterward that she wished it had been her instead.

"We weren't planning this," Hollie said finally. "It was a complete surprise."

The last word caught in her throat unexpectedly, the same choking feeling she got in the middle of the night when she accidentally inhaled spit. She swallowed hard. She was totally uninterested in crying, but her eyes nonetheless started to sting.

Hollie pressed her eyes closed, and she only opened them when she heard Mallory push her stool back. Without saying anything, Mallory moved to the other side of the island so she stood shoulder to shoulder with Hollie.

"I'm so sorry, Holl," Mallory said, sounding like she meant it. Hollie exhaled cautiously, not sure whether she was about to start sobbing.

"We always said we wanted kids," Hollie said. "And I thought I did. I really thought I did, but lately—I don't know." She pressed her eyes closed again, but it was no use. The tears were coming whether she allowed them to or not. "When I took the test, the first thing I thought was that this is the end of my life."

Hollie thought of the little plastic window, how the control line had appeared just a second or two before the test result. The test was so small—just a little bit of paper behind a little bit of plastic—but to Hollie, it was her universe condensed.

"What's wrong with me?" Hollie whispered. She wanted to open her eyes but couldn't, too afraid she would find in Mallory's face what she had seen in Nick's.

"What do you mean?"

"What's wrong with me that I don't want kids?"

Mallory was quiet. Hollie pressed her fingers against her eyelids, attempting to halt the tears. She didn't know if she was crying for Nick or for herself, for the person she had only just discovered she was. She felt broken in some indescribable way, like she was missing some crucial piece to being a woman. Some women were mothers. Some didn't have what it took. And then there was the select group of women who had everything—their kids, their careers, their lives. The latter were strong and capable, doing the most impressive thing a woman could do. Hollie had always assumed herself to be one of them, but now she could see that this wasn't even close to being true.

"Listen," Mallory said finally, the word unexpectedly firm. "I love Fiona, and I'm glad I'm her mom, but being a parent isn't some moral requirement for being human. It's a lifestyle, just like any other lifestyle, and it's bullshit to expect all women to want the same one."

There was a beat. In it, Mallory's face seemed to soften. She moved her hand so that it was covering Hollie's. This was unusual, as Hollie rarely allowed anyone to touch her besides her husband.

"And just because you thought you wanted it once," Mallory added, her voice now gentle, "doesn't mean you're bound to that forever."

There was another silence. Hollie thought of her own mother, who had gotten pregnant with Hollie in college. Hollie had asked her once whether she had considered an abortion. Her mom had said no, of course not, never, but she had paused just long enough that Hollie sometimes wondered whether the real answer was in the silence.

"How cruel would it be," Hollie said, "to make someone who isn't wanted by their own mom?" She thought, then added, "But Nick wants this, and who am I to take this from him?" She looked at Mallory, feeling suddenly desperate. She whispered, "What do I do, Mal?"

Hollie wondered suddenly if this was the reason Mallory had worried—this very specific situation. Maybe Mallory had known what would happen the moment she had received Hollie's text.

"I don't know, Holl," Mallory said. She sounded as unsure as Hollie felt. "It's hard. It's impossible, really, but you're just going to have to do what you can live with—what *you* can live with, not anyone else."

Hollie wasn't crying anymore. She instead felt completely focused. She was acting like Mallory had answers, like there were any answers to actually give.

"But how do I know what decision I can live with?"

"You can't, I guess. Not for sure, anyway. I guess just imagine telling someone what decision you made and see how it feels."

Later, once Mallory was gone, these were the words Hollie came back to, the words that highlighted everything that had gone wrong. Because Hollie had made a career—had made a life, really—of showing people the best parts of herself. She didn't know how to show them the worst.

CHAPTER

22

Hollie

The Morning After
Vík, Iceland

HOLLIE JIGGLED HER knee beneath the table as the officer across from her scanned her spiral notepad. The woman's name was Officer Guðmundsdóttir, which Hollie would not dare try to pronounce out loud. Officer Guðmundsdóttir had the same clear skin as every other woman in Iceland, with straight blonde hair that she had forced into an uncomfortable-looking bun.

They were sitting in the dining room, at a table pushed against the back wall. It seemed as though whoever had decorated the room had changed their mind on the theme halfway through, pivoting from tropical to country. The room was a nauseating shade of pea green, and on the shelf above their table, a toucan figurine sat next to a decorative pail of milk.

"So," the officer said after a moment, looking up. Her eyes were blue and translucent, the color so thin that trying to read them was like grasping at air. "I understand that you and Alabama did not know each other particularly well."

Hollie had one hand resting on each thigh, and hidden from view, she clenched and unclenched each fist like two tiny hearts. Each pulse in her right hand was greeted by a radiating pang, which she ignored.

"We only met a few days ago, yes," she said, which was technically true.

Once, when Hollie was younger, she had come home from school to find her mom in their living room with a bottle of wine and a man with a nose so big and oily, Hollie had noticed nothing else about him. Hollie's mom had given her five dollars and told her to go get some ice cream, forgetting that Hollie—recently vegan—didn't eat ice cream anymore. Hollie had pocketed the money, happy to escape the paddle-nosed man and his big, waxy pores. Instead of ice cream, she had gotten herself a copy of *Cosmopolitan* magazine, which she had read in her room alone.

Later that evening, her mom's actual boyfriend had come over. The boyfriend (Hollie was pretty sure his name was Jake) had ordered a Hawaiian pizza, which they'd all eaten straight from the box in the living room. While they were eating, Probably-Jake had asked Hollie's mom about her day. Her mom hadn't blinked as she'd left the paddle-nosed man out of her answer entirely.

Hollie hadn't liked that boyfriend very much, but how easily her mom had lied to him had bothered her regardless. When she had confronted her mom about it later, however, her mom had been wholly uninterested in guilt. "Everything I said was true," Hollie's mom had told her, and Hollie had nodded, really trying to understand why this answer had felt so wrong. Even then, Hollie had understood something about honesty that her mom apparently did not.

"But I understand you and Alabama did spend some one-on-one time together," the officer said in a way that made Hollie feel as though she had walked straight into a trap. Hollie met her eyes briefly before Hollie's gaze flickered over the woman's shoulder to the wall that glowed with floor-to-ceiling glass.

"We ran together yesterday," Hollie said. "Just a couple of miles before breakfast."

Outside, swirls of gray ocean and black sand beaches seemed to flow into one another, making it impossible to confidently delineate the two. Before coming to Iceland, beaches had always existed to Hollie for the purpose of being enjoyed—tepid water to cradle lazy parades of swimmers, piles of white sand for toes to dig through. It was an idea so disparate from this beach, Reynisfjara, whose sea was violent and indifferent, like it could swallow a human without remorse.

"And can you tell me about that? About the run?"

Hollie forced her attention back to the officer. She thought of Alabama's phone still beneath her pillow upstairs. She tried to imagine the cop's reaction if Hollie were to produce it—the woman's clear blue eyes rounding in surprise or narrowing in suspicion. Hollie couldn't be sure which would be the most likely result.

"What would you like to know exactly?"

The beat that followed seemed excessively long.

"Anything that sticks out to you, really. We're just trying to fig-ure out whether anything about her behavior seemed off."

The woman's eyes bore into Hollie. The officer's stare was unwavering, not even a flash to the clock on the wall that seemed unnaturally loud.

When Hollie had unlocked Alabama's phone earlier that morn-ing, she had been more surprised than anything. Though she had been trying to unlock it, she had not really expected to guess Alabama's passcode. In fact, when Hollie had tapped in her own birthday—oh one, oh six, nine-zero—it had been mostly for some-thing to do with her hands.

Hollie hadn't looked through everything, and she hadn't looked for that long—just a few minutes to scan the last few days' worth of text messages and calls. Anything more had felt invasive, which Hol-lie recognized as ridiculous. As though *that,* of all the lines, was the one Hollie couldn't cross.

Most of Alabama's call history was to her husband, as were her last texts. Those, Hollie had read. Hollie knew very little about Henry Wood besides his name. It was strange to think it was not the same, the other way around.

"I'm sorry," Hollie said. "I want to help, but I don't think I can. I really didn't know Alabama well enough to tell you if her behavior was off."

CHAPTER

23

Hollie

The Morning Of
Reykjavík, Iceland

THE MORNING OF the glacier hike, Hollie opened her eyes to the sound of something scratching. It was so quiet that when Hollie blinked the first time, she thought it might have been part of a dream.

Then she heard it again, this time louder. It was actually more of a knock than a scratch, coming from the bedroom door. Hollie glanced over to the bed Katherine had claimed when they had arrived. In the faint glow of morning light leaking in from behind the blackout shades, Hollie could make out tumbles of red hair across her pillow.

Hollie checked her phone for the time. She had set her alarm for five twenty, as she'd told Alabama she would meet her outside at five thirty to run. That wasn't for another half an hour. She pressed her eyes shut but was not totally surprised when there was a third knock, this one the loudest.

When she pulled the bedroom door open, Alabama's eyes widened as if surprised to see Hollie there. "Ohmygod," she said, all as one word. "I didn't wake you, did I?"

Hollie felt her retort rising. It was five in the fucking morning. Of course she hadn't been awake.

"What's going on?" she said, voice flat.

"I was just up and thought we could get started early." Alabama smiled. She was wearing baby blue biker shorts and a matching reflective tank. It looked like the sort of tacky get-up a lonely person might buy for their dog. Hollie thought of Robin, whose dog wore little knit sweaters when it was cold.

"Well, let me get dressed," Hollie said.

Hollie left Alabama in the hallway as she shuffled around for her running things, navigating the dark room by the flashlight on her phone. Katherine didn't move. "I'm a heavy sleeper," she had informed Hollie when they had arrived.

When Hollie stepped into the hallway a few minutes later, Alabama seemed to buzz with energy. It occurred to Hollie that maybe running with Alabama once would not, in fact, be enough to keep her at bay for the rest of the trip, as Hollie had hoped.

"So, you're on Strava, right?" Alabama said as Hollie motioned them forward. Alabama led the way, shimmying sideways down the hall to keep one eye on Hollie. "I mean, I know you're on Strava. Duh." She giggled. Hollie felt the beginning of a headache forming between her eyes. "Anyway, there's this segment that's, like, a quarter mile long, and not that many people have run it. So I was thinking, wouldn't it be cool if you and I did that? If we ran the segment together, I mean? We could be, like, number one on Strava together."

Strava was a social media app designed for athletes, a way to log workouts on a public forum for other users to see and assess. The idea was to build community, which Hollie supposed it did, in the cutthroat way the mafia could be considered a community. One of the best and worst features of the app was the segments—short routes designated by users as benchmarks so that local runners could compare their times. Hollie personally held several top times for segments around Dallas, although none of them were recent.

"Sounds fine," Hollie said. Alabama beamed.

The damp evening had shifted sometime the night before, and when they stepped outside, sun heated Hollie's shoulders beneath her running fleece. It was a bit breezier than it had been when they had arrived, creating a sheen over the water in the distance like a thin film of oil swirling in the sunlight.

"Should we, like"—Alabama motioned to her leg—"stretch, or whatever?"

"Sure," Hollie said.

It was much warmer than Hollie had expected, and had she been alone, she probably would have taken off her fleece to run. Now, however, the sight of Alabama's sharp elbows stopped her. It was an unconscious decision, no more deliberate than turning away from a loud noise. When Hollie realized she had made it, she was filled with an overwhelming sense of loss.

Never in her life had she been ashamed of her body, because never in her life had her body been so out of her control. In high school, she had whittled it down to nearly nothing with zero-calorie sweeteners and powered diet shakes. In college, when she had started taking running more seriously, her coaches had impressed on her the importance of adequate fueling. They had handed her pamphlets about macronutrients, micronutrients, good and bad fats, which Hollie had consumed with a religious fervor. She had charted and planned her meals with the same meticulous dedication that she had applied to her workouts, and in return, her body had held up its end of the deal. It had been lean, and strong, and efficient. It had been beautiful.

"So," Alabama said after a little while, "the segment starts at the bottom of that hill." She pointed. "Over there by the church."

Hollie followed Alabama's finger to the church's red spire that seemed to pierce the wall of black and green cliffs behind it.

"We can run, like, a mile warmup, and then go?" Alabama's eyes shifted to Hollie, her expression serious. Hollie just nodded in response.

When they took off a few minutes later, down the hill and toward the water, the road blessed Hollie with a steep decline. Even so, Hollie could feel the unfamiliar heaviness of her body with each step. She hadn't run for weeks, and it was very much evident by her labored breathing. Thankfully, Alabama was chattering too quickly and loudly to hear.

"I didn't always run," she said, her breathing unaffected. "I didn't even like it. When I was in high school, I'd always tell my gym teacher I had period cramps to get out of the warmup lap."

Hollie tried to ignore the sensation between her thighs, the clumps of flesh that rubbed against one another like they never had before. At one point, a point not too long ago, she'd had grand plans of winning the race she was planning with Robin that summer. She would donate the prize to charity, of course, and people would remark to one another how gracious and humble she was.

"But running is actually kind of nice," Alabama went on. "I mean, the beginning was hard, but now that I'm used to it, I can run for a really long time." She barely took a breath between sentences, speaking like they weren't running at all. "I listen to podcasts, mainly. Not really music. You know, I only started a few months ago, and I already finished the entire first season of *Serial*. Have you listened to it? *Serial*, I mean? Henry—that's my husband—he says it's basically just true crime TV for podcasts, but I don't think so. It's much more humanitarian, if you ask me."

Here, she paused, as though expecting confirmation. Hollie grunted, unable to manage anything else. Without warning, Hollie was stuck with a great surge of anger—rage, even, to Hollie's surprise. Hollie's success had always felt so personal and exclusive, but Hollie could see now that it was not. She could lose it all in an instant, and there would always be Alabama fucking Wood waiting in line to take her spot.

As they made their way farther into the village, Hollie's attention rose to her chest, which seemed to be wrapped with something invisible and unforgiving. Eventually, Alabama's voice was lost as background noise until she turned to Hollie to ask, "Are you alright?"

Alabama shot her a worried look, and Hollie's anger rose again in a wave. She resented the pity more than anything, especially given its source. And yet, as they started to slow, Hollie felt her body aching for relief. As much as she loathed it, she allowed Alabama to lead them to a stop.

"I'm fine," Hollie said, pretending to study their surroundings—an unmarked road, a pristinely painted fence. The sun was warm, but the breeze near the water felt cooler. It plastered stray hair against her sweaty face. "Just not feeling great this morning."

"Sick?" Alabama said, giving Hollie a knowing look. It was like she was referring to a secret they had shared earlier, which was bizarre, albeit no more bizarre than anything else this fucking girl did.

"Just tired." Hollie didn't look at Alabama and instead kept her gaze deliberately forward, where the church loomed ahead. It looked both bigger and smaller than Hollie had thought it would somehow. It was stocky and discreet, with blank white walls and sharp corners, like a model of a church made by someone who didn't actually know what churches looked like. It was perched on the hill above all the other buildings, a surveyor of the village sprawled out by its feet.

"We don't have to do this if you don't want," Alabama said. She sounded the most normal Hollie had heard her, her voice laced with warmth and compassion and a tiny bit of sympathy. Something in

Hollie roared, and in a way, this comforted her. Maybe people pitied her, but she wasn't so far gone so as to accept it yet.

"No, I want to do it," Hollie said firmly. "Unless you don't."

"No, no, I want to. I definitely want to." Alabama nodded vigorously.

"Let's do it then," Hollie said, her fingers fluttering at her legs. Little fires of adrenaline shot up from unlikely places—behind her belly button, around her sternum, in the space between her nose and lip. They were no different from the nerves she felt before any other race in her life, and in the split second between Alabama raising her hand and starting her timer, it struck Hollie that this race meant just as much to her as any she had run before.

"Okay, and"—Alabama lowered her hand—"go."

Hollie's heel dug into the ground, the soles of her shoes sliding slightly in the loose gravel. Pops of color exploded in her vision, the abrupt shift in velocity apparently more than her body was prepared for.

For a moment, all she heard was the synchronized crunching of ground beneath their shoes. She could see Alabama in her peripheral vision, a flash of baby blue and reflective silver. Hollie willed her body with everything she had in her, demanding from it more than just discomfort, more even than pain.

Beside her, Alabama's shoulder came into better view, the elegant curve where her collar bone came to a point beneath the skin. And then her blonde braid, clapping against her tank.

Something tingled in Hollie, electric shock waves of dissent. The church was closer, nearly in front of them, and Hollie leaned, more falling than running. And still, Alabama was two steps ahead, then three steps, then four.

Hollie saw her own hand reach out like it wasn't connected to her. She didn't know what she intended to do with it. Or, maybe she did. In her mind, she saw her fingers wrapping around Alabama's thick braid, Alabama's neck snapping back as Hollie pulled.

And then there was a snap, but it wasn't Alabama. Beneath her running tights, Hollie's hamstring squealed in pain. She stopped abruptly just as Alabama came to a halt, two triumphant fists in the air.

Hollie, outside herself for an instant, screamed.

Alabama whipped around, her arms still raised by her ears. Hollie was on the ground now. She grasped at her hamstring with one hand, the other palm pressed hard enough into the road that tears welled.

"Are you okay?" Alabama said, sounding urgent. Hollie thought of her own hand reaching forward, how close it had been to Alabama's hair.

She directed her focus to her leg, where her muscle pulsed beneath her hand. She extended her leg backward a fraction of an inch. Her hamstring fired, but not horribly. She had probably strained it, although she could already tell it wasn't nearly bad enough that she had any reason to be on her hands and knees right now.

The air was thick with salt and sunshine. A single bird whistled into the breeze. Hollie wondered if she would have actually grabbed Alabama if her hamstring hadn't stopped her. The fact that she didn't know the answer immediately seemed like an answer in itself.

Hollie heard Alabama move to come closer, and Hollie opened her mouth to scream—*at* her this time. To get away. To leave her the fuck alone. Instead, she turned to the grassy shoulder of the road, and in one violent heave, she threw up.

24

Celeste

The Day Before
Vatnajökull National Park, Iceland

O NCE, BEFORE BELLA was born, when Louis had just started at his advertising firm, he had come home with a futuristic pair of goggles as a gift from a client. "Night vision," he had said with a childlike glee, and he had led Celeste up to their room by the hand. For a second, Celeste had felt like a teenager, nearly giddy with anticipation, but then Louis—fully clothed—had strapped the goggles to Celeste's head and turned off the light, disorienting Celeste momentarily as her previously familiar bedroom had transformed into a strange, brightly colored world.

Amazed, she had waved her hands across her face, and through the lenses, she had watched glitchy red and yellow fireballs shooting across her vision. "Thermal imaging," Louis had explained. She had turned to him, surprised to find her husband also transformed into a psychedelic version of himself. "It turns IR light into visible light," he had said, which had meant very little to Celeste.

Celeste thought of this now as she stared at Alabama's back. They were in the GoIceland front office, collecting gear to start their glacier hike. Alabama had said no more than five words that morning through all of breakfast and the entire car ride over.

Celeste thought of Louis through those goggles—his head a fluorescent red, his hair streaked blue and green—and she wondered what she would see if she could use them now. Something had shifted in Alabama since she had gotten back from her run with Hollie that morning, and Celeste imagined pulling on those goggles and seeing a halo of flaming orange fury enclosing Alabama's body.

Alabama was angry. Celeste didn't know why, but she could feel it. She'd felt it as Alabama had stomped back to their bedroom after her shower, wrapped in a bleach-stained towel, and later, as Alabama had poked moodily at the scrambled egg she hadn't taken a single bite of. Alabama hadn't explained what had happened on the run, and until Hollie had limped into the dining room, Celeste hadn't even known anyone had gotten hurt.

"Now remember," the man at the front of the office boomed, tapping at his head with a thick finger, "if yer not on the bus, do NOT take yer helmet off. I do NOT want to see one helmet-free head until we're back in this office, you hear me?"

Around him, the group of women shifted their weight uncomfortably, but no one said a word. Celeste felt the overwhelming urge to clarify the instructions—could they take their helmets off in the bus or not?—but she decided quickly that this man did not seem like a person who would appreciate clarifying questions.

His name was Tom O'Brian, and he worked for GoIceland— "head of the expedition division," he'd informed them when they had arrived, his barrel chest puffed out. Unlike the other GoIceland employees they had met at the car rental office—each in a pale yellow polo shirt with a GoIceland logo on the breast—Tom was dressed in a white thermal and khaki overalls, which seemed entirely appropriate for his demeanor. He had a gruffness about him that intimidated Celeste, and there was something about his wiry red hair that made Celeste feel as though he was probably very accurate at throwing an axe.

"These helmets are so not on brand," Celeste said to Alabama quietly so Tom wouldn't hear. She had meant it as a joke, but Alabama didn't even turn around. She just slammed the neon green helmet on her head wordlessly, staring forward.

Ahead of Alabama, Hollie was near the front of the group. She too was holding a helmet, pressed between the crook of her elbow and her hip. She didn't seem to notice Alabama sending silent daggers into her back. Or maybe she did. Maybe that was why her back seemed so unnaturally straight as she listened to Tom's spiel.

"When we get off the bus, there's going to be a little *hike* to the base of the glacier," Tom continued. He emphasized the word *hike* for reasons unclear. "Once we get to the glacier, we'll put on our crampons." He waved the medieval-looking device in his hand, a spiked-tooth jaw Celeste assumed would go on their feet. "Benno here will show you how to use them."

He gestured to Benno, who gave a friendly wave. Celeste assumed that Benno was actually a Benjamin, but she agreed that Benno suited him more. He was young—no older than twenty-two or twenty-three, if Celeste had to guess. He had a tan, reedy body that Celeste suspected was stronger than it looked, and he spoke with a darling Australian accent.

Before Tom had started with the announcements, Celeste had overheard Benno talking to one of the other influencers, Emily, who was about his age and was almost definitely flirting. From the conversation, Celeste had learned that Benno's life goal was to start his own outdoor sporting company in Switzerland, which Celeste considered an impressively specific goal for someone so young.

For the next several minutes, Tom and Benno took turns holding up tools—ropes, helmets, shoes—and gesturing in ways Celeste assumed would have been meaningful if she had been concentrating.

Finally, they were directed to collect their helmets and crampons, which Celeste held cautiously away from her body. They all followed the men out to the parking lot, where a minibus idled out front.

The sky had cleared since the day before, the mist evaporating to reveal stretches of crisp blue. The sky seemed endless, but still somehow smaller than the mountain rising up to greet it just beyond the parking lot.

From Vík, they had followed the southern coast of the island to get to the GoIceland office, which was more of a hut than a building at the edge of Vatnajökull National Park. Celeste had driven, and for most of the drive, they had seen almost nothing but gray water on one side and barren black rocks on the other, sometimes speckled with moss, sometimes with ridged channels where water had run through. Celeste had noticed some dark peaks in the distance, but the glacier was different. When it had come into view, she had pulled the car to the side of the road to get a better look. There had been pictures of the national park on the internet, but still, something about the immaculate white of ancient ice reflecting in the sunlight had left Celeste speechless.

Later, when she had checked the itinerary, she had identified the mountain as Kristínartindar, home of the Skaftafellsjökull glacier they were set to traverse. She had seen these words before and had understood them as being significant, but only in a distant and irrelevant sense, like reading random state capitals on a map. On the roadside, however, with seaside breeze sneaking up her neck and into her hood, she had felt for a second the way Moses must have when he had gone up on that hill and talked to God.

In the parking lot, Benno and Tom ushered the women toward the bus with different degrees of fervor. Celeste noticed Alabama hanging back, her eyes following Hollie as she limped toward the open door.

"What's going on, Al?" Celeste said, unable to help herself any longer.

"She's pregnant," Alabama snapped at once. She didn't look at Celeste, and for a moment, Celeste thought she had heard her wrong.

"What?"

"Hollie." Alabama's mouth formed a line so thin and straight, it was almost impossible to tell she had lip injections. "She's one hundred percent pregnant. I can tell."

Celeste's eyes moved to Hollie, now pulling herself onto the bus. Several questions crowded her mind at once.

"Did she tell you that?" Celeste decided to start with.

"No." Hollie disappeared into the bus, and Alabama finally turned to look at Celeste. The intensity behind her eyes was startling. "But I know she is. She's definitely gained weight, and she could barely run this morning because of morning sickness."

Celeste licked her lips as she considered this. Hollie, pregnant—it wasn't out of the question. Well, no, Celeste supposed she had no idea if it was within the question or not. She had even less of an idea why it mattered to Alabama. Hollie being pregnant—if she even was pregnant—seemed so immaterial to Alabama, Celeste couldn't draw a single line between the two.

"And of course," Alabama continued, her voice deadly, "just when I decide I'm going to start running, she goes and does this. A baby announcement." She laughed, the sound mirthless. "I'm just never going to get ahead, am I?"

Celeste stared, which Alabama didn't seem to notice. Something about Alabama's posture reminded Celeste of a cat poised to pounce.

"Ladies!" Tom's voice thundered. Celeste startled, so lost in her own thoughts that she had momentarily forgotten what they were doing. Tom was standing near the bus door, his arm windmilling. "Let's move!"

25

Hollie

The Day Before
Skaftafellsjökull Glacier, Iceland

HALFWAY UP THE glacier, they finally found the Icelandic wind. Hollie gritted her teeth and focused on her feet as they pulled her forward. The sun overhead sprinkled the packed ice around them with a dusting of glitter. If Hollie hadn't been so tired, if her stomach hadn't still been lurching ominously, she might have paused for a moment to take in the beauty of it all.

Tom was at the front of the line, leading them up. Even toward the back, Hollie could make out tongues of red hair licking from beneath his helmet.

Earlier, the bus had dropped them off at the foot the mountain, a quarter mile from the glacier's base. From there, they had hiked to the glacier in a hesitant clump. Tom had seemed impatient, like he had wanted them to move faster. The influencers, however, had not been in any hurry. They had all moved cautiously, avoiding puddles and scaling down small ledges like Amazon explorers. (In their defense, hiking was not easy dressed head to toe in PinkPurse, which was designed more for looks than function.)

The whole time, Hollie had monitored her hamstring for any sign that it was not capable of making the hike. To her disappointment, the most she had felt was a faint twinge every few steps. It made her fall earlier that morning seem that much more pathetic in context.

When they had finally reached the base of the glacier, Hollie had already sprouted a patch of sweat under each armpit and below her bottom lip. The glacier was a sheet of perpendicular ice from years and years of snow packed densely on the slope. That's what Tom had told them, anyway, right before he had spent ten minutes giving them a demonstration on how to properly scale the ice.

Benno—the younger, cuter of the two—had shown them all how to put on their crampons, explaining exactly how snugly their hiking boots were meant to fit inside. He had then started to demonstrate before Tom had cut in impatiently.

"I WANT YOU TO FOLLOW ME EXACTLY," Tom had barked, shouting like he had been instructing them all from a half-mile away. "STAY IN ONE LINE! AND WHEN YOU WALK, YOU NEED TO LIFT THEN STEP!" He had then lifted his own foot eight inches from the ground before moving it forward, like a cartoon character tiptoeing through snow. It had seemed over the top until they had set out on the ice, and Emily had stepped before lifting, causing one of her metal crampon pins to catch on the ground and send her tumbling.

"CAREFUL," Tom had cried while Benno had helped Emily up. It had been both underwhelming and terrifying, because Emily hadn't actually fallen anywhere, but she could have. The glacier was etched with grooves running parallel to the mountain's slope, and when Hollie had craned her neck to peek into one, she hadn't been able to see the bottom.

"IN LINE," Tom shouted now, his swarm of red hair replaced by a bellowing face as he turned around to yell. Hollie watched as the women in front of her also turned one by one. Alabama's eyes landed directly on her, blue and cold.

After Hollie had thrown up on their run that morning, Alabama had initially offered to help Hollie up. Hollie had ripped her arm away, not wanting help, especially not Alabama's. This, apparently, had angered Alabama, who had been stiff and silent on the walk back to the bed and breakfast and had been glaring unashamedly at Hollie since.

Hollie didn't mind exactly. In a way, it was easier having Alabama mad at her than having Alabama bumping into her elbow every few steps. But still, Alabama's reaction was slightly disconcerting, as it seemed completely out of proportion to what had actually happened on the hill. It was almost as though Alabama had sensed Hollie's hand while they were running, like she knew what Hollie had almost done. It made no sense, but Hollie could think of no other reason Alabama would be looking at her the way she was now, as though imagining how she would kill Hollie if given the chance.

Hollie turned away from Alabama to scan the back of the line for the culprit. There, Margot was maybe six inches to the left of Katherine in front of her. Margot's cheeks flushed.

"Sorry," she shouted in a warbly voice.

Tom flicked his hand to the side impatiently, shooing her back in line. Margot disappeared, and when Hollie faced forward again, she tried to ignore Alabama, who remained turned around a few seconds longer than everyone else.

For the next ten minutes, they marched in silence. Skye led the group just behind Tom at the front of the line. She kept glancing back nervously, probably afraid that one of her girls would go careening down the slope. They had taken a few pictures at the base of the glacier, the scenery so striking that those shots alone would probably make the trip worthwhile. Hollie could nonetheless sense Skye's growing agitation. Pictures aside, PinkPurse probably didn't pay her enough to cover a lawsuit if one of the influencers got seriously injured on her watch.

"STOP," Tom bellowed, the sound echoing through the thin mountain air. Hollie froze, one foot still lifted off the ground. She half expected something deadly—a saber-toothed tiger rising up from its icy grave, or maybe an avalanche. But she saw nothing except Tom scurrying forward faster than seemed possible on the ice.

"This is a treat," he said, turning to face them. He waved his arms. "You can gather 'round here."

For a moment, none of the women moved, clearly suspecting a trap. Hollie put her foot down finally, the metal pins planting firmly in the ice.

"This is safe," Tom said, sounding exasperated. He waved again, and finally a few girls appeared from behind Hollie. They all moved forward warily as Tom knelt.

"See this?" He motioned to the chunk of ice. No one said anything. "This crevasse." Tom pointed to the bottom of the ice chunk, which was separated from the glacier by a four-foot gap.

"Oh, that's a good one," Benno said. He had appeared beside the group and was nodding at the crevasse like a proud parent.

Tom waved Benno forward, who lift-then-stepped his way up to the front of the group. Tom produced a rope from his bag and flung it to Benno, who pulled it around his torso and tied it with several quick and efficient tugs. They both then turned to the group like a pair of magicians who had just performed a trick.

"Who wants to go down?" Tom said, looking more cheerful than he had all morning. "We don't normally see crevasses this well-formed." He nodded to the well-formed crevasse. "Benno here will go down first, then we'll lower down whoever else wants to give it a whirl."

No one moved. They all stared in a horrified kind of silence, like they were watching somebody slowly lose their mind.

"I will."

Everyone's eyes moved simultaneously to Alabama, who had taken one large lift-then-step to separate herself from the women behind her. "I'd like to try." Her voice was bold, like she was making a point.

"Excellent." Tom beckoned her forward. "Benno, slip on down there."

Benno gave Tom a small salute before lowering himself to his butt. Without hesitation, he disappeared into the crevasse in one fluid slide.

"Was that a figure-eight that you tied him with?" Alabama said, one finger tracing the rope, now quivering slightly as Benno maneuvered out of sight. She was speaking low enough that she was clearly talking only to Tom, but Hollie could nonetheless hear her, as the chunk of ice shielded them from the mountain wind.

"That it is!" Tom sounded positively jolly. "Are you a climber?"

Alabama shook her head.

"Not really, no. I just . . ." She trailed off for a moment, her finger still stroking the purple rope absently. "I've just seen knots like that before, is all."

Tom patted her on the back, his palm taking up nearly all the space between her narrow shoulder blades.

"Very handy, the figure-eight." He nodded approvingly. "What'd you say yer name was?"

Alabama looked up at him as if just realizing he was there. When she told him, he chortled.

"Haven't heard that one before!" he said, apparently not seeing anything rude in this response. "Well, I'll tell you what, Alabama"—he pronounced her name with an odd rhythm, like a football chant—"if you ever need a job, you'll learn much more than just a figure-eight out here."

A few steps to Hollie's right, she noticed Celeste shifting her weight. She seemed uncomfortable, and Hollie didn't blame her. The whole thing—Tom, the knot, Alabama in general—was fucking weird.

Celeste and Alabama were good friends, Hollie had gathered, which she also found strange. Unlike Alabama, Celeste seemed reserved, maybe a little unsure of herself, but otherwise normal. Hollie half wanted to ask Celeste how and why she had managed to befriend someone like Alabama. The other half of her really wanted as little to do with either of them as possible.

"All good down here," Benno's disembodied voice rose from the crevasse.

Tom patted Alabama on the back a second time.

"Ready there?" he said. Alabama nodded, her face set with resolve.

The group watched in silence as Tom guided Alabama to her butt. Hollie could almost hear their collective intake of breath as Alabama nudged her way down. Her legs disappeared cautiously, her torso a little quicker, and then her head. No one said a word as Alabama's blonde braid slipped out of sight.

26

Celeste

The Day Before
Vatnajökull National Park, Iceland

CELESTE COULDN'T STOP trembling. At first, she had thought it was the cold, but even once they were down from the glacier, the shaking hadn't stopped. They were now back in the GoIceland office, although Celeste's mind was still on the mountain, watching Alabama disappear into the earth.

"I can take that for you." Benno's voice seemed to float from nowhere. Celeste blinked, noticing a beat too late that she was still holding onto her helmet.

"Sorry," she said, releasing it into Benno's outstretched hand. He gave her a crooked smile, which she might have found endearing had she not been so tense.

Celeste couldn't put her finger on exactly why she felt the way she did. After all, nothing bad had happened on the mountainside. Alabama had slipped into the ice, but a minute later, she had come right back out. There was no reason for Celeste to be trembling now, which was part of the problem. With no logical explanation for Celeste's panicky feeling, there was no way to rationalize it away.

Behind her, someone exhaled impatiently, and a second later, Margot scooted past. Celeste stepped back as Margot held out her helmet for Benno. With her other hand, Margot twisted a lock of hair around a gel-manicured finger.

"So do you, like, live here?" she said to Benno in a voice Celeste hadn't heard her use before now. It was both higher and sweeter than how Margot had introduced herself to Celeste the night before. (They had been in the middle of their first icebreaker, an excruciating game of charades from which Celeste was still recovering.) Like the other girls, Margot was clearly flirting. Benno, unfortunately, did not get the hint.

"Sure do, but I get into Reykjavík to see my girlfriend as much as much as I can. She's a therapist. Not much for her to do out here in the mountains," he added good-naturedly.

Celeste turned, but not before catching a glimpse of Margot's reaction. Her plump lips bunched together into a disappointed pout. This struck Celeste as something that Alabama would have found funny. They might have laughed about it later, even though it would have made Celeste feel a tiny bit mean.

Celeste looked around, searching for her friend. On the way down from the glacier and on the bus ride back to the office, Alabama had again been worrisomely quiet. She had stared out the window, her face so close to the glass that when the bus had cleared a particularly large bump, her forehead had collided with it.

Celeste caught sight of Alabama's head over the other women in the small room. Alabama's hair had frizzed in the helmet, creating a slight aura of static that shone where the weak light caught it overhead.

As Celeste approached, she heard the tail end of Alabama's conversation with the bearded guide, Tom. His voice was so deep that the old planks beneath him seemed to shake slightly when he spoke.

"Every mornin' but Sunday," he boomed, sounding jolly. "Mornin' hike starts at nine AM sharp."

"So tomorrow morning too, then?" Alabama said. She was still holding her crampons. As Celeste neared from behind, she noticed Alabama's thumb caressing one of the steel pins.

"Yep. Why? You thinking o' coming again?" he said with a chuckle that quivered at the end of his beard. Celeste stepped to Alabama's side just as she answered, shaking her head no.

"What was that all about?" Celeste said as they crossed the parking lot a little while later. They were far enough away from the other influencers that no one could hear their conversation, although Celeste kept her voice low anyway.

"What was what about?" Alabama was walking a few steps ahead of Celeste.

"You were talking to Tom about something." Celeste trotted to catch up.

"Oh," Alabama said as she rounded the car.

Celeste waited for more to follow, but nothing did. Alabama came to a stop at the passenger side and reached down for the door. She pulled at the handle hard, then pulled at it again even though it was clearly locked. Celeste frowned, trying to read Alabama's face.

"Al, are you sure you're alright?"

Alabama met her eyes. Only her head was visible over the Taurus, beneath the halo of frizzy hair she had not yet fixed. She looked at Celeste blankly for a moment, as though waiting for Celeste to translate the unintelligible question she had just asked. The expression reminded Celeste of Bella, which did not make Celeste feel better.

A sudden gust of wind whipped across the car, shaking it a little. The metal creaked as it rocked back and forth before becoming still. Alabama and Celeste looked at one another over the top, and then, unexpectantly, Alabama's face broke out into a smile.

"I'm fine, CeCe. I feel good. I feel like things are all falling into place for me, you know?"

Celeste shivered, thinking of Alabama's face on the mountainside, where she had produced the same wide, brazen grin.

"You got some balls," Tom had said to her as he had hoisted her from the crevasse. "Not many girls woulda gone and done that like yeh did."

It had been a categorically sexist thing to say, and for a moment, Alabama had just looked at him with a slightly dazed expression—understandable for someone who had just been dipped in and out of the earth. But then her face had morphed—slowly at first, then all at once. She had looked Tom directly in the eye, and she had smiled like something had just clicked.

Alabama looked down to the door again. Wind rustled her hair, sending the baby-fine pieces skyward. She grabbed the handle and pulled at it, three more quick, impatient pulses, even though it was still locked.

They didn't talk much on the drive back. Alabama spent most of the ride staring out the window, checking her phone every so often for service that never stayed for more than a minute or two. Celeste gripped the steering wheel diligently and chewed the inside of her cheek until it was sore.

She thought about calling Louis to ask for his opinion, although she was unable to work out what to say. Louis didn't know what Henry had told her about Alabama, and Celeste felt no desire to bring that conversation up. Besides, even if Celeste did tell Louis, she could imagine his response. *If Henry says she's fine, she's fine,* he would tell her, probably with a shrug.

As their little car finally grumbled its way up the hill into Vík, Celeste had whittled her options down to one. She had to contact Henry. She very specifically did not want to contact Henry, but she could see no other choice.

Alabama didn't ask to shower first when they got back. She simply decided she would. Celeste didn't mind, as this meant she had the room to herself. The sky outside was still as bright and cloudless as it had been when they had left for the hike that morning, although the wind had picked up since. It announced itself with a repetitive *thwack thwack thwack* of something light but irritatingly persistent against their bedroom window.

As soon as Alabama left with her shower caddy, Celeste pulled out her phone, ready to type. Five minutes later, however, Celeste's cursor remaining blinking amid empty space. Her worry felt as real as her heartbeat, but she found herself unable to articulate it to Henry past some vague sense that something was wrong.

Celeste decided to start with Alabama's odd grin. It was difficult to capture the expression with words, but it was something concrete for Celeste to latch onto, something real she had seen with her own eyes. She told Henry about that, and then about Alabama's bizarre reaction to Hollie's possible pregnancy.

As the message zipped off into cyberspace, Celeste brought the phone to her chest and closed her eyes. She didn't know what she wanted Henry to say to her exactly. Did she want his advice or just for him to validate her concern?

She thought of Bella back home in Chicago. Was there a part of Celeste that would feel validated if something was wrong with her too? If a teacher or medical professional confirmed that Celeste wasn't crazy, that she had been right all along? The fact that she couldn't answer this question made her feel as though she had already failed her daughter somehow.

By the time Henry answered, Alabama was back in the room, lotioned and dressed.

You're feeling guilty, Henry had typed, *and that's understandable. But worry is not an effective coping strategy. I promise, Alabama is fine.*

Something gurgled in the back of Celeste's throat, warm and acidic. She couldn't count all the times in her life she had been told not to worry, and yet something about Henry saying this to her now felt borderline cruel. She jammed her thumb against the screen hard. The message, she decided, did not warrant a response.

"Your pics are doing well," Alabama said, drawing Celeste's attention back to her. Celeste looked up.

"Yeah, I guess so." A beat, then Celeste added, "Yours too, it seems like."

This wasn't exactly a lie. Celeste had checked both of their pictures before they had left the GoIceland office, in the brief window she'd had decent cell phone service. Celeste had gathered a few hundred more likes than Alabama by that point, but that was so insignificant in context, it was essentially nothing.

"Not as well as yours," Alabama countered. "You're up to forty thousand likes already. Didn't you see?"

Celeste didn't mean to stare, but she felt herself unable to look away. It dawned on her what she hadn't been able to identify at first: something almost serene across Alabama's face. The expression looked foreign on her friend, rendering Alabama almost unrecognizable.

Celeste forced herself to look down at her phone. She opened Instagram, and true to Alabama's word, Celeste's photo from the glacier had amassed over forty thousand likes, almost twice as many as usual. She felt a tug of dread as she clicked to Alabama's profile.

Alabama's last photo was nearly identical to Celeste's—one white Midwestern body swapped out with another—and yet, Alabama's picture was hovering at twenty-one thousand likes, only a couple thousand more than when Celeste had checked it earlier that day. For not the first time, Celeste wished she could make sense of the discrepancy, although she knew trying to understand the forces that drove social media was like trying to decipher random weather patterns.

Worry is not an effective coping strategy, Henry reminded her from inside her head.

"Anyway," Alabama said, sliding to the edge of her bed, "I'm gonna go for a walk." She bent over to unravel the towel from her hair in one fluid motion before straightening. She was wearing cotton pajama shorts, a cheerful shade of sunshine yellow that provided barely any contrast to the orangish hue of her bottle-tanned legs.

If the thought crossed Alabama's mind to change out of her pajamas, it wasn't persuasive. She slipped into her white Keds, and by the time Celeste thought to ask Alabama how long she would be gone, Alabama had already left.

Celeste stared at the bedroom door for a while before lumbering to her knees. Through the window, she watched Alabama emerge from the front stairwell and into the parking lot. Her back was to the bed and breakfast, so Celeste couldn't tell if she was looking at the car in front of her or something else. She seemed to stand there for ages—silent, unmoving—until finally she turned and started walking briskly toward the sea.

27

Hollie

The Day Before
Vík, Iceland

H OLLIE SHOWERED IMMEDIATELY when they got back from the glacier hike, wanting to wash the day from her as soon as she possibly could. Now Katherine was in the shower, and Hollie was on her bed, glad to be alone.

Katherine had spent the entire drive back from the glacier providing her own unrequested commentary on the day's events. "I'm going to be honest with you," she had said at one point, feet propped up on the dashboard. "How happy Alabama seemed about that crevasse was one of the weirdest fucking things I've ever seen."

Hollie hadn't said anything to this because Hollie had decided she was done thinking about Alabama. In fact, she longed for a time when she would never have to think about Alabama again.

Hollie leaned forward. Her injured leg was extended in a lazy hamstring stretch, although rather than actually tending to her injury, most of her focus was on her phone. After she had tackled a few easier emails—one annoying email from Robin, one less annoying message from her manager—she had opened the message from Nick. She had, genuinely, intended to answer it. So far, she had come up with: *Hi.*

From out in the hall, there was the faint shush of a door creaking open. Hollie looked up, anticipating Katherine storming into their bedroom, dripping wet. Yesterday after Katherine had taken a shower, she had marched back into their room without knocking. She had then proceeded to drop her towel before pulling on her underwear and bra, like they were two men in a gym locker room. (Hollie wasn't a prude, but she also didn't need a full frontal of Katherine Livingston without warning.)

Hollie waited a few more seconds as silence settled back around her. Finally, deciding that it hadn't been Katherine after all, she refocused on the phone.

She had never imagined herself getting a divorce. Perhaps no one did, but Hollie had been especially sure. She had assumed that a failure of this magnitude was impossible in her life, impossible for someone like her.

Hollie had failed in so many ways lately, but a divorce from Nick still seemed unfathomable somehow. How would they even do it? How would they decide who got the house, the Peloton, the car? Would they divvy up the houseplants too, or would they just let them die? How did one draw a line down the middle of something so entwined as their lives?

Hollie had once unintentionally watched a documentary about a pair of conjoined twins. She had just turned on Netflix when the preview had caught her attention. The sight of two tiny bodies with two tiny pairs of arms, two tiny pairs of legs, bound together by a stretch of skin pulling at their two tiny torsos. It had been so easy to see how it had happened, two bodies pulling apart like a sticky piece of taffy in their mother's womb, not quite making a clean break.

Hollie had watched in quiet fascination as the doctors had plotted the separation surgery—mapping out cut lines, creating life-sized models for elaborate practice runs. Documentaries, Hollie knew, were produced like any other movie, and indeed, near the climax, it had come out that the two twins shared a kidney. One kidney, two babies—Hollie had let out an audible gasp.

The decision had been excruciating. Who should get the kidney? The stronger baby? The surgery would be invasive, and in a way, it made sense to do everything possible so that at least one of the twins survived. Or should it go to the smaller, weaker baby? The one who clearly needed it more?

The parents had been useless, understandably so. They had been unable to see the decision with any clarity, although even Hollie— distant from the twins in every way—had been torn. It was an impossible decision because there was no right answer. There were only different versions of wrong.

She tried to imagine herself in couples therapy with Nick, like he had suggested. This was difficult primarily because she knew essentially nothing about therapy besides what she saw on TV. She imagined the office—a Scandinavian-style couch and sterile white walls. The therapist would be a stern woman with thick-framed glasses, and she would smell like sandalwood, probably. Would the therapist make them do something performative and silly, like hold hands? She imagined sitting in front of Nick, her hands in his. She would look him in the eyes and say—what, exactly?

There was nothing to say, and that was the problem. Unless the therapist could go back in time and change things, Hollie could see no way for even the most overeducated person in the world to help them now.

She missed Nick. She missed their lives. She missed happy hour margaritas and mimosas at Sunday brunch. Weekend trips to Austin. Spontaneous shower sex. How had she never before realized how exquisite and fragile it was for Nick to turn off the lamp at night and kiss her in the darkness before they both fell asleep?

But maybe the worst part, the most unbearable part of the whole thing, was that Nick missed her too. After everything that had happened, after everything Hollie had said and done, he was willing to make things work.

Hollie closed the email without typing anything else.

CHAPTER

28

Celeste

The Morning After
Vík, Iceland

"THIS IS QUITE good, isn't it?" Officer Björnsson said. He had already eaten one slice of lava bread and was cutting himself another. Delphine had interrupted them with the loaf a few minutes earlier, to the officer's polite irritation. Officer Björnsson was the sort of person, Celeste had decided, who probably pressed his lips together very tightly when he was caught in traffic but never cursed at anyone out loud.

Celeste nodded. She had taken a single bite of her slice, then set it back down on the napkin, where it had remained since.

Officer Björnsson used the bread knife to move the slice from the platter. He had swept the crumbs from his first slice into a neat little pile beside his napkin. Celeste thought of Henry, back at home in Chicago, and how orderly his cutlery drawer was. Alabama maintained that she had once caught him reorganizing the drawer immediately after she had unloaded the dishwasher, which was only unbelievable because Alabama so rarely did the dishes.

There was a ting beneath the table. Officer Björnsson looked down to his hip, where he had clipped his cell phone, reminding Celeste less of a serious detective than an endearing father. Celeste's own father wore black belts with brown trousers and didn't leave the house without his cell phone secured to his waist.

Celeste tried to decipher Officer Björnsson's expression as he read the message, but the only thing she could detect was the faintest tightening of his jaw.

"Would you excuse me for a moment?" he said. He crossed the room so abruptly, he was still holding the bread knife.

She thought of Henry. She wondered if someone had told him yet. Probably. They would probably alert Henry straight away. She didn't know Henry well enough to know who he would call after that. His mother? His friends? Were his friendships even good enough for that?

Maybe he would call Louis, she thought suddenly. This made her feel very, very cold.

She brought her face to her palms, where she stayed until Office Björnsson returned.

"So," Officer Björnsson said, flipping open his notepad. "I think we've just about covered everything we need from you at the moment." He ran one finger down the lined paper, although Celeste got the impression he wasn't actually focused on the notes in front of him. Whatever had happened, whatever message he had received, it had left him shaken.

This felt like such a human reaction, to be flustered, to be distracted, so paradoxical to being a cop. Of course, Celeste knew cops were people, just like doctors and politicians and ambulance drivers, but Celeste had always let herself think of them as different. They were people, but people in a league just above normal people like her, who managed to always use the wrong toaster setting and burn her toast more often than not. She always felt a bit dazed when she remembered that policemen and doctors and ambulance drivers were nothing more than people who felt things exactly like she did.

Perhaps this was why, without really thinking, she said, "They found her, didn't they?"

There was a beat of silence. Officer Björnsson's face was still cast downward, but his eyes were no longer moving. Celeste thought of Alabama's eyes, wild and angry. What if that was the very last image of her that Celeste had?

"I'm her best friend," Celeste whispered, even if it was no longer true. "Just tell me if she's okay."

Officer Björnsson looked up. His eyes were a light shade of amber, a color Celeste would probably have described as yellow, although that wasn't exactly right. Yellow was bright and cheerful—sunflower petals and lemonade pitchers and sunshine. Yellow was not shallow and sad.

"We found the car," Officer Björnsson said evenly. "Off an embankment. It was"—a tiny inhale—"submerged."

Celeste swallowed. She felt her eyes watering, and for a moment she thought she was about to cry before realizing that she had simply forgotten to blink.

"What about Alabama?"

Celeste barely recognized her own voice for how strained it sounded.

"We haven't found her yet, but . . ."

He trailed off, and Celeste waited for a moment—fixated—until she realized that he wasn't planning to say anything else. And then, the next realization, nearly instantaneous: He didn't need to. He had already said all he needed to say. They hadn't found her, *but*. The *but* was everything. The *but* was all she needed to know.

Celeste felt herself begin to tremble, the shaking starting in her shoulders and spreading outward. She was suddenly freezing. Her teeth chattered, so she bit down on nothing, clenching with every drop of energy she could tap.

"I'm sorry," Officer Björnsson said, sounding like he meant it. He reached over the table. The warmth of his skin against her clammy hands was unexpected, and without thinking, she whipped her hand back. This seemed to startle her more than it did him, and it struck her that Officer Björnsson had probably seen much ruder in his line of work. Maybe he *was* in a different league from Celeste. Celeste couldn't fathom a life where a person encountered this situation more than once.

She wondered again if they had told Henry, and what Henry had told them.

"No," Celeste said, unable to stop herself. "I'm sorry." Beneath the table, her hands were balled into fists. She inhaled, long and deliberate, and then with a voice as steady as she could make it, she looked at Officer Björnsson and finally said it.

"I haven't been completely honest about what happened last night."

CHAPTER

29

Celeste

The Night Of
Vik, Iceland

I T WAS NEARLY ten by the time Celeste got out of the shower the
night after the glacier hike, more than an hour since Alabama had
left. She still hadn't come back, a fact Celeste was doing her best not
to worry about.

The bed and breakfast bathroom was drafty and small, not
nearly equipped for the number of lotions and potions the average
Instagram influencer was likely to bring. Celeste felt she was rather
conservative in this regard, as she only had two toiletry bags—one
for the essentials, and one for her makeup. And yet even she was
having a hard time making it work. She felt like one of those circus
contortionists as she attempted to balance on one leg while applying
lotion to the other, all the while trying to touch as little of the mil-
dewy tile as she could.

The bathroom was on the second floor of the building, with a
tiny window above the toilet, which overlooked the parking lot. The
window was frosted, presumably for privacy, but half open as it was,
anyone on the second floor of a building would be able to see Celeste
through it. (Celeste had tried to close it, but it was stuck.)

She swirled both palms around her calf, spreading the lotion
across her skin. Her legs were covered in goose pimples, due somewhat

to the brisk evening air but also to her tingling anxiety about Alabama. As much as Celeste tried, no matter what Henry had said, she could not stop herself from worrying.

Celeste was struck with a memory from her wedding, right before she had walked down the aisle. She had been standing in the church sacristy—a beige room with a small but tidy kitchenette and a crucified Jesus mounted to the wall—waiting for her cue. She had been so nervous, she had been unable to clasp her bracelet because she had been shivering so badly. The bracelet had been her grandmother's, a tiny silver chain with a minuscule silver latch, and right there in front of Jesus Christ Himself on the cross, she had said the f-word for probably the fifth time in her life.

Alabama—her only bridesmaid—had been peering out at the congregation, but hearing Celeste swear, she had appeared by Celeste's side. Silently, Alabama had latched the bracelet for her, then kissed the top of Celeste's hand. In Celeste's whole life, it had been one of the most soothing things anyone had ever done.

Below the window, Celeste heard the distinct sound of crunching gravel. She looked out and was relieved to see Alabama heading from the road toward the bed and breakfast parking lot. Celeste quickly withdrew from the window, not wanting Alabama to see her watching.

Working quickly now, Celeste shook the bottle of lotion that was nearly gone. The bottle was sample-sized, sent to her by some pretentious "earth-friendly" company in more packaging than seemed particularly earth-conscious, if Celeste was being honest.

She lathered the rest onto her other calf, not caring how evenly the lotion was applied. Even though the bottle wasn't totally empty, she tossed it into the trash can. She then brushed her teeth and ran product through her hair, then searched around for her phone for a moment before realizing she had left it in the room.

She grabbed a second towel and wrapped it around her hair, then moved to open the door. With her hand on the doorknob, however, she stopped, caught by her reflection over the sink.

She was surprised by how old she looked, as she didn't remember looking this old only a few weeks ago. She leaned closer to the mirror, examining herself more closely. The strange thing was none of the individual components of her face looked old. Her forehead was Botoxed smooth, as was the skin around her mouth (although her mouth, thankfully, needed less help). And yet, put together, she felt like she was looking at someone twice her age.

Maybe it was her posture. Her back naturally slouched when she wasn't paying attention to it, which she often wasn't. She straightened her shoulders, and her reflection mimicked the movement. But no, that wasn't it either. She wondered if it was possible for exhaustion to taint one's appearance, if looking old was simply looking very tired.

She turned the knob and flicked off the bathroom light. This was a problem she would leave for a future version of herself, she decided, as she couldn't do much about it now. She seriously doubted there was anywhere in Iceland she could even get a facial peel. The people in this country didn't need it. Everyone she had met so far— every single person—had emanated youth, like they had all slipped into a permanent Instagram filter.

As she shuffled down the hallway, she wondered if it was something in their genes that did it, or if it was the minerals in the water. Probably the minerals, she decided, and then she wondered if she should have splurged on the silica mud mask at the Blue Lagoon gift shop. As she pulled her bedroom door open, she decided she would swing by on the way back and pick up a bottle, even if it cost more than—

THUD.

Celeste let out a small gasp. She wasn't sure if it was the sound that had startled her or the object whizzing past her cheek.

"IT WAS YOU."

Celeste's eyes found Alabama just in time to see her cock her arm. A moment later, a shoe—Celeste's shoe, she realized, right before ducking—flew over her, landing with the same sickening thud against the wall.

"YOU," Alabama shrieked, her eyes wild as she searched for her next projectile. She snatched a tube of lipstick from the corner of the desk and moved more quickly than Celeste had ever seen a person move.

Celeste turned halfway, enough that the plastic cylinder pelted her in the back instead of the chest. She arched forward in pain.

"Alabama!" she cried, her hand reaching for the spot where the lipstick had made contact. "Stop!"

"IT WAS YOU!"

More plastic, this time a tube of highlighter careening past Celeste's face.

"What was me?" Celeste tried to protect her head with her arms as a hair straightener slammed into the bedroom door, which Celeste had unconsciously closed behind her. She wondered how long it would take for someone to hear the noise and come in, and what they would find when they eventually got there.

"YOU'RE THE ONE HENRY'S CHEATING WITH."

Celeste froze. For a moment, it seemed as though Alabama had too, as if hearing the words out loud had caught her off guard. Celeste lowered her arms and turned to look at her friend, noticing for the first time a phone—her own phone—in Alabama's left hand.

Alabama's eyes followed Celeste's, and Celeste flinched, thinking for a second that Alabama was about to throw it at her. When Alabama raised her arm, however, she just waved the phone back and forth.

"He texted you," she said. She wasn't screaming, which Celeste appreciated, but her voice sounded almost deadlier than before. "I saw my name, so I looked at your whole convo." She sucked in a ragged breath. "You bitch."

Celeste felt the words as tangibly as the lipstick pelting her between the shoulder blades. Alabama had said this last part so calmly, like she was simply stating a fact. Which it was. It was as much of a fact as the DNA coiled tight in her cells—inarguable, immutable, a foundational component of Celeste's being. She was Celeste Reed, a bitch.

"Alabama," Celeste started, but Alabama's hand flew up, cutting her off.

"Just tell me," she whispered. "How long? How long have you been having an affair with him?"

Celeste started shaking her head before Alabama had even finished asking the question.

"There was no affair," she heard herself saying. The truth seemed to spew out of her like projectile vomit. "I promise, Al. I wouldn't do that to you."

And here is where Celeste should have stopped. A split second later, this would become overwhelmingly clear, and a few minutes after that, she would wonder why she hadn't. But these thoughts came only after she had added breathlessly, moronically, "It was only that once."

Alabama made a sound like an angry mare—braying, teeth bared. She seemed to use the entire force of her thin body to wind up and hurl Celeste's phone toward her, which smacked decisively on the wall over Celeste's ducked head before falling to the ground.

Celeste straightened and somehow found Alabama's eyes, now shining with tears of fury. Celeste opened her mouth, and Alabama seemed to pause for an instant.

It was possible that if Celeste had been able to summon the right words, if she had been able to inject them into this narrow slice of time, Alabama would have listened. Or maybe not. Celeste would never know because Celeste's brain didn't formulate a single word. All it emitted was a throaty croak.

Alabama was suddenly moving, and Celeste braced herself, sure that Alabama was charging to attack. But then, just as Celeste's arms crossed over her chest, Alabama flew past her. She thrust the door open and stomped out into the hall.

"Alabama," Celeste called out pointlessly as Alabama reached the top of the staircase. Celeste took a step into the hallway after her, close to crying herself.

On the top step, Alabama turned. Celeste felt her breath catch in her chest.

"You don't realize it," Alabama hissed. "But you're the most selfish person I know, Celeste."

And then, without another word, she was gone.

30

Celeste

Three Months Before
Chicago, Illinois

After Bella's soccer game, Celeste had a glass of wine at three o'clock in the afternoon. She didn't normally drink wine in the afternoon. Actually, she didn't normally drink wine period. She liked wine, but she had recently read about the dangers of it in an incriminating article titled "The Last Five Pounds," or in Celeste's case, the last ten.

Apparently, drinking one's calories was the number four reason women were unable to shed those last stubborn pounds, right after late-night snacking, eating too much, and eating too little, in that order. And so Celeste, always appreciative of an actionable list, had decided to drink only water and black coffee except for the occasional, exceptional situation.

And today was one of them.

She was alone in their kitchen. Bella was upstairs taking a nap, so deeply asleep that when Celeste had checked on her a few minutes before, she'd tiptoed over to the bed just to make sure her daughter was still breathing. Bella barely napped anymore, finding no use for it in her advanced age. The fiasco that morning, however, had apparently wiped her out.

Louis was also upstairs in his office, doing work. Or that's what he had said, although Celeste couldn't fight the suspicion that he had only disappeared into the study because it was the one place he knew Celeste wouldn't be.

She had never made a scene like the one she had that morning. Until very recently, she had not even thought herself capable of such a thing. What Celeste had never before considered, however, was that sometimes it wasn't a decision. She had no more decided to shout at Bella in front of those parents than she had decided to wake up with all ten toes on her feet.

A part of her wondered what the other parents now thought of her after witnessing such an outburst. The other part of her—the bigger part—didn't have to wonder. *And you wonder why she acts out.* Louis's words were as clear to Celeste as if he had repeated them in the kitchen. It was as though he had taken her own worst thoughts and said them out loud. *Yes, Celeste, maybe this is your fault.*

And so, the wine.

Celeste swirled her glass, allowing the pale yellow liquid to wink at her in the sunny kitchen. She had never purposefully drunk to get drunk, even in college. It wasn't that she had some moral opposition to it, or even a practical one. It was mostly that drunkenness seemed so . . . audacious, which Celeste was not.

She brought the wine to her lips and took a large, undignified gulp. She then sat back in her chair and stared at her cabinets. They were the expensive kind that didn't make a sound even when you slammed them.

She wondered if Auggie also blamed Celeste for Bella biting her son, and then she wondered why she even cared what Auggie thought. She barely knew the women, for god's sake—except, Celeste felt like she did. It was a pity, really, that the best friendships were oftentimes the ones that never actually started.

Celeste took another long sip. It was a shame she would never be friends with Auggie. It was a shame, but it was not a tragedy, so why did it feel so tragic? She felt like someone had swiped back a curtain to reveal a magical alternate universe filled with all the things Celeste could've had and might've been. And then, in an instant, the curtain had fluttered back, covering it all.

She finished the rest of the wine, then pushed herself up from the table. As she marched up the stairs, she directed an inordinate amount of attention to her hands and feet, making sure she wasn't tipsy enough that they felt tingly. But she was sober, as far as she could tell.

She didn't knock at Louis's door before she pushed it open.

"I'm going to Alabama's," she said as Louis was still swiveling around in his chair. She glanced at the dual monitors behind him. His Outlook inbox was open on one, an Excel spreadsheet on the other. He did appear to be doing actual work, at least.

"Okay," he said simply, and that was it. She wasn't sure what she was expecting—an apology, maybe. An acknowledgment that he had been upset at the game too and that's why he'd said what he had, not because he had actually meant it. For a split second, she thought he was about to say something further. He opened his mouth slightly, his lips parting like he was about to speak. But then he closed them again, saying nothing.

In the car, Celeste thought she could feel the alcohol absorbing into her blood. She still wasn't drunk, but something about her thoughts felt different—sharper. It was like wiping clean a window's dusty glass.

The thing Celeste liked about alcohol was that—to the surprise of some people—it made her think more clearly. She had never understood sloppy drinkers for this reason, how they slurred and rambled. When Celeste had alcohol, the jumbled mess in her head distilled itself down into very basic, very identifiable emotions: happiness and sadness, affection and dislike. Straightforward feelings uncomplicated by her sober self's impulse to manhandle them into cooperation. Clarity. It was worth the extra calories when the situation called.

Spring had started its tentative arrival, and as she flew down the road, mild air whipped in through her open car window. This was soothing to her, almost as soothing as all the messy feelings from that morning starting to disentangle. Sun twinkled off the dashboard as the mood inside her settled, and to her surprise, she realized something with remarkable certainty: She wasn't mad at Louis for what he had said. Not really. She wasn't even hurt. More than anything, Celeste just felt alone.

When Celeste pulled her car to a stop at Alabama's curb, another thought floated through her brain, sharpened by the wine: This loneliness wasn't all that new. Her entire life, she had felt alone in one way or another. How strange, she thought, examining the realization like someone examining an unusual seashell. How very curious that a life as crowded as hers could feel so startlingly lonesome.

She pushed herself out of the car and onto the sidewalk, thinking suddenly how glad she was to have someone like Alabama in her life. A friend. A real one. Granted, Alabama was not the sort of friend Celeste would have picked for herself, but Celeste hadn't been given the option. Alabama had been a random roommate assignment their freshman year in college, and it had been Alabama's decision to become more than that. Alabama had latched onto Celeste immediately, and once Alabama decided something, it was nearly impossible to change her mind.

Celeste ascended Alabama's front steps and rang the doorbell. Through the door, she heard the muffled sound of wind chimes. As they faded and the ensuing silence settled, Celeste considered— probably not soon enough—that she should have called Alabama first to make sure she was home. She pulled out her phone and had one finger over Alabama's number when the door opened.

"Henry," she said, sliding the phone back into her purse. "Hi. Is Alabama home?"

"Hi, Celeste. I'm sorry, but no." Henry used one finger to push his glasses up the brim of his nose. "She's getting her hair done this afternoon."

Celeste nodded, which felt like the right response, although frankly, she hadn't heard a word after no. She hadn't anticipated Alabama not being there, which now felt marvelously dumb.

"Oh. Okay. No problem."

There was a beat. "Are you alright, Celeste?" Henry said.

"Yes, yes. I'm fine." Celeste waved her hand. She didn't understand why he would ask something so presumptuous. "Why do you ask?"

"You're crying," he said. He sounded apologetic, and Celeste instinctively reached up to pat her cheeks, which she was surprised to find wet. She wiped them hurriedly, her face burning.

"Sorry," she said, all of the winey clarity now gone. How humiliating this was, crying in front of Henry. She didn't even know why she was.

"You don't have to apologize," Henry said, and for some reason, this felt like the saddest thing in the world. The alarm bells in Celeste's head screamed out in warning, but it was useless. She felt the sob rise up inside her like a huge, swelling wave, and, unable to stop it, Celeste was suddenly bawling, as helpless against her own body as someone trying to karate kick the tide.

She was vaguely aware of Henry's hand landing on her forearm, and when he started to lead her inside, she felt a half-hearted notion to refuse. But then she thought of going home to Louis, of trying to explain to *him* why she was crying, and that just made her cry more.

She let Henry guide her through the door, down the hall to the living room, where he lowered her to the couch. He seemed to hesitate for a moment before placing one hand on her upper back. It was such a simple gesture, unsure but nice. Celeste continued to cry, the unflattering snotty kind that took her whole body.

She wasn't sure how long she cried for. Eventually, once her body had expelled more water than was probably healthy, she felt her tears starting to slow. In their place, a feeling of tiredness washed over her, the sort of all-encompassing exhaustion that followed a good, long sob.

"I'm sorry," she said, patting her nose with her sleeve. She hiccupped in a way she might have found embarrassing if she'd had any shame left. "I don't know what's gotten into me."

Henry produced a tissue from somewhere, which Celeste took.

"I just . . ." She creased the tissue in half and then in quarters before blowing into it quietly. "I just—I think I might be a bad mom."

She withdrew the tissue from her face and stared at it for a moment, as though it had said the words instead of her. She hadn't even realized she thought this about herself until she had said it, but now that she had, she knew without a doubt that it was true.

"Well," Henry said, sounding thoughtful, "in my experience, the bad moms are usually not the ones worrying about whether they're bad."

Celeste met his eyes. He looked so deeply serious that Celeste wasn't sure whether she felt embarrassed or just uncomfortable having this sort of conversation with him. After all, when you really got down to it, Henry was someone she didn't know particularly well.

"Bella bit another kid at her soccer game today," she said quietly. "And I got so angry with her. I *blamed* her for doing it, like she had done it just to ruin my day."

The words were so ugly. Hearing them, that's all Celeste could think. They were ugly words and ugly thoughts, and she was so ugly for thinking them.

"Which would be horrible all on its own," she went on, picking up momentum, "but the worst part is that I know it's not her fault. I don't know if it's autism or something else, but it's something. Louis doesn't think so, though, and I'm too much of a coward to challenge him. To actually *do* anything about it. I'm . . ."

Celeste stopped, sensing a line being crossed. As hurt as she was, it didn't feel right to talk about her husband like that.

There were a few seconds of silence. Celeste considered her tissue, which was the nice kind with lotion infused into the fiber. Celeste never splurged on this sort of thing, which suddenly seemed overwhelmingly selfish. What was an extra dollar or two so her family's noses didn't get chapped?

"Alabama has been seeing a psychiatrist," Henry said at last. Celeste looked up at him, and he looked right back, his gaze steady. "He prescribed her some medicine, so she's cut back on the appointments recently, but before that, she'd been seeing him weekly for almost a year. She's been having"—he swallowed loudly—"unhealthy thoughts."

Celeste was completely quiet. If talking about Louis had been a betrayal, this sort of information about Alabama was surely marital treason.

Henry said, "It really started last winter when we were watching a documentary about Bethany Hamilton. She's that surfer who lost her arm a few years back. When we finished, Alabama said to me, she said, 'That's a thing—her arm. That's the thing that sets her apart.'" He swallowed again, his Adam's apple moving visibly along his neck. "I thought she was joking, but she wasn't. You know her engagement on Instagram has been down recently, and she thought that if she lost an arm like Bethany Hamilton, it would help." He shook his head, now looking at his knees. "She wouldn't let it go either. She was obsessed with a thing, and I was afraid she was going to hurt herself or somebody else. It was"—here, Henry's voice broke, the faintest crackle—"scary to witness."

Celeste's eyes were now totally dry, her previous outburst seeming years away. If she hadn't felt so gobsmacked, she might have felt embarrassed for crying in the first place, for working herself up about something that was arguably trivial compared to this.

How had she not known? Alabama had always been more intense than most people, her feelings bigger and louder than the norm, but Celeste had never suspected anything seriously wrong.

"What I guess I'm saying," Henry said finally, quietly, "is that I know what it's like to be lonely in a marriage. Even when it's not their fault necessarily, sometimes you just feel alone."

Celeste looked at him—actually looked at him. He had dark green eyes, the color of ivy climbing up a shadowed wall. They looked like they were reflecting back at Celeste everything exactly as she felt it.

From the other room, Celeste noticed a steady hum punctured by the rhythmic clank of something hard against metal. It sounded like the dryer, a zipper banging against the drum. She was suddenly aware that this was Henry's home, not just Alabama's. It was where he did his laundry, where he slept and ate and lived.

It wasn't clear which one of them touched the other first. It was like they had been sitting there one second, two alone people separated by space on the couch, and then they weren't.

It struck her as she was kissing him that she had never thought about kissing him before. At the same time, it was somehow exactly like she would have expected. His lips were slow but deliberate. His fingers grazed her collarbone, the touch light and attentive. None of this surprised her about him, and suspended in this feeling—this feeling of understanding, of being understood—Henry wasn't Alabama's husband at all.

But then, his hands. They were moving along Celeste's shoulder until they were at Celeste's waist, fluttering at the button on her pants. Celeste drew back sharply. Henry leaned back too, confusion lining his face.

A few years ago, Celeste had seen a black-and-white video on Facebook of an atomic bomb—a sudden flash, the instantaneous flattening of trees and buildings and people. It had been horrifying for the obvious reasons, but the most chilling part had been the swiftness of it, how one burst of heat was all it took for decades of life to be obliterated to dust. It had been unimaginable to Celeste, how that sort of damage could happen just like that. And yet here Celeste was, seeing it with her own eyes.

She stood up quickly, feeling dizzy. He stood up too, much more slowly.

"I'm sorry," she said, her first instinct. She wasn't apologizing to him, not really, and maybe Henry understood this, or maybe he didn't. Either way, he flinched at the apology, and something about this sickened Celeste. She felt a wave of visceral disgust.

"We can't tell Alabama," she said, not giving him the chance to respond. "Or Louis," she added, an afterthought.

Henry said nothing for a moment, gave no indication whether or not he agreed. She didn't wait for an answer. She couldn't bear to look at him for a single second longer.

When she got home, the first thing she did was hug Bella, although Bella—impatient and unwilling—shrugged her mother away. Celeste then disappeared into their bathroom for a shower without looking Louis in the eye. She turned on the water, and as it warmed, she stood naked in front of the mirror, examining her body as if she had never before seen it. As if she was Henry, looking at something he desired.

She stood there long enough that the mirror started to fog. Right before steam swallowed her reflection entirely, she realized that she had been wrong, that it wasn't Henry she couldn't stand to look at.

She bit into the skin of her forearm so Bella and Louis wouldn't hear her cry.

31

Alabama

The Night Of
Vík, Iceland

THE THING MOST people didn't understand about Alabama was that she didn't *enjoy* being angry. When she was little, grown-ups had always been talking about her temper like it was something she could control, like it was a pet dog she intentionally let loose. For the longest time, Alabama had believed this too. They were grown-ups, after all, and Alabama was just a kid. The problem, of course, was that grown-ups could be just as stupid as anybody else.

Alabama stormed down the stairs, wanting to feel as comforted by this thought as she usually was. Usually, when someone had wronged Alabama—when she wasn't invited to a wedding or a digital marketing manager passed her over for a campaign—Alabama was comforted by the fact that people, in general, were remarkably dumb.

But this felt different, maybe because she knew for a fact that Celeste wasn't stupid. Even Henry—though he did regularly buy the wrong kind of shampoo and was always losing socks in the wash—wasn't a total moron. This wasn't a matter of a misplaced number or a scattered marketing campaign. Celeste and Henry had done this intentionally, and they had done this to her.

Alabama came to an abrupt stop in the middle of the staircase. The pressure in her head felt so severe, she wondered if it was possible for a person to literally explode when they got too mad. She allowed herself to picture this for a moment—her head popping off like one of those little weeds she had played with as a child. *Momma had a baby and its head popped off.* She imagined blood and brains and little flecks of bone splattering all over the wall. Hopefully Celeste would be the one to find it. Hopefully she would see it and know immediately what had happened, and then wouldn't she feel horrible for what she had done?

Alabama took a deep breath. She liked the idea of vengeance, but she liked it less if she couldn't enjoy it. And how would Alabama enjoy it if her head was oozing down the wall?

She closed her eyes and took another breath, trying to make this one as long as she could. Her stupid doctor had suggested this to her—*mindful breathing,* he had called it, which Alabama still thought was one of the stupidest things she had ever heard. The whole point of breathing was that you didn't have to think about it, and she had told him that. She had asked him why she would waste her time thinking about breathing when she could be thinking about literally anything else.

A few steps below her on the staircase, the wind outside howled against the cloudy window. She thought of the rope in the Taurus, coiled neatly in the trunk. She would have never met her stupid doctor if Henry hadn't found her first rope, or if Alabama had been smart enough to lie when he had. Her mistake—a mistake she could now see clearly—was that she had trusted him. She had thought he would understand. A naïve part of her had even hoped he would be impressed.

Because the plan *was* impressive. The research alone was remarkable. Anyone with half a brain could see that. Alabama had majored in business in college because science had seemed too hard, but now Alabama knew she had underestimated herself. Knots and tourniquets and blood oxygen levels—she understood them all. She knew exactly where to tie the rope around her bicep, exactly how many minutes it would take for tissue death to occur. She knew all about amputation and what the recovery would require. She could have been the next Bethany Hamilton, inspiring millions with her heroic Instagram posts and documentaries made for TV. She could have, and she would have, if it hadn't been for Henry.

Henry hadn't been impressed, maybe because Henry was not quite as smart as Alabama gave him credit for. Instead of acknowledging the research—instead of, God forbid, *praising* her for something—he had taken the rope and made an appointment with a doctor who thought she was insane.

Alabama was not insane, although with some distance, she was able to acknowledge that the plan was not totally flawless. There was the issue of the prosthetic, for one thing, which could do most normal arm things but never looked exactly natural. Also the fact that the plan would generally hurt. She still hadn't figured out how to work around that.

And so, when Alabama had received the invitation to Iceland, she had put a pin in the research and had directed her gumption instead toward befriending Hollie Goodwin. Inserting herself into Hollie's inner circle would solve all of her problems, she thought. She would have a *thing* and both her arms too.

But, of course, she had underestimated Hollie. Hollie didn't want to share her success, which was why she had decided to one-up Alabama with the pregnancy. Alabama had to admit—it was a good plan. People loved babies. And while this had enraged Alabama initially, she didn't even blame Hollie anymore. Actually, if anything, it only proved to Alabama that she and Hollie were not that different. In the end, they would both do anything to get ahead.

Which had led her back to Plan A, which had led her to the only hardware store in the tiny fishing village earlier that evening. There, she had purchased the rope, and the rest she had done already. She already knew how to scale the glacier, and from her weeks of research, she already knew all the right knots. She knew how and where to tie the rope around her arm. Rope to arm, arm to ice block, and her, tangled in between. If she timed it right, if she positioned herself in the exact right spot on the mountain, Tom and Benno would find her, struggling valiantly, bravely, first thing in the morning, when they led a group on their first morning hike.

The hike was the beautiful part. It would provide a ready, captive audience to witness her rescue, her grit. She would wince in pain when Tom and Benno untangled her, but she would not cry. The people on the hike would witness this with wonder and awe. *She was so strong!* they would say later. *She was so beautiful and brave!* They would go home and tell their friends, their loved ones, and when Alabama announced her amputation—a brief and solemn explanation about the rope, the lack of blood to her arm—these people would be aghast. Facebook posts would be written. GoFundMes would overshoot their goals. Strangers would write to Alabama and tell her what an inspiration she was. No one would even notice a boring old pregnancy announcement at all.

For all of this, an arm was a reasonable price to pay.

But now, this. Celeste and Henry, together. The whole goddamn thing. A plan like Alabama's required a sympathetic hero, not a pitiful pariah. Who would cheer on a woman no one wanted in the first place?

32

Hollie

The Morning After
Vík, Iceland

JUST OFF THE shore of Vík, there was a collection of black rock that rose up from the water as columns, darker and more jagged than the mossy cliff walls guarding the village. One of the columns was thin and tall, flanked by two that were squatter and rounder. At their base, surf crashed relentlessly into the stone.

As Officer Guðmundsdóttir scribbled something into her notebook, Hollie gazed out at the columns, thinking of the woman Katherine had told her about the first day of the trip, the one who had swum out to the rocks and died. It was a sad story, but Hollie could not help but think the woman had been asking for it, to some extent. What had she expected to happen, in water like that?

"What are those things called?" Hollie said thoughtfully. She gestured toward the window. "Those rocky columns—they have a special name, don't they?"

Officer Guðmundsdóttir glanced over her shoulder to where Hollie was pointing.

"Reynisdrangar," she said, voice gruff. The word sounded like a string of beads, each foreign syllable colliding into another. "They're basalt sea stacks."

Hollie nodded. She remembered hearing those words before—basalt sea stacks—but she couldn't remember what they meant. She might have asked, but she got the impression that Officer Guðmundsdóttir would ignore her if she did.

It was for this reason that Hollie felt so unprepared when Officer Guðmundsdóttir continued, without prompt, "According to legend, two trolls were trying to drag a ship to the beach. When dawn broke, the trolls turned into needles of rock."

Officer Guðmundsdóttir's Icelandic accent was nearly imperceptible to Hollie's American ears—no more than an odd *w* where a *v* belonged—but for a moment, Hollie wondered if she had misunderstood.

"Oh," she said stupidly.

"Susanna." A male voice, startlingly deep in the quiet room. Both Officer Guðmundsdóttir and Hollie looked up at once.

Hollie inhaled sharply, barely stifling a gasp.

Officer Guðmundsdóttir's partner was in the doorway between the kitchen and the dining room. He was using one foot to prop the door open, one hand to beckon Officer Guðmundsdóttir with him, toward the hall. In the other hand, there was a knife.

The bread knife.

Hollie felt all the air leave the room.

Officer Guðmundsdóttir exhaled impatiently but followed her partner through the door. Hollie pressed her palms on the table, attempting to steady it, to steady herself. The gash across her right hand throbbed. A different knife might have made a clean cut, but the blade of the bread knife was jagged. Though not deep, the cut on her hand had ugly, ragged edges.

When Officer Guðmundsdóttir returned, Hollie's hands were still pressed flat against the table. No time had passed since the officer had left her, and an entire lifetime has passed as well. Hollie had always wondered what she would do in times of true emergency. It turned out that her natural impulse was to freeze.

"Apologies," Officer Guðmundsdóttir said, barely noticing Hollie. She gathered her notepad without sitting back down. "I appreciate your patience and cooperation. It has been very helpful. I think we can be done here for now."

The officer sounded distracted, and Hollie couldn't help herself.

"Did you find something?" she said. "Did you find Alabama?"

This seemed to get Officer Guðmundsdóttir's attention. She looked at Hollie as though only noticing her for the first time.

The officer appeared to consider her answer for a moment.

"A car," she said carefully. "The one we think Alabama was driving. It was off an embankment on the southern coast."

"And Alabama?"

"We haven't found a body yet."

Hollie closed her eyes. It felt like she was drunk, that sickening feeling of her body gyrating although she was perfectly still.

A body. Alabama was now officially a body. A body lost, a body to be found.

She thought of Alabama's eyes—bloodshot, confused, but alive. Alive, at least in that moment.

Even now, even after everything, Hollie found it breathtaking that things could change so fast.

CHAPTER

33

Hollie

The Night Of
Vík, Iceland

I F IT HAD been dark, Hollie probably wouldn't have ventured out after the glacier hike, but the summer sun in Iceland didn't set until after ten, so Hollie went for a walk.

She hadn't told Katherine where she was going when she had left earlier that evening, mostly because she hadn't known for sure herself. She had instead let her feet carry her down the front stairwell of the bed and breakfast and along the slope of the hill toward the beach, hoping they would take her where she needed to go.

Heading back to the bed and breakfast now, every few steps were met with a squelch as her bare toes slid inside her shoes. At the beach, she had taken off her socks, which were now balled in one hand. In the other, she held her phone, where her draft email to Nick still sat unsent.

She had brought the phone with her on her walk hoping for some clarity, or at least some courage. Instead, she had found herself ankle deep in the ocean, the frigid water splashing up her calves. For one brief but serious second, she had imagined flinging her phone out into the waves and the sound it would make, a soft plunk that would be inaudible over the rush of surf and wind. She had imagined how light she would feel afterward, seeing it disappear beneath the surface.

When she reached the bed and breakfast's front stairwell, she stopped to brush off her calves and ankles, now covered with wavy lines of dried sand. Hollie tasted salt as she ascended the steps, and her stomach rumbled. She had been deliberately eating less during the day, mostly to make a point to herself. *See?* she felt like saying. See? She still had some willpower. In a way, the emptiness that echoed in her gut felt like a small triumph, which she recognized as unhealthy at best.

She pulled the front door open, and as she stepped into the silent hall, her phone chirped out from her hand. Hollie's mind immediately flew to Nick. She wasn't sure if she wanted him to email again, much less what she wanted him to say. And yet, when she saw Robin's name instead of his, she could not help but feel let down.

Hollie closed the door behind her and debated ignoring Robin's email, as she wasn't in the mood to talk race logistics. Her thumb hovered over Robin's name for a moment, and then—curiosity winning out—she clicked so the message expanded on her screen.

Hi, Hollie! Hope your trip is going FANTASTIC! I just wanted to check in to see if you'd heard from LoneStar about the starting line? If not, no worries, but I do want to send a follow-up email soon. Looking forward to seeing you when you get back! Let's go for a run?

Hollie skimmed the rest of the message before closing it. Their race was approaching quickly, and most of the planning was done already. Only a few details remained—the starting line from LoneStar Inflatables, for one, and the exact design of the participant shirts. Robin had coordinated nearly everything, assigning Hollie duties only as needed.

The race, Hollie knew, meant nothing in the grand scheme of things. And yet, after Nick had left, the race was what Hollie had thought of, in bed by herself. She had imagined winning it, feeling so full that all the empty parts of her life would no longer matter.

Hollie's stomach growled again, and suddenly, the emptiness felt searing, like it was burning a hole from the inside out. She thought of Robin typing out the message, her humongous teeth bared in a smile, knowing that Hollie wouldn't run with her—*couldn't* run with her in this exact moment in time, at least not the way she had been able to run before.

Which was ridiculous, Hollie knew, not to mention impossible. There was no way Robin could know that, not without Hollie telling her. Which Hollie hadn't. In fact, she'd done the exact opposite—the old photos on Instagram, the misleading captions, painting a picture of life as usual. She had stopped using Strava altogether, unable to work out a way to fake runs she had never actually done.

A familiar heat in Hollie's stomach spread outward toward her limbs, causing her palms to sweat. She imagined Robin's face the next time they saw one another in person, which Hollie had managed to avoid for weeks before the trip. It would have to happen eventually, and when it did, Robin's smile would only falter for a second as her eyes traveled across Hollie's padded stomach, to the disgusting flesh squeezing from the armholes of her bra. Robin would wonder how Hollie had gained so much weight in such a short period of time, but she wouldn't ask. She wouldn't say anything, just give Hollie a kind, pitying smile.

Before Hollie knew what she was doing, she was in the bed and breakfast kitchen. She felt the sensation again of being a passenger in her own body, her nose pressed up against the window of a train as she watched the scenery around her rush past.

The refrigerator door made a suction cup–like sound as she pulled it open. None of the food inside looked particularly good, but that didn't really matter. Her arm reached out. Her fingers clasped around a brown cardboard container of blueberries, a plastic tub of hummus, a half loaf of lava bread wrapped in tinfoil.

As her legs carried her back to the table, she thought of Nick the last time she had seen him in person. She had gotten home early from a hair appointment and had found him in their bedroom, rummaging the drawer where he kept his socks and undershirts. "Sorry," he had said, apologizing for being there, like he had trespassed in her space. *Her* space. Not theirs—hers.

She barely even chewed the blueberries, swallowing most of them whole. Over the kitchen sink, a thin curtain fluttered against the cracked window, and through it she could hear the sound of the waves in the distance. She thought of earlier, standing in the surf, the current so intense that water had splashed occasionally to her thighs.

The truth was, she had imagined throwing her phone out into the water only after she had imagined jumping into the water herself. She had imagined what it would feel like for the rough surf to envelop her body, how weightless she might feel as the waves shook her around like a rag doll. She had wondered whether this would be freeing or if she would just feel scared. This question was the only thing that had stopped her from going in.

She rose from the table to locate a bread knife in one of the messy drawers. She cut a slice of the lava bread, then another. She brought both back to the table with her, barely tasting either before they were gone.

She reached for the hummus. For a moment, she considered dragging her finger across the oily surface and scooping it into her mouth, but that seemed disgusting even for her, so she pushed herself up again and crossed the room to the pantry.

One of shelves held a box of crackers, and without pausing to see what else the pantry offered, Hollie grabbed it and moved back to the table. She tipped the box over so two sleeves rolled out. She ripped one open and dug a salty circle into the hummus.

She wasn't hungry. The heat in her stomach was gone, quenched by the food she had eaten already. Before she knew it, the first sleeve was gone. She tore into the second without thinking, without even feeling. It was like she had left her body entirely.

"Hollie?"

Hollie startled, dropping the cracker she was holding. It landed hummus side down on the table in front of her, a tiny explosion of goop. She blinked once before turning around in her chair.

Alabama stood in the kitchen doorway. Her eyes moved slowly from Hollie's face to her hands, to the food spread out in front of her like a crime scene. She had one hand on the doorknob, the other holding her phone.

Hollie could see the recognition unfurling across Alabama's face. Each new connection resulted in a slight twitch of understanding, a new realization being made.

"What's going on, Holl?" Alabama said slowly, taking a step into the room.

Hollie rose from her chair, a low ringing in her ears. She recognized the disgust in Alabama's face immediately. It contorted Alabama's otherwise generic features into something ugly.

Hollie turned back to the table. She could not look at Alabama, even if the disgust was nothing new to Hollie. For weeks, the same expression had sullied Hollie's own reflection each time she looked in the mirror.

"I'm fine," Hollie said, although her voice shook slightly. She swallowed and closed her eyes, directing every iota of willpower toward steadying herself. "Please just leave me alone."

Not knowing what else to do, Hollie bent down and gathered the food, which was really too much to hold at once with any sort of dignity. The ringing in her ears was louder now. She could barely hear anything besides her own breathing.

She held her chin high as she walked over to the trash can. She pressed her foot down on the pedal and dumped all of it in—every disgusting morsel.

"Hollie," Alabama said, sounding far away through Hollie's racing thoughts. Hollie heard Alabama crossing the kitchen. She spun around.

"Leave me alone," she hissed, but her voice was barely audible. Alabama either didn't hear it or didn't listen. She continued forward. She was at the table, then a step away from Hollie. She was reaching out for something—a hug?—when Hollie felt any semblance of control vanish.

"God damn it, just leave me alone, you fucking weirdo," Hollie snapped, overcome with a wave of fury. Without thinking, she used both hands to shove Alabama as hard as she could.

Alabama made a small gasping sound as she stumbled backward, nearly falling but catching herself on the back of the chair just in time. Hollie was breathing heavily, and her heart was racing. In her head, she could not find a single coherent thought through all the noise.

She watched as Alabama straightened up slowly, looking stunned. Hollie too felt surprised by her sudden outburst—surprised, but not sorry.

There was a second of silence. Two.

Finally, Alabama's eyes found Hollie's. The shock across Alabama's face had vanished, and Hollie felt her own fury dissipate as well. Instead of anger, Hollie's neck prickled with fear.

Without thinking, she took a snap inventory of her surroundings—a utensil crock by the refrigerator, a fire extinguisher hanging by the door. The bread knife lay balanced on the edge of the sink, surrounded by a halo of lava bread crumbs.

For a moment, there was no movement, no sound except for their breathing. Alabama seemed to be winded. Her nostrils flared.

Then she lunged.

PART IV

Not a Surprise

CHAPTER

34

Hollie

Two Months Before
Dallas, Texas

A MONTH AFTER HOLLIE's positive pregnancy test, she had her first prenatal appointment. Nick insisted on driving her even though he hadn't driven Hollie anywhere—hadn't spent more than ten minutes with her—in weeks. He pulled into their driveway like a personal chauffeur, and Hollie, who had been waiting by the front window, slipped out to meet his car before he could get out.

Nick had seemed surprised that the first appointment wasn't until she was seven weeks along. She had told him the date, and he had gone silent for a second on the other end of the line.

"You don't have to come if you don't want to," she had said, mostly to be kind, although a part of her had wanted him to say no.

"It's not that," Nick had said at once. "I just thought you'd go in earlier than that."

The weeks between that call and the appointment had been rife with surprises for both of them. Hollie was relatively informed thanks to Mallory, although some things had still caught her off guard. Mallory had talked about cravings, but never had she described food aversions like the ones Hollie had experienced—a passionate loathing toward oatmeal, for example. The fact that peanut butter could make her literally gag. Thankfully, that had lasted only a couple of weeks, and now, almost two months in, the only physical symptom to complain about was the cramps—nothing like her monthly cycle, but enough that she had needed to google whether acetaminophen was safe.

"Hey," Hollie said as she slid into Nick's passenger seat. She felt strangely unsure of herself, like she was fifteen being picked up for a date.

"Hey," Nick said, his smile completely confined to his lips. This wasn't like him, the eternal optimist of the pair. It made her feel even more out of sorts.

Nick waited until she had clicked her seat belt in place before he pulled backward out of their driveway. The sky was cloudless, the sun white as it climbed further and further from the horizon. Hollie thought about saying something about the weather, but the thought of small talk with Nick felt so wrong, she couldn't bring herself to do it.

Nick turned on the radio, filling the cab with some Top Forty beat. It was peppy and fun, a cruel contrast to the mood in the car. Hollie leaned her head against the headrest and closed her eyes, willing the universe to give them only green lights until they arrived.

"So," Nick said after a few minutes, "have you decided for sure whether you're going to . . ."

He trailed off, although Hollie didn't need to hear the rest of the question to know what he was asking. She didn't open her eyes as she shook her head.

"Not yet," she said, knowing that this wasn't fair to him. But it was true. She still truly had no idea what she was going to do.

The problem was that Hollie felt wholly incapable of imagining either scenario. When Nick had left the first night, she had tried—really tried—to imagine life with a baby. She had stood in their guest bedroom and tried to picture a white slatted crib, a tiny bookshelf, and she had wondered if it would really be so bad. She didn't know because she couldn't see it. She couldn't even imagine a baby's bedroom, let alone a child to put in it. She couldn't imagine herself doing the most basic things a child would require.

And yet, when she tried to imagine the alternative—a life where she had aborted Nick's baby—she couldn't picture that either. She couldn't picture the loneliness, for one thing, or living with the knowledge that she was capable of hurting someone that deeply.

When she had told Nick about the first appointment, they had been separated for a couple of weeks—long enough that the conversations had chilled with distance, not out of spite necessarily, but more in self-defense. They were preparing themselves for the possibility that this was permanent, that someday, maybe someday soon, they would be actual strangers who spoke this way.

But on that phone call, for just an instant, the spell had been broken. She had told him she had made an appointment, and when his voice had spilled through the speaker, it had been filled with warmth. "Does that mean you're keeping it?" he had said, whispering the way someone whispers a wish.

"No," she had said firmly. And then, "I don't know, Nick. I just don't know."

The waiting room at her doctor's office was over air-conditioned and nearly full. For every man folded in a plastic seat, there were at least three women.

A nurse called them back five minutes before her scheduled appointment time. She was young and talked chattily as she took Hollie's vitals.

"A lot of women are nervous about their first appointment," she said, pulsing a bulb in her hand. Around Hollie's upper arm, the blood pressure cuff squeezed. "So don't be surprised if your pulse is a little high today." In the doorway, Nick's expression hardened. Maybe he, like Hollie, was imagining a world not so unlike reality where Nick and Hollie might have chatted back happily.

Hollie had switched health insurances only a few months prior, which had meant changing doctors, so she wasn't sure what to expect when she got back to the examination room. Nick pressed his back against one of the straw-colored walls while Hollie stared straight ahead to the parking lot out the window.

"Good morning, Mrs. Goodwin," said the doctor when she entered the room a few minutes later. She was a heavyset Black woman with a thick ponytail at the base of her neck. "I'm Dr. Powell." Her voice was husky but kind, and Hollie had the immediate impression that this woman was decent. This did not help anything for Hollie.

"Hi," Hollie said, attempting to return the smile. "Call me Hollie. And this is my, uh"—an inhale—"Nick."

If the doctor registered the brief intake of breath, if she found it odd, she didn't let it show. She shook Nick's hand the same way she had shaken Hollie's, then lowered herself onto a wheeled stool by the computer desk. Hollie's eyes found Nick, and there she saw the recognition. He had heard the pause and had understood what it meant.

The doctor started with some questions. Earlier—on the drive over—Hollie had planned to ask about abortion before the doctor could get started. Now, though, Hollie just shook her head and nodded, confirming her age, her diet, her exercise routine, her travel. No, she had never been diagnosed with anxiety or depression. No, no recent trips outside of the country or any STDs.

As the doctor prepared for the examination, Hollie decided she would wait until the end of the appointment to broach termination. She would let the doctor think of Hollie as a specific kind of person before revealing which kind she really was.

The doctor eventually disappeared into the hall to find the ultrasound machine, leaving Hollie and Nick once again in silence. Hollie's chart was open on the computer screen, her entire existence reduced down to a page.

The doctor came back a few minutes later wheeling an elaborate device with a screen and a keyboard. She squeezed clear lube onto the wand, and Nick looked away as she inserted it inside Hollie. Hollie closed her eyes as the machine moved around inside her, searching for the organ that Hollie now shared.

The office door was heavy, so the only sound in the room was the humming A/C and the echoey swish of Hollie's insides. After a few seconds, curiosity got the best of her. She opened her eyes to peer at the screen, where she was met by a galaxy of grainy white swirls. She squinted, trying to decipher what she was seeing—which part of the image was her and which part wasn't.

The doctor continued to move the wand, which didn't hurt but was slightly uncomfortable. Hollie waited, feeling impatient. She glanced at the doctor's face, and it was only then that Hollie noticed the woman's face.

"Is everything okay?" Hollie said. "There's a baby in there, right?"

The doctor moved the wand again, the screen shushing back.

"There is," she said. "But I'm afraid I can't find a heartbeat."

For a moment, Hollie forgot that the woman was holding a plastic wand against her organs, forgot that Nick was there in the room with her, watching the whole thing. She stared at the doctor like she had started speaking in tongues.

The doctor, apparently feeling Hollie's eyes on her, finally looked away from the screen. Hollie took in the woman's expression, and suddenly, something clicked. There was no heartbeat. There was a baby, but it was not alive. She felt awash with a swift wave of embarrassment for not having considered this option, that keeping or not keeping a pregnancy might have never been her choice at all.

The doctor pulled the wand out and turned off the machine. Hollie sat up, the lube still dripping between her legs. The doctor said something apologetic, speaking to both Hollie and Nick equally. Hollie caught only fragments of the sentences, albeit enough to get the general gist.

It was possible—improbable, but possible—that she had misdated the pregnancy. They might come back in a week and all would be fine. More than likely, however, Hollie would start bleeding. It could last hours, or it could last days, and if she didn't, they would schedule a surgery to remove all the tissue.

The tissue. And that was that.

"I'm sorry," the doctor said a final time. Hollie nodded, feeling numb. They scheduled a follow-up visit, and with nothing else to do, they left.

When they got back to the house, Nick offered to stay for the first time in weeks.

"If you want to," Hollie said, "but don't do it for me. I'll be fine."

And Nick believed this, because he had no reason not to. She was, after all, getting exactly what she wanted. The universe had heard her thoughts and deemed her—for whatever reason—deserving. So he didn't come inside.

The first thing Hollie did after that was set out on a run, although she made it only a half mile before turning around and walking home. Her body felt foreign and bloated, making the effort more agonizing than anything else.

When she took a shower later, she stared at her reflection for a long time, analyzing every curve and line. It was like she was looking at a stranger. She had never felt so separate from her body, so betrayed by it. It seemed so unfathomable that something could be dead inside her and she had no idea.

That evening, Hollie sat in her kitchen alone until the sun set and the kitchen grew dark. She had no right to feel as though she'd lost something, as though something had been stolen. And so that night and for many nights after, she chose not to feel anything. Instead, she ate.

CHAPTER

35

Celeste

The Day After
Vík, Iceland

S KYE CALLED THE entire group into the dining room after they
found Alabama's car.

"The decision has been made to end the trip early," she said once
all the influencers had situated themselves. From one corner, the
Emily-Margot complex took a collective intake of breath. The noise
was faint but noticeable enough for Celeste to look over at them.
She watched with a sort of numb fascination as their faces rounded
with the same stricken expression, harmonizing with their identical
loungewear sets.

Celeste thought of Bella, whose eyes widened similarly in the
face of setback, as though she could simply not believe the disappointing way her life sometimes turned out. Celeste couldn't tell if
Emily and Margot were upset about the turn in the investigation, or
whether they were more upset about the abrupt end to the trip.

"We're working with GoIceland now on rebooking your return
flights," Skye said. Her voice was oddly formal, and Celeste wondered if PinkPurse briefed their trip coordinators about situations
like this as part of their trip coordinator training. She imagined a
group of faceless executives passing out pink pamphlets with a script
for each conceivable tragedy the coordinators might face.

"Some of your flights have been booked already," Skye continued, expression grim. "I'll be in touch with each of you after this
meeting to confirm."

There was a rustle through the room, although none of the
women actually said anything. Celeste could not look at any of them.
She instead stared at the worn rug.

"In the meantime," Skye said after a moment, after the initial
surge of anxious energy had cleared, "we would appreciate if you
could please hold off on posting about the trip for the time being."
There was a beat before she added, "Given the circumstances, as I'm
sure you understand."

The only people in the room to appear unmoved by this
announcement were Hollie—whose expression was completely
vacant as she stared at the wall—and Katherine, who was seated
beside Celeste. Katherine was chewing loudly on a piece of gum that
smelled like spearmint. The combination of the smell and the sound
was nauseating, and it crossed Celeste's mind that she was closer to
throwing up than not.

Thankfully, Celeste did not throw up. After the meeting was
over, she confirmed her flight details with Skye before leaving the
room in a disembodied sort of trance.

She didn't know who had come to collect Alabama's things, but
when she got back to her bedroom, Alabama's suitcase was gone. She
crossed the room in silence and lowered herself onto the bed across
from Alabama's, which was still unmade. For no real reason, she
leaned over and picked up one of her shoes, the first article of clothing
Alabama had aimed at her the night before. The only thing Alabama
had actually hit her with was the tube of lipstick, and it occurred
to Celeste that maybe this had been on purpose. Maybe Alabama
hadn't actually wanted to hurt Celeste, hadn't really believed Celeste
was capable of doing what she had done.

The shoe in her hand started to blur as the tears formed, reduc-
ing it to a white smudge. She wiped her eyes, annoyed with herself
for crying, for having the audacity to feel sorry for herself.

She wondered whether she would have confessed to Alabama
eventually if Alabama hadn't figured it out first. Celeste had for-
mally confessed once in her life, although the situation had been
much different from this. That time had been from inside a Catholic
confessional, which was really just a phone booth with an elaborate
air vent. She had confessed along with the rest of her RCIA group.
(Louis was a hand-me-down Catholic who had inherited Christmas

and Easter masses from his parents, something he treated like any nonfunctional heirloom. For the sake of tradition, however, he had wanted to get married in the church, which had required RCIA for Celeste, as she hadn't been baptized before.)

For eight months, Celeste had met with other middle-aged men and women in the basement of their local church, learning about Catholicism while eating powdered donut holes. Celeste had found the subject matter either suspect or downright terrifying—sometimes both—but the idea of confession she had liked. She had liked enumerating her sins, molding an abstract cloud of guilt into a triable list. She hadn't taken confession literally the way she was supposed to, as per her RCIA workbook. She hadn't actually thought of the priest as a middleman for God. But still, there had been a certain comfort in running the rosary beads through her fingers for penance, knowing exactly which words to recite for her sins to be absolved.

And maybe this was her penance now, she thought. If Officer Björnsson was to be believed, she would not be in any real trouble, at least not in the eyes of the law. After all, infidelity wasn't illegal. Neither was betraying your best friend. The only tangible repercussions would be losing Alabama and possibly losing Louis, and the latter was still avoidable, depending on what information got out.

The only other consequences were those in her head—knowing that Alabama had driven off alone into the brief Icelandic dark and careened off an embankment. Knowing why she had been upset enough to do something like that.

Celeste rose from the bed, suddenly unable to sit still. She gave a sweeping glance to the room, now only half as full as it had been the day before. She was set to leave the bed and breakfast in less than two hours for her rebooked flight home, and she still had to pack. But it didn't matter. She couldn't be in this room right now, just her and her guilt.

She picked up the second shoe and slid them both on, then shrugged on a windbreaker as she stepped toward the door. Thankfully, no one was in the hall. All of the other influencers were likely in their rooms, packing and gossiping. Celeste wondered if any of them knew what had happened between Alabama and Celeste, if they had heard the screaming or the various objects hitting the wall. She realized almost immediately that she didn't care. No one in the world could judge her as harshly as she had already judged herself.

The clouds that afternoon were thick and low, a motley ceiling hung from the sky. Celeste pulled her windbreaker around herself more tightly and flipped her hood up over her head. It was windy, with powerful gusts rolling from the ocean like waves, smashing Celeste with the smell of salt and seaweed. She trotted down the front stairwell to the road, which she followed toward the beach.

As she walked, she studied the buildings around her, looking for something that probably wasn't there. The previous evening, Alabama had walked this very same road, and it was almost as if Celeste now expected to find absolution in one of the windows, something that pointed outward, casting the blame away from Celeste.

Most of the houses were residential, simple block-like formations in red, yellow, and white. The road was mottled, the wider holes rippling with brown water, tiny wakes in the wind. She passed a small convenience store. A hardware store. An unmarked building with painted metal siding. She tried to imagine Alabama on this road but couldn't. Alabama with her balayage hair and stiletto-shaped nails. The gold chain she wore around her neck, a diamond-encrusted *A* resting against her collarbone. Some people needed only a soft bed and central heating to be comfortable, whereas Alabama required at least a Starbucks and a nail salon nearby. With enough time, the simpleness of this village would have been enough to kill her, if the cold water hadn't first.

Celeste veered from an elbow in the road, where the pavement below her bled into gravel. The closer she got to the water, the more difficult it was to distinguish the rush of wind in her ears from the sound of the tide colliding with the beach in the distance. Eventually, the gravel turned to dark sand, a cross between dirt and flaky ash. In the distance, the moss on the cliffs looked electric against the powder-white sky.

She passed through a parking lot with only one car. Beside it, an older couple in matching plastic parkas rearranged camera bags and hair. They waved cheerfully as Celeste passed, and Celeste raised a hand in acknowledgment.

She finally stepped out onto the stretch of beach, where nothing separated her from the water but sand. Up close, with the village behind her, she felt like she was the only person on the planet—in the universe, even—with nothing in her life but boundless space.

36

Hollie

The Day After
Vík, Iceland

WITH EACH STEP Hollie took, she could feel the sand rubbing between her toes and against the soles of her feet. She had taken off her shoes when she had gotten to the beach, not because she hadn't wanted to get sand in them, but because she had felt a sudden, dire need to feel the grit against her skin.

The wind whipping against her face was making the walk less than pleasurable, although Hollie hadn't set out looking for pleasure. She had walked all the way down the beach to find the Reynisdrangar, those odd columns in the water.

Up close, the basalt sea stacks had looked nothing like trolls—just heaps of black rock, piled like the insides of an egg timer gone hard. This wasn't all that surprising, but still, Hollie had felt a sense of disappointment looking out at them, like she had expected to meet a friend only to find that she was alone.

She was on her way back now, heading toward the parking lot. She still needed to pack for her return flight, something she probably should have done straight away. Instead, Hollie had set out for the beach after their meeting with Skye in the dining room, as being alone in her bedroom with Katherine had sounded like torture.

Her mind wandered briefly to her still-unpacked luggage, to the folded cardigan stuffed at the bottom of her suitcase. The sweater was probably still damp where she had done her best to rinse it. In her mind, she could see everything so clearly from the night before. The water running pink beneath the knitted fibers, the slight sting of peroxide on her wound. The serrated edge of the bread knife. How easily it had cut her skin. Cleaning the knife had been both easier than cleaning the cardigan and, in some ways, much harder. With the fabric, at least, it was familiar. Every woman, at some point in her life, had done it, salvaging clothing from leaky tampons and surprise periods. Not everyone had cleaned blood from the toothy edge of a knife.

And yet she had done it. Or, it certainly seemed like she had. Because there the knife was, back in the drawer, beside the rubber tongs and mismatched silverware. Hollie had checked after their meeting, slipping away from the group, holding her breath. And to her amazement, she had found it. Unfathomably, unbelievably, the cops had just left it there.

A wave rolled in, and Hollie didn't flinch as water rushed up to her ankles. She could no longer imagine jumping in it. She couldn't imagine the energy it would take to fight the waves long enough to wade into deeper water, to hold her breath as the current batted her around.

"Maybe they'll still find her," Hollie had heard one of the influencers saying at the meeting. The girl, Emily, had sounded so hopeful, so optimistic. Hollie had bit the inside of her cheek so hard, it had tasted raw. It had annoyed her, how stupid and naïve some people had the luxury of being. What did Emily hope they would find exactly? Hollie had seen a drowned body once on TV, on a show that was more graphic than she had realized. It had all been makeup, of course, but the sight had been nonetheless shocking—marbled white skin, a bloated body saturated with water. Emily had no idea what she was hoping for.

A gust of wind swept in from the water. Hollie shivered as she trudged along. She had both hands in her pockets, each clutching a phone. She wasn't sure why she had brought Alabama's out with her. It was a needless risk.

But maybe that was the point. Maybe she wanted someone to catch her, to give her no option but to come clean. She almost had with Officer Guðmundsdóttir. She had been so close, her mouth full with the confession. A minute longer, maybe less, and Hollie felt sure the whole thing would have come out.

Hollie looked up, searching for the parking lot, hoping she was close. There had been two cars when she had arrived, but now she could only see one. Parallel with the parking lot, she noticed the dark outline of someone standing near the water ahead of her. She squinted but couldn't make the person out.

She continued walking, moving from the water's edge to the middle of the black stretch of beach, not wanting to cross paths with the person. She didn't want to be close to anybody, not even for a passive wave hello.

As she neared, however, she realized who it was. Without thinking, she called out.

Celeste turned at the sound of her name. She moved slowly, the way Hollie had seen drunks sometimes do. Celeste placed one hand to her forehead even though there was no sun, and her face pinched together in the middle like she didn't know who Hollie was.

Hollie changed directions and headed back toward the water where Celeste stood. The closer she got, the worse Celeste looked. Her hair had succumbed to the wind, stray pieces frizzing chaotically in the humidity. She hadn't put on makeup, and her complexion looked as anemic as the colorless sky around them.

"Hey," Hollie said, coming to a stop a few feet from her. Celeste had her arms crossed over her body like she was hugging herself. Hollie wished suddenly that she hadn't said anything. Celeste's expression was so distant, there was not a doubt in Hollie's mind that she could have snuck right past her without Celeste having any idea.

"What's going on?" Hollie said, injecting a casualness into her voice that probably wasn't appropriate. Celeste's expression didn't change.

"Oh, I was just . . ." Celeste motioned to the water. She didn't seem to notice that the sentence floated away unfinished, but Hollie got the point anyway. Hollie followed the sweep of her hand to the ocean, momentarily mesmerized by the whitecaps racing across the surface. The wind bellowed at them loudly enough that if Hollie angled her body just right, she could convince herself she was standing there alone.

Hollie thought of the previous night, how she had stood at the water's edge, looking out. She had never felt as small as she had in that moment, and the irony of this was maddening. So much of her current situation could be traced back to smallness, or at least her pursuit of it. It was ironic how her smallness now was excruciating.

She wondered what would have happened if she had jumped in yesterday when she had thought about it—not to harm herself even, but just to swim, just to feel the sharpness of cold water against her skin. Would that have changed Hollie in some small but fundamental way? Would that have changed what had happened?

"Was Alabama a good person?" Hollie said, filled with a sudden and unexpected urgency. As soon as the words came out, however, she recoiled, disgusted with herself for asking.

Celeste was quiet. Hollie held her breath, hoping her question had been lost in the wind.

"She was a complicated person," Celeste said. She sighed, deflating herself further.

One gust of wind ebbed, and before the next one took its place, there was a space of near silence for Celeste to add softly, "She didn't deserve for things to end like this, though."

Hollie nodded, understanding. And then, for reasons she could not explain, she found her hands rising to her stomach.

She had always privately judged pregnant women who did this, their hands gravitating to their bumps any time someone looked their way. What Hollie hadn't considered before was that perhaps women weren't looking for attention. Maybe they did it instinctually, their bodies naturally converging on the most fragile part. Hollie was surprised to learn that she could be one of these women, even when she was no longer pregnant at all.

The truth was, Hollie had thought something very similar to Celeste a few months ago, in the middle of her miscarriage. There had been blood—so much blood, more than Hollie had expected. Hollie had looked at it in the toilet, and her first thought had been, *she didn't deserve this.*

Hollie closed her eyes and turned toward the ocean, allowing the wind to pelt her in the face. She had always thought of herself as a good person. Perhaps everyone did to some extent, but Hollie had always believed it to her core. She wondered how many bad things a person had to do before it defined them, before they were forced to admit that they had never really been a good person at all.

"I kissed her husband," Celeste said, shaking Hollie out of her thoughts. Hollie opened her eyes and was surprised to see tears now streaming down Celeste's face in noiseless lines. "That's why she left last night—because of me. Because of what I did."

When Celeste met Hollie's eyes, Hollie had to look away. She was no more able to look at a pain that raw than stare into the sun.

Hollie thought to say something, but nothing came out. She wanted to be the type of person who could help Celeste, but she knew now that she was not. Instead, she simply stood there as Celeste continued to weep, until after a while, the sound was indistinguishable from the raging ocean, as impersonal as the roaring wind.

A little while later, Celeste decided to leave. She made a half-hearted attempt to have Hollie join her and seemed relieved when Hollie declined. Hollie continued staring at the water as Celeste walked back toward the parking lot, focusing on the chaotic patterns in the waves, how the gulls overhead seemed to float in the wind rather than fight it.

When enough time had passed, Hollie looked over her shoulder. The parking lot was empty now. Hollie was totally alone. She turned back to the ocean and walked to the edge of the water, pulling Alabama's phone out of her pocket.

She wound up and threw it as far as she could.

CHAPTER

37

Celeste

Two Days After
Chicago, Illinois

B Y THE TIME Celeste's plane touched down at Chicago O'Hare International Airport, she had been awake for over twenty-four hours. She had gotten a window seat for the return flight, which should have been more comfortable than being crammed in a middle like her flight there. And yet she hadn't slept a wink.

Her redeye from Reykjavík had connected in Boston, so the people around her stirred with a hum of distinctly American accents. The layover had been three hours, enough time for a quick stop at Apple's genius bar. The geniuses had seen much worse than Celeste's cracked screen, apparently. Replacing it had taken no more than an hour.

Celeste unfastened her seat belt and swiped the newly installed glass, bringing the device back from airplane mode. It took a moment for her phone to locate service, which was followed by a hemorrhage of alerts. It was less than she was used to after flying, which didn't surprise her. She hadn't posted anything since the glacier hike, and now even her Instagram stories had expired.

She wasn't sure if she had expected a certain reaction to her abrupt silence, but from what she could tell by the alerts, none of her followers seemed alarmed. She wondered if they even noticed that she had stopped posting or if it was possible for her to vanish entirely without anyone realizing she was gone.

The terminal was uncrowded and bright when she stepped off the jet bridge. The long hall was illuminated by commercial lighting and midmorning sun through the windowed ceiling overhead. She had texted Louis from Boston to let him know that her flight was leaving on time, to which he had responded with a single emoji, a hand in the "okay" sign. Celeste had bristled at this, then felt promptly disgusted with herself. As if she was entitled to feel irritation with anyone, let alone him.

She followed the stream of passengers down the terminal hall, past storefronts waiting eagerly for the day. Ahead, a brachiosaurus skeleton loomed, the replica's skull nearly skimming the ceiling.

"Such a weird thing to put in an airport," Alabama had said before they had left for Iceland, sounding bored. She'd had a mouthful of gummy worms, which she had gotten from the Hudson News next to security along with an egregiously overpriced pack of gum. Celeste had said something in agreement. Or maybe she had just nodded—she couldn't remember. She wondered how many memories with Alabama she had already started to lose.

Celeste's phone tinged with a message.

I'm here, it read, and Celeste felt another passing wave of annoyance.

Where is here? she started to type back, although she only made it to *is* before she saw him ahead.

Louis didn't normally come into the airport to pick her up. He usually waited in the cell phone lot before looping around to the curb. As she approached, she noticed the dusting of gray along his hairline fighting valiantly through his color-correcting shampoo.

"Where's Bells?" she asked as she approached him, her version of hello.

"Your mom's at the house."

He held out for a hug, and without thinking much about it, she walked into it. He smelled like home, like their actual house— oranges and a touch of chimney smoke, reminding them to clean the flue. She was surprised to find herself burying her head in his chest and was slightly less surprised when he wrapped her up more tightly. He had always been a good hugger, which wasn't a quality people usually put much stock in when choosing a partner. Celeste, though, had always found it important. Maybe it was why she had married him.

When they finally separated, Celeste was crying again. If she had been wearing any makeup, it would have been lined with streaks. Louis held her upper arms just below the shoulders and studied her for a moment before using one thumb to swipe away the tears.

"You're tired," he said. In another lifetime, she probably would have found this insulting. Now, she nodded, grateful that he understood.

"I just can't stop thinking about it," she said, patting her sleeve against the bottom of her nose. "I can't stop wondering if I could've done something to help her, you know? To stop her from having a breakdown. I thought something was wrong, but I didn't think . . ."

She trailed off, shaking her head. She could feel herself flirting with self-pity, which was not her intent. She didn't want sympathy. She wouldn't even know what to do with sympathy, where to put it, but she couldn't articulate this to Louis without revealing too much about what she and Alabama had fought about that night.

"CeCe," Louis said, the solidness of his voice catching her off guard. She looked up, meeting his eyes. "You can't let your mind play these games with you. Alabama was a grown woman with agency. However bad you two fought, there was no way for you to predict something like this."

He squeezed her arm gently, as if to put a period at the end of his thought. She tried to be comforted by these words but wasn't, not even a little.

When she didn't say anything else, he pulled her in again and kissed her forehead. Then he grabbed her bag, and they held hands for a little while until Celeste's hand got too sweaty and she let go. They didn't talk until they got to the parking garage, where Louis asked if she wanted to stop on the way home for coffee. She didn't but agreed anyway because she knew he wanted to.

As they pulled away from the airport, she thought again of what he had said in the terminal. *There was no way for you to predict something like this.* She turned these words over and over in her head, like a kid flipping rocks hoping to find one with some truth she could hold onto.

38

Hollie

Two Days After
Dallas, Texas

Nick wasn't waiting for Hollie at the airport because she had told him not to come. And yet, as she was heaving her enormous suitcase from the rotating luggage track at Dallas Love Field, she nonetheless felt disappointed at his absence.

Before leaving Iceland, Hollie had finally returned Nick's email—not with an answer about couples therapy, but to tell him about what had happened on the trip. He had replied immediately, offering to pick her up from the airport and take her home. She had thanked him, told him it was nice, but that she didn't think it was a good idea.

It was an effort to get all of her luggage into her car by herself, but she managed. The afternoon air hung hot and heavy in the parking garage, and by the time she slipped into the driver's seat, the tiny hairs around her forehead were stuck to her skin. She turned the air conditioning on full blast and sat there for a few minutes, staring at the concrete pillar in front of her.

She didn't cry on the drive home, and as she pushed herself through the garage door and into her kitchen, she didn't cry then either. Maybe she would have if she hadn't been so exhausted, but as it was, Hollie could not produce the energy it would require for making tears.

She left her suitcase standing upright by the door as she crossed the kitchen to the island, where she had placed a note for Mallory before she had left. It was plain white cardstock with *thank you* pressed in gold foil across the front. In it, Hollie had scribbled a note thanking Mallory for house-sitting along with some brief instructions for watering her most temperamental plants. She had also slipped a crisp fifty-dollar bill inside. *Treat yourself with this, please,* she had written, although Mallory hadn't. The money was still there on the counter beside the envelope, as though Mallory had considered it for a second before setting it back down.

Hollie exhaled heavily and leaned over, pressing her forehead into the cool counter surface. She was so exhausted, she could barely imagine unpacking her suitcase in her huge, empty house alone. She thought about Officer Guðmundsdóttir back in Iceland, doing whatever it was she did after big breaks in a case. It took everything in Hollie not to close her eyes and melt onto the floor.

She stood like this for almost five minutes—limp and lifeless, her forehead pressed into the countertop—until across the house, the doorbell rang out. For half a second, Hollie considered ignoring it. Instead, she picked her head up.

As she started toward the door, she attempted to smooth her hair. This was mostly pointless, as it was an oily mess from too little sleep and too much recirculated airplane air. When she caught a glimpse of herself in the hallway mirror, she barely recognized herself for how disheveled she looked. She wondered what Nick would make of this if it was him at the door. Would he feel bad for her, or would he just be grossed out?

It wasn't Nick. Mallory stood on Hollie's front step with a bouquet nestled like a baby in one arm. In the other, she held a bottle of wine.

"Oh, good," Mallory said, sounding relieved. "I was worried you might not be home yet."

Hollie nodded but couldn't muster an actual response. Mallory seemed to understand this and took a step into the house without waiting for an invitation.

"Coop was adamant about bringing you flowers," Mallory said, nodding to the bouquet. Cooper was Mallory's husband. He had always been an uncommonly thoughtful guy. "I, on the other hand, thought you might prefer wine."

At this, Hollie felt a small but genuine smile rise.

In the kitchen, Hollie rummaged around in her silverware drawer for a corkscrew as Mallory extracted a vase from below the sink.

"You didn't take the money," Hollie said, nodding at the uncreased bill on the counter.

Mallory scrunched her nose. "Did you think I would?"

"I would've."

"I don't believe that."

Hollie thought about this for a second. Then, deciding Mallory was right, she took a healthy sip of the rosé. It was still cool. Hollie closed her eyes, savoring the bubbly sensation for a moment before swallowing.

"I seriously don't know how pregnant people don't drink wine for nine entire months," she said. "It's insane to me."

Mallory didn't say anything, and when Hollie opened her eyes, she was giving Hollie an odd look, like she was studying a newly painted room, trying to decide whether she liked the color or not. Hollie felt immediately self-conscious in a way she rarely felt around her friend. She looked away, her gaze landing on her wineglass instead.

"You know," Mallory said, setting her own glass down. "It's okay to be sad. Or pissed. Or whatever. Anything. You can be not okay about everything you've gone through recently."

Hollie searched her wine for something she knew she wouldn't find. She thought of Alabama again, the last time Hollie had seen her. Alabama could have meant nothing to Hollie. She could have been nothing, no one, and instead her face was the one Hollie would think about for the rest of her life.

Hollie looked up at Mallory. Mallory gave her a half smile of encouragement, and Hollie realized why Mallory's words—as kind as they were—meant so little. Mallory was giving Hollie permission to falter, to struggle, but Mallory didn't know that Hollie already had. And not just with regard to Alabama. Hollie had failed at all of it. Mallory didn't know about the bingeing, about Hollie's losing struggle to maintain control. She knew about the miscarriage, but she didn't know how Hollie had leaned over on the toilet and cried out for the baby she had never wanted in the first place. She didn't know these things because Hollie hadn't told her. She had lied to Mallory the same way she had lied to everyone else.

"Do you want to talk about it, Holl?" Mallory said gently. Her voice was cautious, as though she sensed the things Hollie could not say out loud, and Hollie was surprised to realize that she did want to tell her. She wanted to breathe all the air from her chest and tell Mallory every single thing, even—especially—the worst parts. The truth was a heavy burden to bear alone, and Hollie was suddenly so tired that she didn't know whether she could anymore.

And yet she had been honest once, with Nick, and because of that, she might lose him for good.

Hollie met Mallory's eyes. The kindness in her friend's face was unbearable. Mallory loved her, Hollie could tell, and it was for this reason that Hollie whispered, "Not yet."

CHAPTER

39

Celeste

Two Days After
Chicago, Illinois

L OUIS LEANED TO one side as he carried Celeste's suitcase up the front
stoop. He was clearly doing his best to keep her oversized luggage
from slamming into his knee as he walked, which was easier for Celeste,
who gently lifted her little carry-on up and over each step with ease.

Celeste waited anxiously behind him as he fiddled with keys on
the front mat, and as he pushed the door open, she strained to hear
over his shoulder. "They might be out back," Louis murmured as
he set Celeste's suitcase down by the stairway. Celeste nodded and
hurried past him. All of a sudden, her need to touch her daughter
felt visceral, like someone crossing a desert and seeing water for the
first time. She didn't care if Bella didn't want to hug her. She didn't
care if Bella threw a tantrum, if she bit every single kid in the state
of Illinois. Celeste didn't care about any of it except the fact that she
could hold Bella, warm and ornery and alive.

As she approached the kitchen, she heard the murmur of voices
that hadn't been audible from the hall. Celeste stepped into the room
and was greeted by the back of two heads, separated by a foot of
space and fifty years.

Celeste's mom heard Celeste before Bella did. She turned around.

For as long as Celeste could remember, her mom had kept her hair short. Her "Jamie Lee Curtis cut," as Louis liked to joke about it. Celeste's mom never seemed to laugh.

"Hi there," Celeste said, attempting a smile. From her mom's expression, the smile didn't look much more genuine than it felt. Her mom nudged Bella, who held up one hand like an impatient businessman. Celeste shook her head. Her mom smirked.

Celeste stepped to the counter, where Bella was hunched over a sheet of paper. A mess of crayons was fanned out in front of her, scattered with the hasty chaos of an artist deep in work. Celeste leaned down so her face was even with her daughter's, close enough that she could feel the heat of Bella's concentrated breathing.

"A bottleneck?" Celeste said.

Bella finally looked up. "Bottlenose," she corrected.

Celeste nodded and pulled her daughter in for a hug.

Bella tensed for a moment, but then, with a movement small and deliberate enough that Celeste almost cried, Bella leaned in a fraction of an inch so her head rested against Celeste's stomach. Celeste squeezed tighter, overcome with an intense, teary emotion. She couldn't tell if she was stricken or euphoric or both.

Finally, when Bella had reached her threshold, she patiently unwrapped Celeste's arms from around her and resumed her work. Celeste straightened as Louis appeared in the kitchen doorway.

"Hi, Deb," he said, giving Celeste's mother a small salute. Celeste's mom nodded in acknowledgment. "Do you want this upstairs, CeCe?" he said, gesturing to her bag.

"Yes, please," Celeste said, glancing up at Louis briefly before refocusing on her daughter, who was now again in her own world. Celeste didn't know if it was her imagination or if Bella really had grown in the few days since Celeste had left her. It was astonishing how everything in their lives was capable of changing so fast.

Celeste reached out and touched a lock of Bella's hair. Bella, so deeply absorbed by her drawing, didn't seem to notice. She didn't even bat her mom's hand away.

"I'm glad you made it back," Celeste's mother said, reminding Celeste that she was still in the room. Celeste inhaled, searching for the powdery scent of her daughter.

"It was a long trip," she said simply. She hadn't meant to clip the answer, but she also didn't know how to explain what had happened, where to even begin.

"I'm so sorry to hear about Alabama," her mother said, sounding like she meant it.

Celeste nodded once, appreciative. "I'm still processing it, I think."

Celeste had once blamed her mother for their lack of connection, but now, as an adult, Celeste no longer believed that the blame sat with either of them. Really, the older she got, the more she suspected that there was no blame to be had—just two people who had tried but could never quite make it work.

There was a beat of silence except for the sound of wax on paper as Bella filled in the dolphin's torso with meticulous shading.

"I would imagine her husband is having a very hard time with it," her mother said finally, and Celeste felt an uncomfortable tingle at the base of her neck. She studied her mom's eyes, so dark that they were almost black. The darkness gave away nothing, no hint as to whether the inflection Celeste thought she had heard had actually been there or not.

"Mama," Bella said, sitting up abruptly. "Mama, look."

Celeste drew her eyes away from her mother slowly to look at the piece of paper now inches below her nose. A bottlenose dolphin stared back at her with a blank expression. Bella hadn't filled in the background of her drawing with ocean or other fish, so the dolphin was suspended in sterile white air.

"Bottlenoses are carnivores," Bella said with a sage nod. A few years prior, Celeste might have looked around for the source of this information. Now she understood that these things were printed on the inside of Bella's mind in some mysterious, permanent ink.

"I didn't know that," Celeste said, her mind flitting back and forth between the carnivorous bottlenose and her mother sitting patiently beside her. No, she decided. No, there was no way her mother could possibly have known about Henry, not unless Henry or Alabama had told her, and that seemed highly unlikely, even in this new universe where the highly unlikely was her new norm.

"I'm going to show Daddy," Bella said. She didn't wait for acknowledgment from her mother or grandmother before scampering out of the kitchen and toward the front hall. Celeste looked at the doorway for a long moment, even after Bella had disappeared through it.

"Louis tells me she's been having nightmares," her mom said, nodding toward the empty doorway. Celeste raked her fingers through her hair, now stiff with too much dry shampoo.

"Yes. It's becoming sort of a problem, actually."

"You know, you used to have nightmares when you were around her age too."

"Hmm," Celeste said, frowning. She remembered the nightmares vaguely, although it was so long ago that the memory had blurred from specific images to just a general feeling—low-grade dread, a distrustfulness around sleeping. Most of the nightmares had been a by-product of what she would later self-diagnose as a mild case of anxiety and four brothers who exhibited a borderline obsession with blood and gore.

"And, you know," her mom added, speaking softly, "I handled them terribly, looking back."

"I'm sure you did the best you could," Celeste said, even though she really had no idea. She tried to think back to her mother's reaction to the dreams, although she couldn't come up with a single one, good or bad. It was like her mother had been absent from that part of her life entirely.

"That might be true, but I don't think it was enough. Not as a mother, anyway."

Celeste didn't know whether to argue with this, if only to ease whatever guilt her mother still harbored. Luckily, her mother didn't wait.

"All I did was tell you that it wasn't real," she said. "I said the dreams were all in your head."

"Well, that doesn't sound too bad."

Her mom smiled sadly. Celeste noticed the parentheses around her mouth, how much deeper the grooves were there than between her eyebrows. She wondered whether her own wrinkles would follow the same pattern eventually, if the balance of joy and sorrow in one's life was simply a matter of genes in the end.

"No, what I should've told you is that it *was* real. Not the monsters, but the feelings. Your feelings are real in the way that matters."

Before Celeste realized what was happening, her mom reached out and put one hand over Celeste's. The sensation was cool and unexpected, not least of all because it was not a language they often shared.

"Some feelings are there for a reason," her mom said, her voice quiet but deliberate. "I wish I would've learned that much sooner in life." She squeezed, letting the pressure linger against Celeste for a long moment. Her skin was much thinner and splotchier than her daughter's, although with one hand stacked on top of the other, Celeste realized they were almost exactly the same size.

40

Hollie

Two Days After
Dallas, Texas

HOLLIE HAD EVERY reason in the world not to go on a run the day she got home from Iceland. She was jet-lagged for one thing, and her hamstring still stung. Perhaps most glaring was her body's complete incapacity for anything more than a glacial jog.

And yet, here she was.

It was almost seven, but the sun still beat down like it was the middle of the day. Hollie tried to ignore the sensation of chafing skin between her legs where her thighs rubbed against one another.

In her earbuds, the sound of a text message tinged through her music. It was probably Mallory. Mallory had texted Hollie as soon as she'd gotten home earlier that afternoon and nearly every hour since, as though Hollie was on suicide watch. Hollie wasn't, although the constant check-ins nonetheless put her on edge.

She ignored the message and wiped her forehead using the back of her hand, doing not much more than spreading the sweat around. Nick had also checked in on her, but unlike Mallory's messages, Hollie had not replied to his. *Get back okay?* he had texted her. Hollie hadn't meant to ignore it on purpose. She just didn't have an answer. Yes, she had gotten back. The okay, on the other hand, was arguable.

She was running along a leafy residential street that didn't see much through traffic. A dog barked from one of the yards, chasing Hollie along the fence until it couldn't any longer. Hollie thought of Robin's goldendoodle and wondered if it was still shitting on Robin's indoor rugs.

The thought of Robin sent a jolt of something unpleasant through Hollie. Somehow, Hollie had managed to go nearly two days without thinking of Robin, not since the last night in the bed and breakfast kitchen. After that, Robin had faded into nothing but a minor, distant worry, as irrelevant to Hollie's present situation as the overdue oil change in her car.

Hollie wanted to speed up. She tried to, and her body made an honest attempt. Instead of soothing her, however, the change in pace only made Hollie feel worse. Her hamstring in particular resisted the effort.

Hollie tried to imagine Mallory's reaction if Hollie had told her the truth about Iceland. In the hours since Mallory had left, Hollie had turned the situation inside out in her head, searching for some way that her fears about a confession would not become reality.

Hollie thought of Nick the night she had started miscarrying. That night, he had slept at their house for the first and last time since he had left. They hadn't discussed it, nor had they talked about it after the fact. He had lain down beside her—not touching her, but there—and through the pain and the cramps of miscarrying their child, she hadn't protested. They had both fallen asleep with their clothes still on, and when they had woken up early the next morning, she had migrated just far enough over that her limp head had touched his ear. "We can't do this," he had said, his voice full of something she could not bring herself to identify.

And then, she felt it, her hamstring like a rubber band—taut, taut, taut, then snap. Unlike in Iceland, Hollie didn't cry out at the pain. She didn't make a sound as she came to an immediate halt. Instead, she sank to the ground, feeling any semblance of strength leave her entirely.

She lowered her head between her knees and pressed them into her temples, which pounded back with her pumping blood.

There had been so much blood throughout her miscarriage. Days of blood, to the point where Hollie had started wondering if it was too much, if something was wrong. She had never told Mallory how much blood there was. She had never told anybody, not even Nick.

She thought of her last night in Iceland, the pink bloody water that had dripped down onto the ceramic sink bowl. She had watched it fall and thought of the baby she had never wanted in the first place, of all the babies she still didn't want now.

Hollie pulled her phone from its running sleeve. It was indeed Mallory who had sent the last text, which Hollie ignored. She went instead to her contacts, scrolled for a moment, then pressed down. As she brought the phone to her ear, the thought crossed her mind that she had no idea what she was calling to say. Or maybe she did.

"Hollie." Nick's voice was somewhere between surprise and worry. "Are you back?"

Hollie raised her head and looked up to the sky, where a lone cloud had crossed over the sun.

"Yeah. I got back this afternoon."

"Oh. That's great," he said, except it didn't sound great. The word sounded like someone releasing a last breath, all thin and weak.

Hollie thought of the bread knife in the bed and breakfast kitchen, how naturally she had reached to grab it. She thought of it in the officer's hand the next morning, how thin the air in Hollie's chest had felt. There were things about Hollie that no one knew, but the most surprising thing was all the ways Hollie had never really known herself.

"Do you think you could be happy without having kids?" Hollie said. "Like, say we try couples therapy and get to a good place. Would you be okay knowing I might never change my mind?"

Nick was silent on the other end of the line. Hollie couldn't tell if this was because the question had surprised him or if he just didn't want to say the answer.

"I don't know," he said finally. He sounded unsure but mostly sad. "Maybe I could. I mean, our life is pretty great. Maybe I don't need anything else."

Hollie opened her eyes and stared across the street to where someone was rolling their trash can down to the curb. Despite the heat, the lady was wearing stockings beneath her skirt, which were the wrong shade for her skin.

When Hollie hung up the phone a few minutes later, she didn't stand up right away. She thought of her life with Nick, the way it had been. It had been great. Wonderful, even. She wasn't surprised that Nick also thought this, although she was surprised by how he had chosen to word it. "Our life *is* pretty great," he had said, in the present tense. It was so at odds with the way he had sounded, the hope in his voice so forced, it didn't sound like hope at all.

"Excuse me," someone said behind her. Hollie turned to where a woman was standing at her garage door. She looked down her driveway at Hollie, who probably looked odd on her curb. "Is everything okay?" Hollie could tell that the woman was trying to determine if Hollie was a threat, although she was nice enough to mask this as concern.

"Yes. Sorry," Hollie said, pressing her hand into the concrete for leverage. Her hamstring squealed in response. Hollie winced but stood up anyway, swaying a little as she did. "I was just running and pulled a muscle, so I needed to stop."

"Oh my." The worry in the woman's face this time looked genuine. She took one step down the driveway, her hand on her chest. "Do you need help? Should I call someone?"

"No, no." Hollie waved. Standing, her hamstring hurt, but not so badly that she couldn't manage the half-mile walk back to her house. "Really, I'm fine," she said, knowing that she wasn't. Maybe she had never been fine this whole time.

CHAPTER

41

Celeste

Two Days After
Chicago, Illinois

CELESTE LAY IN bed the night after she had returned from Iceland with no real expectation of falling asleep.

She wanted to fall asleep. Her tiredness was so deep in her bones that she could feel it in her teeth. Whenever she closed her eyes, however, all she could see was Alabama.

Louis lay silently beside her, but he wasn't asleep either. Celeste could tell from his breathing, which was still light and nearly soundless. She wondered what it was about sleep that turned his perfectly normal breathing into the labored gasps of a drowning person. She usually nudged him when he got too loud, forcing him over, but he generally didn't wake up enough to register why. He probably had no awareness of the situation past the drowsy sensation of a limb in his back.

Celeste wondered if her own mother had ever lain awake when Celeste was younger, ears primed for the sound of her name. That was one thing about being a mother that none of the websites ever talked about. They talked about the lack of sleep, but they didn't mention how unsatisfying the sleep she did get would become. Since becoming a mother, Celeste was no longer capable of total unconsciousness like Louis. She always had one foot in reality, waiting for Bella to shout out for her mom.

Celeste didn't remember screaming at her own nightmares, although it was very possible she had. All she remembered was sleeping with her head under the comforter, which was stuffy and uncomfortable but at least provided her some form of protection from the darkness outside. To this day, she still couldn't sleep on top of the blankets. She would turn on three different fans before slipping a leg outside the sheets.

She didn't know what she was afraid of now. It was impossible to articulate, even to herself. She thought of Louis in the airport earlier that morning. *There was no way for you to predict something like this.* He had said it like it was true, but he was wrong. Perhaps she could not have predicted the exact details of Alabama's final hours, but that also didn't make the outcome a surprise.

"Louis," Celeste said. She was whispering because half of her hoped he was actually asleep. There was a second of silence when it seemed like maybe he was.

"Yeah?"

Celeste swallowed. The shades in their bedroom were not nearly as good as the ones in Iceland. The glow from the streetlight outside cast a long shadow across the ceiling from the armoire beside their window.

"You know at Bella's first soccer game, when she bit that kid? What you said right before we left?"

Louis was quiet. She could imagine what he was thinking—that she was really going to start a fight this late at night.

"Yeah," he said finally. The word floated upward at the end like it was meant to be followed by something else, although nothing more came.

"Did you mean it? Do you really think I'm the reason Bella acts the way she does?"

She didn't realize how badly she had wanted to ask this question until the words were out.

"No," Louis said, after a long pause. "No, I don't think that at all." Another beat, and then he added, "I think I was just scared."

The silence settled over them again, hugging them both in the dark. She tried to remember the last time Louis had admitted to being scared of anything, but she couldn't. How was that possible? Surely Louis had admitted to some fear, even something generic. She knew he was afraid of Celeste or Bella dying, for example, but even when he'd told her that, he hadn't framed it as a fear. "I don't know what I would do," he had told her, and Celeste remembered thinking how different the two of them were.

What would he *do*? What would there be to do? What control did he possibly think he would have?

This was what Celeste was thinking when she felt it—Louis's hand on her stomach beneath their sheets. It was not a sexual gesture. It was barely even a friendly one. It was just his hand, warm on her body, a reminder that he was there.

She didn't move for a moment, unsure what to do. Then she rolled over to him because it felt as right as anything else.

"I'm scared too," she whispered. She didn't explain what she meant by this, but somehow she felt like he understood. Without a word, he leaned over to kiss her forehead, and Celeste felt suddenly sure that she had the capacity to hurt him. She could tell him about Henry and the kiss, and it might wound him beyond repair. This seemed like something that should have comforted her, the realization that her husband loved her enough to be hurt by her betrayal, but it didn't at all.

PART V

Alabama, Totally Alone

CHAPTER

42

Celeste

Two Weeks After
Chicago, Illinois

Celeste never knew what to wear to funerals, but she felt particularly helpless when it came to Alabama's. Part of the problem was that Alabama's mother refused to even admit it was a funeral in the first place. *We'll be hosting a prayer service,* she had explained on Facebook, sandwiched between various photos of Alabama ranging from birth to a few days before they had left for their trip. She had not actually used the word "funeral" the entire post.

Alabama's mother, Penny Babinski, sold Mary Kay makeup. She introduced herself as a "beauty consultant" in regular conversations with more pride than when Celeste's father told people what he did. (Celeste's father had worked as a pulmonologist for the last thirty years.) Mrs. Babinski generally used Facebook for sale announcements and transformation pictures. The departure from expensive eye creams and lip balms had made the announcement that much more jarring in contrast.

In the church pew now, with the organ groaning out a tune that was both foreign and depressing, Celeste was glad she had decided to wear what she had—her blazer and pant set. She had debated a deep blue organza dress, which was tasteful and solemn but not quite drab. Standing in front of her mirror, however, something about the dress had felt wrong. Maybe it was too ordinary. Maybe it was not ordinary enough. It had seemed appropriate for a prayer service, but still, Celeste had unclasped it and hung it back up.

Celeste glanced over at Louis, whose back was ramrod straight in the pew beside her. She was surprised by how painfully Louis seemed to be absorbing Alabama's death, although perhaps it really wasn't all that surprising. Maybe Louis had never liked Alabama, but in the grand scheme of relationships, Celeste knew that liking someone hardly mattered. Louis and Alabama had been like siblings—grudging siblings, but family—and he seemed to be digesting her death accordingly.

Celeste's eyes moved past him to where a group of influencers sat together across the aisle. There were four total, including Emily, Katherine, and Margot from the PinkPurse trip. Celeste had witnessed Margot and Emily outside the church earlier taking pictures, which were now amassing likes on Instagram. Celeste could not decide if the women's tributes to Alabama were sincere or self-serving, although in either event, they had managed to get #SweetHomeAlabama trending, a play on words that seemed only distantly relevant to Alabama or her death.

Hollie was also sitting with the influencers, although she seemed somehow totally separate. Celeste still didn't know if Hollie had liked Alabama, but she knew Hollie cared in some inscrutable way. Celeste could see it in the way Hollie didn't blink as much as the people around her, as though transfixed by the ridiculously large picture of Alabama that Mrs. Babinski had arranged up front.

Above, the music shifted to something even more depressing, and along with the rest of the congregation, Celeste's attention moved to the center aisle, where Alabama's family had appeared. Mrs. Babinski led the way. She was a petite woman with Alabama's nose and blonde hair. She was not beautiful, though not for lack of effort. Her face was an expensive combination of Mary Kay makeup, fillers, and an undisclosed number of surgeries.

Beside her, Alabama's father, Mr. Babinski, looked as bulky and uncomfortable as a grizzly bear stuffed into a suit. Even yards away, Celeste could see a patch of sweat on the back of his thick neck.

Henry followed behind them, looking somber. When he passed Celeste and Louis, Celeste stared at the seat back in front of her.

Celeste spent the next forty-five minutes in a state of dissociation, barely registering the words of the priest. Alabama's aunts spoke, as did Alabama's only two cousins. Celeste had also been asked to say a few words.

When it was her turn, Celeste ascended the stone steps to the pulpit feeling the strangest sensation of watching her body from above. She adjusted the microphone, and when she spoke, she heard the words like they were someone else's. When she gathered her note cards to leave, she caught Mrs. Babinski's eyes, which were filled with tears.

When it was all over, people rose from the pews slowly. The sound of low conversation filled the room again, more sober than when they had arrived. Across the aisle, some of the influencers were crying loudly. Emily had one arm wrapped around Margot, who was wearing a black dress with ruched tulle sleeves and was weeping expressively.

"I think I should go talk to the Babinskis," Celeste said to Louis, unable to draw her eyes from Margot. "I didn't get to say hi when we got here."

"Do you want me to come with you?"

Celeste looked at him. He hadn't cried the entire service. Neither had she.

"It won't take long. Maybe you can go get the car?"

He nodded, looking relieved. Celeste couldn't hold this against him. She didn't particularly want to talk to the Babinskis either, but it felt like something she had to do.

"It's almost over," he said quietly, leaning over to kiss her on the cheek. She felt the urge to grab his arm and hang onto it, but she didn't. She let him turn and disappear down the aisle. Though not feeling entirely ready, she turned toward the front.

And there was Henry, at the end of her row.

He was as clean-shaven as usual and wearing a scratchy-looking tweed jacket with leather elbow pads, every bit the teacher he was. In the overhead lighting, it was clear that his hair was thinning along his hairline. She hadn't noticed this before now.

"Hi," he said, sounding hesitant. Celeste said hi back, which was followed by an uncomfortable pause. Celeste had wondered what it would feel like the first time she saw him after Iceland. It was strange but not surprising that she felt nothing at all.

"That was a really nice speech you gave," he said finally. "It would've meant a lot to Alabama to hear you say all that."

"Oh. Thanks."

Her pew was empty now, as the people on the other side of her had filed out toward the windows. If Celeste wanted to leave, she would have to go that way too, as Henry was blocking her exit into the center aisle. This seemed unfair in some unspecific way.

"She knew what happened with us," Henry said, his voice now low. "Alabama. She knew what we did. She texted me before she drove off."

It struck Celeste as Henry was talking that he was likely only telling her this to ease his own conscience, unloading his guilt onto her. Celeste felt the passing notion to hate him for it, but she didn't. The truth was, she didn't feel a single emotion toward Henry Wood at all.

"I didn't read the messages until I woke up," he went on. He said this tentatively, as though expecting Celeste to cut in. "And I knew right away that something was off. I think . . ." Here, he seemed to struggle for a moment before saying, "I think you were right."

Celeste waited for these words to wash over her, for the validation she knew she should feel. But it didn't come. Hearing this, she felt absolutely nothing but the deepening pit in her stomach that Alabama had left behind.

"I've decided I'm not telling Louis," she said at last, standing up straighter. "And I hope you won't either. He's my husband, and I'm committed to fixing things with him."

As she said it, she felt faintly reassured by how true the words sounded to her ears. She wasn't sure when she had made the decision, or if it had even been one decision or many little ones over time.

Henry didn't say anything for a moment. Celeste got the impression he was waiting for a further explanation, which Celeste would not give. She didn't need him to understand. She didn't need anyone to approve of her decision but her.

"You know," he said, when it was clear that nothing more was coming, "Alabama loved you. I think she loved you more than she loved anyone else, even me."

There was something in his voice that made Celeste feel sure that this would be their only goodbye.

CHAPTER

43

Hollie

Two Weeks After
Chicago, Illinois

HOLLIE FLEW TO Chicago for Alabama's funeral even though she didn't want to. Like most people, Hollie didn't like funerals, and while this was technically a "prayer service," it was hard to see how it would be anything but a funeral in essence. So she packed a black sheath dress and was not at all surprised to find everyone else at the church wearing black too.

The service was over now. Hollie was surrounded by people out on the sidewalk but felt an odd sense of separation from them all. Even with the other influencers, Hollie had felt separate, as though they were operating on some plane just above her own. At one point, all of the girls had been sobbing, each with varying levels of fervor. Hollie had looked at them blankly and wondered what was wrong with her that she felt totally emotionless.

Hollie glanced down at her phone, checking on the Uber that was still seven minutes away. Part of her wanted to start walking just to escape the crowd, but she had no idea where she was in relation to her hotel.

Her gaze wandered to the church, which was still releasing people dressed in black from its front doors. The church was small and out of place on the otherwise bustling block. It was nestled near one end of the Magnificent Mile, Chicago's shopping district, and was noticeably squatter than the surrounding skyscrapers, its intricate spires only reaching midway up some of the taller buildings. Ivy climbed its face, obscuring the stone and giving the impression of an overgrown ruin, particularly compared to the surrounding shops, which were all straight edges of steel and glass.

Hollie didn't know enough about Alabama to know what she would have wanted for her funeral, but she suspected that this church was not it. Inside, the church was dark and cold and smelled like incense. It seemed so contrary to everything Hollie knew about Alabama Wood. The only thing that had seemed remotely close was the picture someone had set up near the pulpit, Alabama's face enlarged to the size of a small horse.

"Hollie."

Her name sounded halfway between a call and a question. Hollie searched for a moment before finding Celeste Reed a few steps behind her in the crowd. Celeste was wearing a navy blazer and matching slacks, both in some heavy-looking fabric. Hollie's first thought was that it was too hot out to be wearing that. Her second thought was that Celeste looked noticeably bad.

"Celeste. Hey." Hollie tried to smile, and Celeste mimicked the attempt. They both stopped almost immediately, perhaps sensing at the same time how ridiculous it was.

Celeste hesitated for a moment before stepping in for a hug. They were briefly caught in an awkward dance as they simultaneously went for the upper-arm position, then for the lower position at the same time.

Celeste pulled away first. "Alabama would've been thrilled you came," she said, tucking some hair behind her ear. "She really admired you, you know."

Celeste looked like she hadn't slept since Iceland. Her eyes were padded with tiny yellow half-moons, and her skin was sallow and sickly looking, which looked even more dehydrated in the harsh midmorning sun.

"It's such a shitty thing," Hollie said.

"Total shit," Celeste agreed. She said this like someone who didn't curse very often.

Hollie was brought back to the last time she had talked to Celeste at Reynisfjara beach before they had left Iceland. It was funny— well, not funny, but interesting—how their reactions had been so opposing. Celeste had confided in Hollie as though unable to resist the words pouring out of her. Hollie, the exact opposite. Hollie wondered what Celeste would have said if Hollie had told her the truth at the beach, if both of them had cast their confessions out into the wind at the same time.

"Alabama's mom thinks they still might find her," Celeste said. She was gazing up at the church, which looked down on them like a stern parent. "She didn't want this to be an official funeral just in case Alabama shows up." She gave Hollie a wan smile. "She made it pretty funeral-like for it not being one, don't you think?"

Hollie wasn't sure whether she was supposed to laugh or not. She looked down at the sidewalk instead. She could understand this irrational hope for closure, although at this point, finding Alabama would bring only that. If they were still looking for Alabama now, it was a recovery mission, not a rescue.

People bubbled around Hollie and Celeste on the sidewalk. Celeste stepped closer to Hollie to get out of their way. Hollie wanted to say something comforting, but she couldn't think of anything.

"Listen," Celeste said, the seriousness in her voice catching Hollie by surprise. "About what I told you at the beach before we left." Celeste wasn't quite whispering, but her voice was low enough that Hollie had to strain to hear her. "I haven't"—she inhaled—"told my husband about it. About exactly why Alabama and I fought. I know that sounds horrible but . . ."

She trailed off. Hollie noticed her hair, how Celeste had tied it back into a sloppy braid which frayed, with stray pieces that she had either not noticed or not cared to tame. Hollie thought of herself that morning, brushing her argon oil spritz through her own hair before moving to her styling devices—two different curling wands for different sections of her head. Looking at herself in the mirror, she had felt totally separate from her reflection, and yet she had gone ahead with the whole elaborate process anyway.

"Don't worry." Hollie kept her voice low too. "I haven't told anyone, and I don't plan to."

The relief across Celeste's face was immediate. Hollie could relate to the reaction, although it was more difficult to imagine herself in Celeste's situation to begin with. She didn't know if it was bravery or a lack of self-restraint that had caused Celeste to confess to Hollie in the first place, but whatever it was, Hollie didn't have it.

"I want to apologize too," Celeste said, looking sheepish. "That was probably a lot to unload on you." She grimaced. "I can't believe I said it, actually."

In the sunlight, Celeste's makeup looked even sloppier than her hair. Hollie could see the line where her foundation met the skin below her chin. Celeste hadn't even bothered to blend it in.

"You were in shock," Hollie said, shrugging. "People do things they regret when they're in shock." She didn't know if this was true, but she hoped it was.

Celeste appeared to be chewing on the inside of her cheek. Hollie thought of Mallory when she had returned home, how Mallory had bit her lip at one point as though not wanting to say something that was fighting to get out.

Hollie wondered if she could have been friends with Celeste in a different life. Were things like that already set in some obscure way? Maybe nothing about Hollie's life was truly hers. Maybe it was all just robotic hair styling before a funeral.

"That's true," Celeste said finally, speaking slowly. "But I don't know. I probably shouldn't have burdened you with it, but it felt good to tell someone, you know?"

She looked so earnest that Hollie was forced to conclude that Celeste meant this, that she really had felt better after admitting her mistakes out loud. Hollie nodded in agreement, as though this was something she might understand somehow.

CHAPTER

44

Celeste

Two Weeks After
Chicago, Illinois

AFTER ALABAMA'S FUNERAL, Celeste stood in front of the bed-room dresser, staring at herself in the mirror. Downstairs, Bella was talking to Celeste's mother, who had come to babysit that morning. Celeste and Louis had returned from the funeral to find the two of them with their heads pressed together—not like grandmother and granddaughter, but two equals deep in conversation.

In the mirror, Celeste's reflection moved to touch her blazer. The blazer was the same one she had worn to dinner with Alabama and Henry a few months prior. It was heavy—probably too heavy for late spring—which Alabama would have been quick to point out. Celeste wondered how long she would continue to think this way, imagining Alabama's impossible reactions to situations like this.

Behind her, the bedroom door opened, and Louis appeared in the doorway. Louis hadn't worn black to the funeral. He instead wore a plain white dress shirt and a solemn slate tie. Fashion could be so much easier for men, as Alabama had once lamented. "It's like they get the multiple-choice questions, and we have to write a whole dang essay," she had said.

"They're just finishing up downstairs," Louis said, nodding over his shoulder. "It appears they're making a dolphin encyclopedia?"

Celeste smiled, mostly at Louis's expression. He said this with the same sort of dumbfounded amazement he had received Bella's first words as young child. For a while there, it had seemed like Bella would never learn to speak. Celeste had been so relieved when she finally had.

Celeste looked back to the mirror. It struck her that the last time she had worn the blazer was in her first life—the one before she had kissed Henry, the one before Alabama had died. She thought of Henry at the funeral. Henry, the first person to admit that Celeste had been right. Hearing this had not made her feel better. It had felt instead like confirmation of all the things Celeste had suspected about herself but had managed to ignore until Alabama was gone.

"What's that?" Celeste said, nodding to the paper she had just noticed Louis holding behind her. In the mirror, Louis held it up.

"The short-beaked common dolphin, as I've been informed."

Celeste turned to study the drawing. As usual, the dolphin was floating in blank, white space. The animal itself, however, was remarkably detailed. Celeste suspected that if she were to get out a ruler, she would find that all of the dolphin's various fins were in perfectly accurate proportion.

"It's pretty good," Celeste said, taking the paper.

"Unusually good," Louis agreed.

Celeste brought the page to eye level, marveling at the shading of the animal's torso, which reflected a true understanding of how light and shadows worked. It was like this for so much when it came to her daughter, catching Celeste somewhere halfway between amazement and concern.

"How're you holding up, CeCe? I haven't had a chance to really ask you yet."

Louis's voice was so quiet that at first Celeste wasn't positive she had heard him. She looked from the paper to her husband, whose expression was unfamiliar. It took her a second to recognize the frown as one of concern, and then another to understand that it was directed at her. She had not realized how much she had longed to be looked at this way by him until just now.

"I'm . . ." Her voice floated off, as she truly didn't know. Up until that morning, she had felt like she was balancing on some precarious edge, about to tip. That feeling wasn't gone, but at the moment, she felt marginally more stable somehow.

Louis stepped over to her, and without saying anything, he wrapped her in a hug. Celeste sank in easily.

They stood like this for a little while—longer than they normally hugged. When Louis finally stepped back, he kissed her on the forehead like she was a child. Rather than patronizing, the action was incredibly comforting. Celeste closed her eyes and tried to commit the sensation to memory for later.

Louis retreated to the bathroom after that, and Celeste turned back to the mirror. With one finger, she traced the line of silver buttons down her chest.

Celeste's mother had once had a coat with elaborate buttons like these, except hers had been gold. Each had been the size of a quarter, with flowering vines formed from intricate, embossed grooves. The buttons were what had made the coat seem so lavish, which was not something Celeste had been accustomed to as a child. (It was difficult to feel lavish in a family of five children, even if they were the five children of a pulmonologist.)

Much of Celeste's childhood had blurred over time, but for some reason, the memory of her mother's coat remained perfectly intact. She remembered running her fingers over the buttons as it had hung in the closet, feeling the cool metal details against her skin. She had never done this with her mother around to see her, but her mother must have seen anyway, because for Celeste's ninth birthday, her mother had bought her a coat of her own. It had been ruby red tweed with a thick standing collar and two rows of large gold button starting from the breast. Celeste had lifted the heavy cardboard lid and felt sure for a moment that it was a trick, that the coat in the box could never be hers.

When Celeste thought about this now, she wondered whether she and her mother had actually been closer than she had realized, at least in some ways—ways she hadn't noticed at the time. She thought back to her mother two weeks ago in the kitchen, to what she had said about Celeste's nightmares as a child. *I don't think it was enough.* How many times had Celeste thought this very same thing of herself? It wasn't enough. She wasn't enough. The question was her constant refrain.

Louis came out of the bathroom just as the conversation downstairs shifted. Celeste heard the distinct sound of a stool against hardwood, and she knew that in a matter of seconds, she would hear her daughter moseying up the stairs.

"Lou," Celeste said, turning to face him. His cheeks were blotchy pink, as though he had just splashed them with water. "We have to get Bella checked out for autism. I know you want to wait, but I really think there's something going on here. I have this feeling, you know?"

Louis's eyes moved between hers for a moment. For a second, she thought he might protest. She didn't know if she had the courage to press the matter if he did.

Instead, he nodded slowly. "Okay," he said. "Okay, yes, I think you might be right."

CHAPTER

45

Hollie

Two Weeks After
Dallas, Texas

THERE WAS A new café in Dallas's Bishop Arts District called Pearl's, where Hollie currently sat in a stiff rattan chair waiting for Robin Sinclair. It was two days after Alabama's funeral, and Hollie didn't want to be getting lunch. However, when Robin had reached out that morning, inviting Hollie for a catch-up run, Hollie had been quick to suggest Pearl's instead, as she wanted to run with Robin even less.

It was nearly one now, when they were set to meet. Robin had texted a few minutes prior to apologize for running late. Hollie squirmed in her chair, lifting one butt cheek, then the other, peeling her skin from the palm stems of her seat. Rattan was chic, but it was uncomfortable as hell.

She took a sip of her drink, which was already sweating. The hostess had seated Hollie up front, near the glass overhead door that had been cranked up toward the ceiling, blurring the line between inside dining room and patio. A fan oscillated back and forth over Hollie's shoulder, fighting through the humid afternoon.

Robin finally arrived ten minutes after one, appearing breathlessly beside the table.

"I'm so, so sorry," she said, sounding flustered.

Hollie stood and waved her away. They hugged briefly before Robin looped her purse around her chair and Hollie lowered herself back into hers. Hollie noticed that Robin had done something different with her hair. Before, Hollie had only ever seen it tied back, usually with a large bow or scrunchie, but now it hung loose around her face in soft waves that just skimmed the top of her shoulders. She was wearing a white tank top with tiny shoestring straps and a shade of raspberry lipstick that Hollie would probably have avoided if she'd had Robin's teeth. Still, something about the cumulative effect was pleasant—pretty, even.

Okay, Robin Sinclair looked pretty. Hollie could admit it.

"I had a dentist's appointment," Robin explained, motioning to her mouth. "It ran way over."

"Don't worry about it," Hollie said.

"I just hate to keep you waiting."

"I wasn't waiting that long."

Robin smiled, her recently cleaned teeth looking extra big and bright against her lipstick.

"Did you order already?"

"Not yet." Hollie looked down. "I'm thinking about this chickpea salad, though."

For a few minutes, Robin and Hollie considered their menus in silence. Hollie wondered how many calories were in the vegan ranch dressing and whether it was more or less than the vinaigrette. By the time the waitress came to take their order, Hollie had decided that even if the ranch dressing wasn't more caloric, it was certainly more fattening, so she went instead with the house salad—add grilled tofu, hold the croutons. Robin annoyingly ordered a pimento grilled cheese sandwich, which was only annoying because it sounded much better than Hollie's salad.

"So," Robin said, leaning forward in her seat. "I bet you're still recovering from your trip." She had a scrunchie around her wrist that was nearly the exact same shade of pink as her lipstick. Hollie's mind flashed to Alabama Wood's bubblegum pink jacket slipping into the crack of the glacier the day before she had disappeared.

She took a long drink of water.

"Yeah, I'm still pretty burned out."

"I bet." Robin gave her a knowing nod.

There was a brief pause. Hollie knew she should say something further, but she couldn't manage anything else. She could feel Robin hesitate, rightfully expecting Hollie to elaborate.

Finally, Robin said, "It's so shocking about Alabama Wood." She tugged at the scrunchie, rotating it around her thin wrist. "I saw an article about it on Facebook. It's so sad."

Hollie knew there had been articles written, but she hadn't read any. She had no desire to know what they said.

"Yeah, it is."

"Do they know what happened to her? Like, where she was going when she drove off?"

Hollie shook her head, her throat swelling. She coughed, trying to clear it, horrified at the idea of breaking down in public.

"I don't think so," she said thickly.

"I'm so, so sorry, Hollie," Robin said for the second time that afternoon. Her eyes were round and apologetic. "Were you—close with her?" She sounded sincere and nice enough that Hollie actually considered the question for a moment.

"It was sort of complicated," she heard herself saying, which Robin received with another somber nod. Hollie thought of Celeste Reed, who had said more or less the same thing on the beach—that Alabama was a complicated person. It had felt like an answer coming from Celeste, but from Hollie, the same words sounded like just another lie.

Hollie was struck with a sudden wave of exhaustion. It was so tiring, the lying, and Hollie was so tired.

"She wanted to be friends, but I was honestly kind of a bitch to her," Hollie added, unsure even as she said it why she was telling Robin this. "And I think that's why I've been having a hard time with it. I mean, it's obviously horrible, but I guess I also just kind of feel"—her eyes flickered away from Robin's, landing on the wall over her shoulder—"guilty, I guess."

The wall was painted brick, a trendy German schmear. It was dotted with a handful of wire planters, each flowing with succulents and golden pothos. Hollie stared at the plant's dangling green limbs as she waited for Robin to say something, not knowing what she expected or even wanted to hear.

"I get that," Robin said, which again was nice, although Hollie seriously doubted Robin understood anything going on inside Hollie's head. "I don't think I told you this, but you know the Josie Project? The charity we're racing for?" Hollie nodded despite knowing little about the charity past its name. "Some of my high school friends started it our senior year. We named it after this girl we went to school with—Josie Summerland. She died by suicide when we were juniors."

Hollie refocused on Robin, surprised, although Robin's gaze had now traveled somewhere distant over Hollie's forehead that only she could see. She was smiling, but the expression was small and sad, and the rest of her face didn't match it. Hollie wondered if Robin even realized she was smiling at all.

"Oh," Hollie said, feeling stupid. "I didn't know Josie was someone you knew." She also didn't know what the charity was actually for, but she didn't say this, not wanting to seem like a complete asshole.

"Yeah. I mean, my friends and I, we weren't, like, super close with Josie before she died. It was kind of like what you were saying about Alabama. Josie was always on the fringe, and—I don't know. I guess we just weren't that interested in her. We had a pretty tight-knit friend group, and we didn't care for any more, you know?"

Hollie nodded again, although Robin wasn't looking at her. Hollie wasn't sure which surprised her more: that Robin could be part of an exclusionary group, or that Hollie was able to relate to Robin about anything.

"When she died, we were all really messed up about it. We thought it was our fault. Like, if we would've just been a little kinder to her, she wouldn't have done it or whatever."

"But you guys were just kids," Hollie said, feeling an unexpected yet genuine swell of defensiveness on Robin's behalf.

"Josie was too, though." Robin had stopped smiling. "But yeah, I don't think it was our fault really. I mean, we could've been nicer, but with things like that, there's usually a million reasons why it happened." A pause, then she added, "It's weird, though, what grief can make you believe. Even if you don't realize you're grieving."

She met Hollie's eyes. Robin looked tired suddenly, just as tired as Hollie felt. Perhaps Hollie would have reveled in this before, as Hollie had spent months wanting nothing more than to beat Robin at everything. Hollie had been self-aware enough to recognize herself using Robin as a stand-in for all the other losses she could not control, and yet this had somehow only made her want to beat Robin more. Now, however, looking at Robin across the table, Hollie could no longer feel it. She could not come up with a single reason why beating Robin might make her feel good.

Hollie thought of Celeste at Alabama's funeral, how tired she had looked. And yet, in some ways, Celeste had looked much better than Hollie had felt. Celeste was in the thick of her grieving, but still, she was grieving. She was living and breathing and feeling. She was not a shiny, empty shell.

"The thing is, I don't think this is grief lying to me," Hollie said, and at once, her heart started hammering. Every edge of her body tingled with self-preservation, demanding she stay quiet. Or maybe it was the opposite. Maybe the only way Hollie could survive this was getting it out. Either way, Hollie took a deep breath, and not quite believing what she was doing, she said out loud the thing she had thought she never would.

"Alabama is dead because of me."

46

Hollie

The Night Of
Vík, Iceland

Hollie didn't think when Alabama lunged for her. She reacted on instinct alone.

Alabama jolted forward with a hard step, her foot thundering in the space between them as Hollie's hand flung sideways, grasping at the only thing she could reach: the bread knife. "FUCK," Hollie yelped immediately as the knife's serrated edge jammed into the meaty part of her hand. She dropped it, the sound startling them both. Alabama faltered as the knife made a slight clink on the floor by Hollie's feet.

For a moment, both of them stared down at Hollie's hand, which she held at the wrist with the other. Across her palm, on the padded section right beneath her thumb, a line of separated skin pulsed with her heartbeat. The cut was colorless for only a split second before the blood appeared, rising in drops.

Hollie's stomach rolled. Without thinking, she pressed her hand into her cardigan as delayed pain erupted. She was shaking with adrenaline. Alabama appeared transfixed by Hollie's hand, which was now throbbing in her shirt.

For a few seconds, neither of them moved. They were both breathing heavily, although the sight of the blood seemed to have reset them. Alabama licked her lips, then finally looked up. Her eyes were bloodshot. It looked as though the whites of each were traced with tiny red hairline cracks.

"You never wanted to be my friend, did you?" Alabama said. The question caught Hollie so off guard, she felt momentarily unable to speak. She had expected Alabama to pounce again, to fight.

Hollie opened her mouth, her lips parting just slightly, but she found nothing there. So unprepared for the question, she could formulate nothing but the truth: No, she had not wanted to be Alabama's friend. She had never even considered it actually, but she did not dare say this to Alabama now.

In Hollie's hesitation, Alabama seemed to find her answer anyway. She swayed, and Hollie braced herself again. But then, before Hollie even realized what was happening, Alabama swept around on her heel. Hollie watched breathlessly as Alabama disappeared through the kitchen door, out of sight.

Hollie stared after her for a moment, feeling shaken. Finally, gingerly, she unwrapped her hand from her cardigan. Blood rose from the wound immediately, creating webs of red across her palm. The sight was nauseating, which was not helped by the enormous amount of shit she had just consumed.

She pressed her hand back into the cardigan and examined the table. She had cleared most of the evidence of her binge except for a wrapper and the cracker she had dropped. Hollie stared at the cracker and was filled with sweeping waves of shame. It wasn't just about the food either. Why hadn't she just lied to Alabama about liking her? What was it about Hollie that made her to look Alabama in the eye, take in the entirety of her desperate fury, and remain silent?

She looked back to the door Alabama had disappeared through. With Alabama gone, the vacuumed silence seemed to relent. Wind rocked the tiny window behind her. The rafters above her creaked with movement, one of the other girls in her room.

Finally, she leaned over for the knife by her foot. She cleaned off the blood, returned it to its drawer. Swept up the wrapper and the cracker and threw both away.

When she was finished, she flicked off the lights behind her and headed toward the stairs. The hallway was draftier than the kitchen. The chill sent a jolt down her arm all the way to her injured hand, which was still pressed into her cardigan. Hollie shivered as she crept toward the stairway as quietly as she could.

When she reached the bottom step, she heard a sound—a faint *shush* like someone had exhaled. Hollie froze, the tingling sensation intensifying to every corner of her body. Her mind sprang immediately to Alabama. She imagined Alabama emerging from the shadows, the sharp corners of her elbows as she raised an arm over her head to strike.

But nothing happened. Hollie's eyes had adjusted to the dimmer lighting, and with a sweep of the hallway, she saw that she was totally alone. The source of the sound was only the front door, which Hollie hadn't noticed at first. It was cracked just slightly, as though someone had pulled it closed but not all the way shut.

The door was heavy, and it put up a valiant fight against the windy night swirling behind it. Every so often, however, a gust snuck through the crack, finding its way into the hallway.

Hollie looked over her shoulder, then inched toward it, her entire body tense.

There was no one at the door either. Hollie opened it and peered out into the night, which was purply black but not all the way dark. Her eyes moved from the parking lot to the small village before eventually landing on the sea beyond it. It felt like the bottom of the ocean—not lifeless exactly, but nonetheless lonely.

As Hollie was pulling the door shut, her eyes caught on something, a glint on the concrete landing. She looked at it for a moment before stepping toward it and crouching down.

She did not touch Alabama's phone right away but instead examined it like an archaeologist staggered by an unexpected find. When she finally lifted the phone from the ground, the screen lit up. It was filled with notifications—Instagram alerts, at least three emails. Hollie rose slowly, her eyes not straying from the device.

There should have been no question about what to do next. A good person, a decent person, would have searched for Alabama, would have found a way to return the phone. A good person would have used this opportunity to apologize for what she had said in the kitchen and for all the unkindness she had shown in the days before.

Hollie had thought of herself as a good person. Maybe she had been one at some point. But in that moment, all Hollie could think about was herself. She thought of Alabama's eyes and how they had flashed. She thought of Alabama's slender fingers, how quickly and furiously she would be able to type out a message, relaying information to the world with the click of her phone.

Hollie stood there in the doorway, partway between the dim hallway and the blustery night, and then she dropped the phone into her pocket and closed the door.

In the upstairs bathroom, Hollie found a first aid kit beneath the sink. As she poured peroxide across her palm, she bit the inside of her cheek but made no sound. She was relieved to find that that cut was not terribly deep. With a little pressure, the bleeding had already stopped.

Cleaned and bandaged, Hollie then scrubbed at her cardigan in the sink. When the water beneath ran from pink to colorless, she turned the water off and returned to her room.

That night, Hollie's sleep was fitful and unsatisfying. She had slipped Alabama's phone into her suitcase, just beneath a folded pullover, and all through the night, she jolted awake, sure it had lit up. The room, however, remained dark and nearly silent except for Katherine's even breathing and the faint whistle of the wind outside.

The first hint of sunlight appeared just after three, barely visible in the space beneath the blackout shade. Hollie stared as it turned from syrupy orange to a muted yellow. When she was unable to stand it any longer, she slid from her bed and pulled Alabama's phone from her suitcase, the device still mostly charged. Silently, she crept out of her room and padded to the one Alabama and Celeste shared.

Hollie knocked and waited for only a second with bated breath before Celeste pulled it open. Hollie could not ignore the disappointment in Celeste's face.

Hollie kept it brief, generic: She had seen Alabama the night before, had noticed Alabama looking upset. She just wanted to check and make sure everything was alright. At this, Celeste's face blanched. With an unsteady voice, Celeste told Hollie that Alabama wasn't there, that she hadn't come back the previous night.

Hollie nodded wordlessly, and Celeste—clearly shaken—didn't seem to find this odd. It was not until Hollie was back at her own door a few seconds later that she realized Alabama's phone was still in her pocket. She had forgotten about it entirely, hearing the fear in Celeste's voice.

The phone was what Hollie would keep coming back to later. She would analyze and reanalyze what exactly it meant—why she had decided to keep it, why she had later decided to look through it and hide it from the police. She would search for some complicated explanation, some justification for how she could do something that seemed so wrong. None of it was like her—unless, of course, that's exactly who she was.

Once she allowed herself to admit it, the explanation was actually very simple: Hollie had been given the choice between saving Alabama and saving her reputation, and she had made a decision. It was a decision she would now have to live with for the rest of her life.

47

Alabama

The Night Of
Vík, Iceland

ALABAMA WAS BREATHING like she had been in a fight, even though she had not thrown a single punch. For a second, she had thought about it. She had thought about charging Hollie—hitting and grabbing and clawing. She had imagined the feeling of Hollie's hair twisting around her fists, the way her scalp would turn white where each little follicle popped from the skin.

She almost had, but then she hadn't, because unlike most people, Alabama had self-control.

Outside the kitchen, Alabama came to an abrupt stop. To her right, wind clattered in the small, cloudy window. To her left, the long stairway disappeared into the upstairs hall. Alabama turned her head to gaze at the staircase, her thoughts running wild. She thought of her brains splattered against the walls, the mental image so vivid it was as though it had actually occurred.

Alabama didn't like blood. It made her feel dirty.

She pulled out her phone. The letters on the screen danced and swayed like little witches in a merry circle, casting a magic spell. She noticed with a detached sort of interest that her fingers were trembling as she maneuvered the screen, as she found Henry's name.

The words came easily. In a way, they weren't even her words at all. They sprang up from somewhere deep within her, some part of her body that was completely outside her control:

I KNOW WHAT YOU DID.

And then:

I KNOW THE WHOLE THING.

And then, in rapid succession:

YOU THINK I'M NOT GOOD ENOUGH.
I KNOW YOU NEVER DID.
WELL, GUESS WHAT? NO ONE'S PERFECT.
EVEN HOLLIE GOODWIN IS A DIRTY, GROSS BINGE
    EATER.
DID YOU KNOW THAT?
SHE'S A LIAR.
SHE'S A BINGE EATER WHO PRETENDS SHE'S
    PERFECT.
I BET YOU THOUGHT SHE WAS PERFECT TOO,
    DIDN'T YOU?
I BET YOU THOUHT CELESTE WAS TOO.
YOU THOUGHT YOU'D FIND SOMEONE BETTER.
WELL, GOOD LUCK FINDING ANYONE BETTER
    THAN ME WHEN I'M GONE.

As the words poured out of her and onto the screen, she felt a slow but steady release. She did not send the message all at once, but as individual sentences as they came to her. She imagined each one zipping out into cyberspace like a little bullet finding Henry's chest.

When she was finished, she looked up, assessing the staircase in front of her. She imagined Celeste fast asleep in one of the bedrooms. The thought made her breath feel hotter, burning her nostrils on the way out.

She turned from the stairway and started walking toward the front door. She moved with a deliberate slowness, aware that running would wake the other women up, which she did not want to do. The control this took was excruciating, and at the last second, she took two furious steps forward and used both hands to push herself out the door.

She emerged from the bed and breakfast in a surge of energy and was immediately throttled in the face by wind roaring past her ears. In a way, this comforted her, the violence of the night. It was as though nature felt her anger and approved of it, of her.

She thought of Hollie in the kitchen, surrounded by all that food. It was almost funny, the more Alabama thought about it. Hollie, the fittest, the healthiest, the most beautiful of them all. She wasn't pregnant. She was just a pig. It was so unoriginal, so *hilarious* in its irony, that Alabama couldn't take it. In the swirl of violent wind, Alabama threw her head back and laughed.

Actually, she was glad for what had happened. When Hollie had reached for the knife, Alabama had known immediately that Hollie could hurt her. No, not just could—Hollie had *wanted* to hurt her. Oddly, it hadn't been scary, just exhilarating for what it had revealed. In the kitchen, Alabama had understood finally that there was no winning over people like that—like Henry, Celeste, and Hollie. She could not make them love her the way that she deserved.

Wind ripped through Alabama's hair. And then, all at once, Alabama understood something so deeply, it was like the truth had come straight from her bones.

She paused, both shaken and amazed by the sensation passing through her. The realization flew through her at first, then rained down in soft and fluttering pieces, like little bits of snow. It was a beautiful feeling, transcendental in its clarity, and for just a moment, even the wind around her seemed to grow reverently still. Alabama sometimes found her thoughts frustrating, as though she was constantly searching for connections that were just out of reach. This was not like that. This was every loose end of her life coming together at once.

The keys to the Taurus were still in Alabama's pocket, and earlier, Alabama might have chalked this up to good luck. Now, Alabama understood this as the universe speaking to her. She could all but feel the cosmos gently urging her along.

Serenity filled her as she approached the car. Once inside, she didn't bother with the radio, as there was no need for outside noise. The headlights flickered on, casting dim wedges of white across the gravel, now dark in the day's last dusky light.

Her only regret was that she had not thought of it sooner, when Celeste had first said it back home. "It's not like anybody at my funeral is going to be talking about my Instagram engagement when I'm dead," she had told Alabama, clearly not realizing the profound truth of what she'd said.

With more time to plan, Alabama could have orchestrated it better—perhaps planned her own funeral, which would surely have been better than anything Henry could do. Then again, it was possible that ideas like this one were not meant for invasive plotting. Maybe an idea this brilliant could only be captured on a whim.

It felt like mere seconds before she was approaching the glacier. She knew she was close because she recognized the mountain, the one with the long, clunky name. She then tried to remember exactly what Celeste had said about the iceberg lagoon, which was somewhere past it.

Icebergs were different from the glacier, apparently—a fact Alabama had learned against her will before they had left. Unlike the glacier, the icebergs were suspended in water. Celeste had shown Alabama pictures of them, some tourist spot she had almost dragged Alabama to.

Alabama thought of the picture now, the luminous chunks of brilliant blue ice floating along its surface. It had been beautiful, but at the time, Alabama had been uninterested, as a boat tour through chunks of ice had sounded boring and cold.

Now, thinking of those images, Alabama couldn't help but marvel at how dazzling the blue ice would look behind reporters, faces grim as they reported Alabama's death.

It didn't take more than ten minutes before Alabama whizzed by the entrance to the GoIceland parking lot. She glanced at the clock, noting the time. She wasn't sure exactly how far the lagoon was from the glacier, although she remembered Celeste saying it was a matter of single digit miles.

With each minute that ticked past with no sign of the lagoon, the soothing clarity seemed to leave Alabama in chunks. In its place, the annoyance grew louder. She felt annoyed with herself for not mapping it out beforehand, although she redirected this annoyance to Celeste for not being more clear about where the lagoon was.

Wind continued to pound against her car, shifting it from side to side in her lane. She gripped the wheel tighter, bending forward like she was a professional race car driver. In her head, she cursed Celeste with all the worst words she could think of, which made her feel better, but not by much.

Although it was the dead of night, a faint glow remained around her car, dust-sized bits of daylight trapped eternally in the air. Past the national park now, there was only nothingness, vast and empty. There were no buildings, no people, no light pollution. The stars overhead were crisp, tides of faraway galaxies now clear. But instead of beautiful, it felt claustrophobic, like she was trapped in a barren snow globe all alone.

For the first time since she had left, a thread of hesitation snuck into her thoughts. She feared that if she pulled it, the whole thing would come undone, and she would lose her resolve. She glanced at the clock—eight minutes. She didn't know how much further she was willing to go.

She pressed her foot harder against the gas, propelling the dinky car faster than it was built to go. Outside, the wind seemed to be picking up. Twice the car swerved, and she ripped the steering wheel back, barely keeping herself on the road. She felt wild. She kept going. For the first time, she felt a little scared.

Ahead, she saw the road converging into one lane, and as she sped closer, she recognized the shimmery sheen of water on either side of the single-lane bridge. She pressed down on the gas, her foot nearly reaching the floorboard. As she burst onto the narrow stretch of gravel, a mighty gale pummeled the driver's side door.

The tires squealed beneath her, the front of the car making small zigzags across the loose ground as she braked. Her knuckles were white against the wheel, her eyes wide and unblinking.

Finally, the car came to a stop.

She sat like this for a moment, breathless, as wind continued to rock her car. It took almost all of her strength to finally push the door open, and even more to keep the wind from ripping it from the frame.

The road was narrow and straight, balanced on an embankment that seemed to go on ahead of her for a while. She took a few steps toward the guardrail and peered over. Below, inky black water shimmered with traces of moonlight.

Not an iceberg lagoon. Darker. More foreboding. But maybe foreboding was good.

Her eyes traced the angle of the embankment, noting where it sank below the water. Then she turned, looking back in the direction she had come.

Her hair swirled madly. Her eyes watered in the cold. She dragged one shoe across the pavement, observing the little pebbles quivering beneath her toe, then ran her hand across the guardrail like a mother stroking her child.

Slowly, calmly, Alabama walked back to her car. The engine shuddered back on as though already fearing its fate. Alabama rolled down all the windows, and then with one hand on the passenger seat headrest, she reversed quickly, back onto the main road.

Wind barreled through the car, now a wind tunnel. She shoved the shifter into drive, her foot still heavy on the brake.

She paused, staring forward. She felt cold with the windows down, each gust forcing itself upon her—around her neck, down her spine. She was stronger than the average person—she had always known that—and she had complete confidence in herself. Even so, for a second she wondered whether she was overestimating the capabilities of any human being. She wondered whether even the strongest person in the world could do what she planned to do.

She groped around for her phone but, after a full minute, still couldn't find it. Had she dropped it? The thought seemed to ricochet around her head like a pinny dropped in an empty well.

She closed her eyes and pictured herself driving back to the bed and breakfast and looking for the phone. Finding it. Slipping back up the stairwell and into her room. She could get there before anyone had woken up. No one would even know she had left, let alone what she had almost done.

Her eyes flipped open at the same time that her foot moved from one pedal to the other. The car groaned but obliged, creating a whir of metal and fury as it accelerated. She didn't look at the speedometer, didn't need to. Wind slapped at her face, unleashing angry streams of tears down her cheeks. The car moved faster, faster still. She let out a high-pitched scream, a mix between a laugh and a yell.

Then she yanked the steering wheel, and everything went silent.

She experienced it in slow motion—her car slipping on the gravel, then regaining traction. Approaching the guardrail—slowly, slowly—before bursting joyously through the barrier. The water was in front of her, coming closer and closer for the longest time. And then . . .

The world seemed to resume its normal speed all at once. Her head hit something. She heard it before she felt it, a sickening thump. She had no time to process this, however, before the icy water stole the breath right out of her chest. She gasped with the most primal desire—oxygen—as water replaced air faster than seemed possible. She could hear her heartbeat, could hear her own panic. Around her, water poured in through the open windows, furious that a foreigner had breached its surface.

And that's when it hit her: This was how it felt to die. This, right here, in the frigid dark water. It wasn't vengeance. It wasn't beautiful or particularly profound.

It was just Alabama, totally alone.

PART VI

Someone She Knew

48

Hollie

Six Weeks After
Dallas, Texas

H OLLIE HAD SEEN Nick a handful of times since she had returned from Iceland, but she hadn't actually *seen* him. Last week, for example, he had come to the house to pick up his golf clubs, and like always, they had chatted briefly about surface-level things—his brother's wife and how fervently she recycled, the air conditioning, which was making a funny noise.

A few times, they had skirted around the issue of couples therapy, albeit never quite making it all the way in. At first, the excuse had been Iceland. The trauma was still so fresh, Hollie's emotions still too raw for a conversation like that. As the weeks had passed, however, this excuse had become increasingly more flimsy, although neither of them had acknowledged this out loud.

It was now the evening before the race Hollie and Robin had been planning, and Hollie was waiting in a coffee shop that would close in an hour. Most coffee shops didn't even bother staying open this late, and Hollie was grateful that this one did. Coffee seemed less intimidating than dinner or even dessert. Meeting for dinner was a commitment, even if you only got appetizers, and dessert gave off the impression of something light and joyous, which this was not.

Hollie took a small sip of her decaf latte. In any other universe, Hollie would not have dreamed of a coffee this late the night before a race. She would worry about the caffeine, that even the small amount in decaf would disrupt her sleeping, and she would be even more concerned about dehydration the next day.

Hollie, however, did not plan on running in the race tomorrow, which had come much to Robin's surprise. "My hamstring's still bothering me," Hollie had explained, which wasn't a complete lie but close enough that it essentially was.

When Nick entered the shop, he did not see Hollie right away, providing Hollie four or five seconds to appraise him on her own. He looked tired, and not in a good way. Not in the dazed but delighted way he had looked when they had moved into their first house, when they had spent all night transporting boxes despite no real reason for the rush other than their excitement. They'd eaten pizza on an overturned storage bin, then made love on the mattress in the middle of the empty master. They had been so happy. They had been so young.

Nick kissed her on the cheek before he sat down.

"Thanks for coming," she said to him, regretting it almost immediately after it came out. It sounded like something she would say to Robin Sinclair when they met for lunch. Hollie thought of Robin, how her face had remained unchanged as Hollie had told her about that night with Alabama. It had never occurred to Hollie that she felt lonely before that moment, but looking at Robin, she had realized she was.

"Of course." Nick said this like he hated the exchange as much as she did. "You look well."

Hollie looked down at herself, surprised. She wondered if he meant it, and if it was true. She had not noticed herself feeling better since Iceland, but she had paused in the bathroom earlier that morning, struck by her reflection in the mirror. She still didn't look like herself—still puffy and bloated where she usually was not—but that morning, she had noticed a pinkness in her cheeks in place of the pale, sallow color they usually were.

"Thanks," Hollie said. She didn't bother lying to Nick about how he looked. She was making a conscious effort to lie less for one thing, and she didn't think he would believe it anyway.

For a moment, Hollie considered bailing. She had come to say a very specific thing that now felt as impossible to her as climbing from the table and jumping to the moon.

She said, "So I wanted to talk about couples therapy." She still felt uncomfortably formal, but she made herself go on. "I know things were a little crazy right after Iceland, but I think it's time."

Nick nodded. His face was one tight knot. She had told him what she wanted to talk about when she had asked him to get coffee, but maybe he had expected a buffer, some small talk before they jumped right in.

"Okay," Nick said. He looked like he wanted to say something else, but instead, he just sat back in his seat. Hollie thought of that day in the kitchen when she had first taken the pregnancy test. His first reaction had been to lean into her, to touch her. She wondered how soon after that conversation this had changed.

"I don't think couples therapy is a bad idea," Hollie started, remembering the lines she had practiced on the car ride over. "I think it can be really helpful in the right situation, and it'd be a good suggestion normally."

Nick nodded like he knew what she was about to say next.

"It's just, I don't know." Hollie's eyes fell to the table before she could help it. She tried to remember the next line in her soliloquy but suddenly couldn't. All she could think about was Nick's eyes fluttering slightly on the pillow beside hers, midway through a dream.

She closed her eyes and swallowed.

"You're not going to change your mind about kids," Nick said, catching her by surprise. Her eyes flipped open. He was looking at her like he had heard every thought running through her head.

Hollie didn't say anything. She hadn't planned on crying, but maybe she should have.

Nick ran a hand through his hair, his gaze out of focus. She hadn't answered his question, and they both knew what that meant. She thought of the conversation they'd had the day she had returned from Iceland. "Maybe I don't need anything else," he had said over the phone. When she had pictured him saying this, she had imagined his expression looking exactly like this one, like he was trying to convince himself of something that he knew wasn't true.

"I love you, Nick," Hollie said, not remotely on script. She couldn't help it. She reached partway across the table but stopped with her hands in the middle, resting on the laminate. She looked at him, not wanting to say it but knowing she had to.

"I love you so much, and that's why"—she struggled—"that's why I can't do this. I can't make you happy the way you deserve."

Her voice broke at the end, but even so, Nick's eyes didn't waver. He had always been so good like that. He was a good man, a good person. He was exactly the man most women prayed to find. Losing him was a failure by any objective measure. And here Hollie was.

Nick didn't say anything for a moment. It crossed her mind that he could argue, although she felt sure that he would not. Indeed, when he finally spoke, his voice was quiet but resolved.

"I understand," he said. He blinked, and Hollie realized he was crying too. "I just hope you know this didn't make me stop loving you. All of this, it never made me love you any less."

He met her halfway across the table, taking her hand in his. He lifted them both to kiss hers goodbye.

CHAPTER

49

Celeste

Six Weeks After
Dallas, Texas

THE SILENT STANDOFF occurring in hotel room 843 was nothing new to Celeste. Bella sat on the edge of one bed, her little legs pressed against an unmade tangle of linens. The crumple of glorious white sheets beneath her was the type of simple luxury that could make Celeste lie awake at night and wonder whether she should have put more effort into being fabulously rich.

Bella hadn't said anything about the sheets when they had woken up that morning, which Celeste supposed was a positive review in itself. Bella didn't like hotels, largely because of the bedding, which she considered too "crumply."

Now, Louis was across the street picking up Starbucks, leaving Celeste with the job of wrangling their daughter into her athletic gear for the race later that morning. The race was at nine, although the prerace packet had "suggested" all racers arrive at the race site by eight. This seemed excessive to Celeste, but then again, she really didn't know much about racing. Earlier that week, she had unearthed the athletic sneakers she had bought after her first (and last) barre class two years prior in a delusional fit of motivation. There had been two tiny balls of tissue paper still jammed in the toes.

"Bells," Celeste reasoned, keeping her voice calm, "the race is the whole point of why we're here. Remember?"

Bella stuck out a lip. It was a plump little thing, clearly inherited from Louis's side of the family.

"I know that," she said with an impatient hmph. "But I changed my mind."

Celeste exhaled and sat down on the bed opposite Bella. As a mother, Celeste's goal had always been to raise a strong, autonomous female, although she did wonder now if she would have done better to wait a bit before introducing to Bella the freedom of changing one's mind.

"This race is for Alabama, Bells. Don't you want to support Alabama?"

It struck Celeste that this was possibly an immoral bargaining chip, using Alabama to coax Bella into compliance. Then again, this was the reason why Celeste—the reason why any of them—were in Dallas to begin with. Celeste could think of a very short list of scenarios in which she would willingly start running, and even fewer that didn't involve some sort of bodily threat.

Bella narrowed her eyes as she considered Celeste's words, something clearly working inside that beautiful, mysterious brain of hers. "Bright girl," the school psychologist had said to Celeste and Louis a month earlier, nodding kindly. Celeste had decided in that moment that she liked the woman.

"Alabama died," Bella said finally, although she didn't sound confident.

Celeste wondered for not the first time if they had done the right thing by telling Bella the truth about Alabama's disappearance. It could have been easy to sweep the details into the murky, un-talkable place where all difficult things had been formerly swept. Celeste, however, had decided that honesty was important. She was committed to no longer sticking her head in the sand, no matter how appealing the option was, so she and Louis had sat Bella down and told her the truth, in the gentlest, most honest way they knew how.

And the truth was, no one knew exactly what had happened that night. The police could only tell them what the evidence suggested, their best educated guess based on Celeste's account and Alabama's last texts. No one knew where she had been going, however, although they had found a rope in the trunk, suggesting nowhere good.

"Yes, she did," Celeste said, injecting a softness into her voice. She had decided on honesty, but she could still try to cushion mortality when she could. "Remember when we had a funeral for Miss Bubbles, though?" Bella nodded, eyes suddenly round. "This is like that."

Bella thought about this for a second. It had been months since the untimely passing of Miss Bubbles, whose brief inclusion in the family had started with Louis hooking a ring around a milk pail at a fall fair and ended a few days later for no obvious reason.

"Is Alabama going to get buried?" Bella said. And then, upon further reflection, "There's no shoebox that big, you know."

Celeste managed to fight back a smile. She could only imagine the mental image Bella had concocted: Alabama, wrapped in toilet paper, nestled in an oversized shoebox. Their heads all bowed as Louis gave an impromptu eulogy, summoning as much reverence as he could for a carnival goldfish.

"No, this is more like"—Celeste looked up—"like a party. Like a going away party for Alabama from all her friends."

"A party with running?" Bella said, raising a dubious eyebrow.

Celeste couldn't help but smile this time.

"I know. But Alabama liked running. And you know what?"

"What?" Bella sounded suspicious.

"I think it would really mean a lot to her if she knew you were there."

Bella chewed on this for a moment. It struck Celeste that they had never had a real discussion on what happened after death, whether it was possible for Alabama to have any actual feelings about Bella at this point in time. It was the sort of discussion Celeste feared, more so even than the sex talk they would have to have one day. Sex, at least, was fact-based, so there seemed like less of a margin for error.

"Okay," Bella said finally, quietly, and Celeste watched in amazement as she slid off the bed. She walked over to her suitcase, which was as immaculately packed as Celeste's own, and crouched down.

"I'm a bad runner," Bella said, her back to Celeste.

"No you're not," Celeste said reflexively as Bella extracted items from her suitcase one by one.

"Yes I am." Bella turned around, a pair of white socks in hand. "My feet are different from other people's feet. Same with my brain, too."

She walked back over to her bed and had to jump a little to project herself onto it. Her bare toes wiggled as she unwrapped the socks and bent one leg to reach her foot.

Celeste stared in silence. She thought again of the school psychologist, a black-haired woman with a wiry frame. "We believe Isabella is a candidate for services under IDEA," she had said to Louis and Celeste equally.

Louis had asked for clarification, but Celeste had prepared for the appointment with hours of online research, so she had already known exactly what the woman had meant. IDEA. Individuals with Disabilities Education Act. It was not the outcome Celeste had necessarily hoped for when she had made the appointment, but it was the one she had prepared for. She would pursue a formal medical diagnosis as soon as possible, one from a specialized clinic in the city, but the waiting list for that was months, and Celeste didn't want to delay. And so there they had been, in front of the school psychologist—her office a touch too warm, a fingerprint turkey taped to her desk— receiving an educational diagnosis first.

"What do you mean?" Celeste said now, speaking carefully. Bella's mouth was screwed in concentration as she worked on inserting one foot into uncooperative cotton.

Bella just shrugged, finally managing to pull the first sock on.

Celeste hadn't told Bella about the diagnosis or the IEP—the individualized education program—they planned to pursue for her. Celeste and Louis had agreed they would tell her once they had returned from Dallas together, as a unified team.

"Did Daddy say something to you?" Celeste said, trying very hard not to sound accusatory.

"No." Bella did not look up. She struggled with her second sock.

"Why do you say that then, honey? Why do you think your brain is different?"

Bella gave an exasperated sigh.

"Because, Mama"—she looked up at Celeste with an unusual directness—"because I know."

She made a small sound, like she was clucking her tongue, before resuming her struggle with the sock. Celeste felt momentarily flustered, although she had the passing thought that this should not have caught her off guard. After all, Bella was on the spectrum, but she wasn't stupid. She was actually quite bright, as the school psychologist had pointed out. Of course Bella had noticed the differences between her world and everyone else's.

Celeste watched her daughter for a moment, about to help, but just then, Bella managed to tug it on. She wagged both feet in front of her like windshield wipers, clearly pleased.

Celeste glanced at the hotel door, hoping Louis might miraculously walk through it exactly when needed. But the door remained shut, and even though she had agreed to have this talk together, she could tell that this moment would not happen twice.

She turned back to Bella, who had shimmied off the bed once again and was now squatting by two Velcro sneakers with lights in the heels. Her face was angled down, leaving Celeste a view of only the crown of her head.

"Bella," Celeste said, speaking gently, "do you know why we went to see Dr. Jackson a few weeks ago? When me and you and Daddy went to your school?"

Bella's shoes were much easier to maneuver than the socks, apparently. She already had one on.

"No."

"Well, we went to talk about your thinking. The doctor at your school, remember how she talked to you so much?"

Bella nodded again as she strapped the other shoe in place. She straightened and gave one confirmatory stomp, her heel light blinking in response.

"Dr. Jackson is going to help us figure out the best way for you to learn. When we're home, I promise Daddy and I will answer all your questions. But, Bells." Celeste paused. "Bella, look at me."

Celeste reached out and touched Bella's arm. Bella looked up, seemingly puzzled—whether about the conversation or the sudden, unexpected contact, Celeste wasn't sure.

"I want you to know that you're right," Celeste said, speaking clearly. "You do think differently from other people, and I want you to know that it's good, okay? It makes you very special."

Bella pulled her arm away slowly, like a parent unwinding herself from a clingy child. Then, to Celeste's surprise, Bella reached out and cupped Celeste's cheeks with her hands, like the roles had been reversed and Bella was the mother, not the other way around.

"I know, Mama," she said. She nodded solemnly, then dropped her hands and pranced toward the television to watch her blinking heels reflect in the dark screen. And just like that, Bella was again a child, and Celeste, her mom.

50

Hollie

Six Weeks After
Dallas, Texas

WHEN HOLLIE WOKE up the morning of the race, she was alone in her bed, as she had been for weeks. For the first time since returning from Iceland, however, she was surprised to find herself filled more with anticipation than dread.

She poured coffee into a travel mug after breakfast, not even thinking of Nick's identical cup somewhere across the city, and drove to the parking lot where the racers had been instructed to meet. It was barely dawn, the morning sun no more than a glow of pink across the city skyline. Robin was there already with four volunteers, none of whom Hollie recognized.

As the hour passed, more volunteers trickled in, arriving in groups of two or three. Robin did most of the directing—bustling around the lot as an inflatable starting line was erected, as biodegradable paper cups were spread across a foldout table beside an industrial-sized water cooler. Hollie finished her coffee and wished she had another, although she didn't leave to pick one up. She felt a responsibility to stay there even if Robin clearly did not need her help.

At one point, Robin bounded up to Hollie, rubbing her hands together like someone in front of a campfire.

"Looks good, doesn't it?" she said, sounding breathy.

"Looks awesome."

"And the shirts are bomb too, right?"

"Totally."

By the time the first racers arrived—two women a few years younger than Hollie, with the creeping hesitance of someone arriving early to a party—Hollie had already started to sweat from the humidity. She checked her makeup in her phone to make sure it was still in place. Hollie didn't normally wear makeup to races, but she wasn't planning on running in this one. What was the point, when there was no chance she could win?

Mallory arrived a little before eight. She waved at Hollie across the parking lot, and Hollie felt an immediate sense of relief.

"So many people," Mallory said, coming to a stop. She wrapped Hollie in a quick hug, then motioned to the crowd already growing around them, most of whom blurred together as a mass of pink cotton race shirts. Mallory was holding a cardboard coffee cup in one hand and handed a second to Hollie.

"God bless you," Hollie said, taking it. "And yeah, there should be around four hundred."

"People?" Mallory raised her eyebrows. "That's how many registered for this thing?"

"That's how many prerace welcome packets I packed. Four safety pins a bag, if you're wondering." Hollie shot her a look. "I packed more than a thousand of those little fuckers Thursday night."

Mallory snorted into her coffee.

For a few seconds, they stood there in silence, watching the people around them. From what Hollie could tell, there seemed to be an equal number of men and women with more than a few children, likely there for the one-mile walk rather than the 5K run. The speakers had crackled on a few minutes ago, pumping the clear morning with bass, and something about the sound mixed with the smell of warming asphalt sent a feeling of melancholy through Hollie. She had never been to a road race that she didn't plan to run in, that she didn't plan to win. It was like walking into a childhood home that was now someone else's.

Hollie raised her phone above her head and took a panoramic video of the crowd, starting at the water table before swiveling to the starting line, where the most committed of the racers were already trotting back and forth in prerace strides. She brought the phone back down and used one hand to shield the screen from the sun, although still she could barely see the video she had just captured.

Hardly looking, she typed out the words for her Instagram story: *This one's for you, Alabama.*

It had been Robin's idea to name the race for Alabama. It was one of two suggestions she had made at Pearl's after Hollie's confession. The second had been for Hollie to start therapy—for the bingeing and also for the trauma. Internally, Hollie had taken this as badly as any other criticism, but she had not protested to Robin's face. Instead, she had taken a sip of water and said she would think about it, having absolutely no intention of thinking about it again.

It was not until Hollie had confessed to Mallory that she had seriously considered talking to someone. It had been more difficult telling Mallory than Robin, as Hollie actually cared what Mallory thought. It had happened late one night in Hollie's big, empty kitchen. Mallory had listened silently, then wordlessly pulled Hollie in for a hug. Hollie had cried then. She had cried a lot over the last several weeks.

"You have to learn to forgive yourself," Mallory had told her. "You have to, do you hear me? I need my best friend back."

Hollie had started therapy the following week.

When Robin Sinclair called out for the start of the race, she sounded very unlike the bubbly, pink-scrunchied woman she actually was. "RACERS," her voice boomed across the parking lot, the sound somewhat scratchy over the megaphone. "THIS IS YOUR TEN-MINUTE WARNING. START MAKING YOUR WAY TO THE STARTING LINE NOW."

"I guess that's me," Mallory said. "Wish me luck." She gave Hollie a small soldier salute before turning, allowing the crowd to carry her toward the starting corrals. Apparently, Mallory had starting running again just for this race, even though it had meant, some days, a four thirty AM alarm.

Across the parking lot, Robin handed the megaphone over to one of the volunteers who was not racing. She climbed down from her makeshift podium—an overturned crate that had previously transported dozens of pink RUN FOR ALABAMA race shirts—and tightened her ponytail before Hollie lost her in the crowd too.

The morning heat smelled like sunscreen and asphalt. Hollie felt a swelling sense of anticipation, as though her subconscious hadn't yet gotten the message that she wasn't racing. She rolled her neck and started off against the crowd, toward the finish line on the other side of the lot.

Hollie took another video as she walked, hoping to capture the energy that buzzed around her. She brought the phone back down and started to type quickly.

Love the energy! Reminds me a lot of Alabama.

She thought about it for a moment, trying to decide whether this was too corny or—worse—slightly crass. Deciding it wasn't, she posted the video to her Instagram stories, tagging Alabama's now defunct profile, which had grown to over a million followers since the Iceland trip. Hollie was surprised that Alabama's family hadn't deleted her profile, or at least set it to private. It was possible that they enjoyed reading the comments on Alabama's last posts, which now served as a memorial of sorts. Whatever the reason, it seemed as though the page was heavily moderated, as most trolling comments didn't last more than an hour or two before silently disappearing from the page.

"Hollie."

Hollie looked up. In the flurry of pink cotton, it took her a moment to recognize Celeste Reed in front of her. A part of this was how much better Celeste looked than the last time Hollie had seen her, at Alabama's funeral. She had cut her hair, for one thing. It was not terribly short, but it was short enough that it bordered on trendy. This surprised Hollie. Out of all the influencers Hollie had met, Celeste gave the impression of being the least interested in fashion.

"Celeste. Hey. You made it."

Hollie hovered awkwardly for a moment before stepping in for a hug, which Celeste seemed to receive with an equal amount of discomfort. Celeste was less bony than the typical influencer. Hugging her felt more substantial, like Hollie was holding onto something real.

"Did you come on your own?" Hollie said, stepping back. She glanced over Celeste's shoulder, where people continued past them without a second look.

"My husband and daughter are here too. They went to go get some water before we get in line for the walk." Celeste gave Hollie a bashful grin. "We don't normally do stuff like this, and I didn't want Bella to get overheated."

Hollie nodded. It took her a moment to register that Bella was Celeste's daughter. For some reason, Hollie had thought it started with an A.

"Well, I really appreciate you guys coming all the way out here for this."

Celeste shrugged. "I couldn't miss it, you know?"

Celeste didn't sound sad as she said this, but there was a note of wistfulness in her voice. Hollie was reminded once again why the race had garnered so much attention. Robin had spent an exorbitant amount of time on advertising—she had somehow corralled Hollie into handing out flyers outside an LA Fitness just last week—but the real reason for the race's success was Alabama. After they had announced the race's dedication, online registrations had ballooned overnight. Part of Hollie wondered how much of the interest was genuine and how much was the same kind that caused people to slow on the interstate after a car crash. Regardless, the outcome was the same.

"I just wish Alabama could be here to see it," Celeste said. She was no longer looking at Hollie. Her gaze had wandered somewhere just beyond, her eyes glassy.

"I wish she could see all these people out here to support her. Maybe she could've—I don't know . . ." Celeste sighed. "Realized that her life was so much bigger than Instagram, you know?"

She refocused on Hollie, her expression so intent that Hollie couldn't tell if she expected an answer. Hollie hoped not, as she didn't have one—at least not one that Celeste would want to hear.

"I just hope this race helps someone else," Hollie said. "Maybe it'll stop another girl from being the next Alabama."

As soon as the words came out, Hollie regretted them. They had not sounded so insensitive in her head. To her relief, however, Celeste did not appear offended. She simply gave Hollie a thoughtful nod.

"Definitely. It's such a great thing for you to be doing. You're really making a difference, you know?"

Hollie smiled but didn't say anything.

"I've been thinking about changing my brand up a little bit," Celeste added. She didn't seem to notice that Hollie hadn't spoken. In fact, it was almost as though she was no longer talking to Hollie at all. "Maybe focusing a little less on fashion and more on parenting. My daughter was just diagnosed as being on the spectrum— the autism spectrum, I mean." Celeste's eyes shot to Hollie. Hollie attempted an encouraging but mostly neutral smile.

Celeste said, "Anyway, there's not a lot of resources out there for parents of girls on the spectrum. You'd be surprised how little there is, actually." She seemed to be talking to herself again. Hollie got the impression that if she backed away quietly, Celeste would have no idea. "I'm still learning, but I think I could use my platform as a starting point. You know, like a resource for other moms like me."

Above them, the loudspeaker crackled. "FIVE MINUTES," a voice called, sending a ripple through the crowd.

"Anyway," Celeste said, coming back from wherever she had floated off to. "I'll let you go. I'm sure you're racing."

Hollie's hand moved instinctively to her hamstring, which was more or less healed but nonetheless provided a ready excuse for why she still wasn't running in the race. The truth was, while therapy had helped her get a handle on her bingeing, she still hadn't run since returning from Iceland. This bothered her much less than she had expected, but she still felt a certain amount of embarrassment when anyone brought it up.

"You know, I might actually do the walk today," Hollie said, making a snap decision. "I think the walk sounds nice."

"Oh." Celeste looked surprised. "Well, maybe we'll catch you out there then."

"Hopefully." Hollie mostly said this to be nice.

As Celeste disappeared into the crowd to find her family, Hollie turned toward the starting line. She thought about what Celeste had said and her obvious regret for Alabama. Hollie understood where she was coming from, as it was a shame that Alabama couldn't see the race. It was a shame that Alabama had died thinking her Instagram images could stand in for an actual life.

Without realizing what she was doing, Hollie came to a stop. Around her, people continued to flow toward the starting line, moving more quickly now that the person on the megaphone had cried out a two-minute warning call. Although the crowed bustled, Hollie felt suddenly still. She closed her eyes for a moment, allowing herself to bask in the warmth of the sun, and then she pulled out her phone. She had a tendency to regret her impulsive decisions, although really, this decision didn't feel very impulsive at all. This felt like an end to something, or maybe a beginning—something she had been moving toward for a while now.

I've made a decision, she typed into Instagram, not overthinking the words as they poured out. *After today's race, I'm going to be stepping away from the internet for a while. I've learned so much through this journey, and I think my next step is to say goodbye.*

Hollie bit her lip. On the screen, the cursor flashed. Someone called out a sixty-second warning from the megaphone. Hollie felt herself sweating, although it had nothing to do with the heat.

The truth is, I've been struggling a lot behind the scenes lately, and I think I've used social media as a crutch for too long. One inhale, and then she kept typing. *Before I log off, I'd like to open up with you all about what's been going on.*

CHAPTER

51

Hollie

One Year After
Chicago, Illinois

I T WAS ROBIN Sinclair's first time in Chicago and only Hollie's second, so while they were there for business, they had both agreed to take a tourist stop at Millennium Park.

Over Robin's shoulder, a group of children shrieked as a fountain erupted across the pavement. The fountain was unusual, like nothing Hollie had ever seen. Instead of a reservoir, water shot straight out from two spigots directly onto the sidewalk. Each spigot was situated on the side of its own rectangular structure, and the side of each structure was illuminated by a massive screen. The screens showed giant faces that shifted every few seconds—a graying man, a younger woman. Every so often, the screen projected a stream of water from the image's mouth.

If you asked Hollie, the fountain was unnecessarily creepy. The children, however, were not deterred. Groups of them stomped around the wet concrete between the structures as parents sat cross-legged on a ledge in the distance. Every few minutes, the fountain drenched the soaking kids to their uproarious delight.

"Alright," Robin said, looking up from her phone. She had the faintest dusting of freckles across her nose, which made her look younger than she was. "After we meet your friend, I think we should bop into Bloom Studio one more time. Just to double check, you know?"

Hollie nodded in agreement. Bloom Studio was a yoga franchise headquartered in Chicago, where Hollie and Robin had met yesterday with the communications manager. The office building had exposed ducts and metal beams across the ceiling. Hollie and Robin had come out of the meeting empty-handed and smelling like rose oil.

"And if they say no"—Robin shrugged—"then they say no. We don't need them. Honestly, PinkPurse alone is more than enough."

She looked back down to her phone, where she had pulled up their list of potential partners for the Josie Project's next race that fall. Registrations for the race had already tripled their last turnout, which Robin attributed primarily to Hollie's hard work. Hollie didn't know if she deserved the credit, but it nonetheless felt good. Since joining the Josie Project full-time, she had put more effort into the charity than she had anything else in a long while.

Hollie was the one who had suggested meeting with the Pink-Purse execs about sponsoring the race, even though Hollie had not partnered with PinkPurse in over a year. Luckily, her past reputation had put her in their good graces. They had agreed to invest enough that the Josie Project was set for a while.

"Sounds good to me," Hollie said. She raised her thumb to her mouth and ripped a hangnail from her finger. She still had a faint scar on her palm, although it seemed to lighten every day. Now, it was nearly invisible unless you knew where to look.

Hollie was nervous about meeting Celeste for lunch, although when Hollie's therapist had asked why, Hollie had been unable to give a clear answer. Hollie had not seen Celeste since Alabama's race, at least not in person. All Hollie knew was what she had gathered over Instagram, the few times Hollie had checked since logging off.

It had surprised Hollie, the first time she had looked up Celeste. Celeste didn't do fast fashion anymore, apparently. Her most recent partnership was with GWMHA—Girls' and Women's Mental Health Association. Hollie had watched an interview Celeste had done with the organization. Celeste had looked directly at the camera the whole time.

"It's a big step," Hollie's therapist had said when Hollie had told her about the lunch. "It's a big step that you're seeking out closure." Was that what Hollie was doing? Hollie didn't know, but she supposed she would find out.

When Hollie and Robin rose from their table a little while later, the fountain showed a picture of a woman with blue eyes and blonde hair much like Alabama Wood's. Hollie looked at it for only a second before they cut through the park, down the concrete steps toward Michigan Avenue.

As they approached a bustling crosswalk, Hollie thought of Alabama, as she had so many times since touching down at Chicago O'Hare. Chicago was Alabama's hometown, a fact that seemed to be following Hollie around. She could not help but imagine Alabama beneath a café umbrella, picking through an overpriced salad. Alabama emerging from a Nordstrom in a waft of air conditioning and expensive perfume.

Sometimes Hollie wondered if she would ever move on from Alabama. Her therapist had been unable to answer this question, or perhaps she simply hadn't wanted to tell Hollie the truth: that no, Hollie would never leave Alabama completely behind.

Just ahead of them on the sidewalk, the crosswalk sign illuminated. A group of people at the corner jostled as they began collectively to cross the busy street. Robin said something else, something Hollie didn't hear because Hollie had stopped abruptly. The back of her neck prickled as she whipped around.

People moved past her on either side. A shoulder bumped into her own. "Hollie?" Robin said behind her, a few steps ahead. Hollie scanned the crowd, feeling breathless. The woman's hair had been brown, not blonde, but still—the small upturned nose, the pouty lips. The way her eyes had flitted every which way, hunter indistinguishable from hunted. It was a woman Hollie recognized. It was a woman Hollie knew.

"Hollie," Robin said again, this time sounding worried. Hollie finally turned back to her.

"Sorry," she said, shaking her head to clear it. She still felt pinpricks beneath her skin as she trotted a few steps to catch up with Robin, who looked concerned.

"What's up?" Robin said as Hollie motioned them forward. The crosswalk sign was now blinking, and around them, people started to scuttle.

"Nothing," Hollie said. She felt the urge to glance back over her shoulder but instead continued moving forward. "It's just, I swear that woman back there looked exactly like Alabama Wood."

CHAPTER

52

Alabama

One Year After
Chicago, Illinois

ALABAMA WONDERED WHAT her new doctor would think about
Chicago.

For Alabama, she had only ever lived in Chicago, so she didn't
know what it felt like to be in it for the first time. Her first time had
been wrapped in a little lace blanket her grandmother had made
for her, which Alabama's mom had used to transport a newborn
Alabama home from the hospital. By the time Alabama had started
remembering anything, she had already lived in Chicago for five or
six years.

The train swayed back and forth beneath her, making the comforting *click click click* sound of wheels against track. Her car was
nearly empty except for a woman a few rows up with a young child.
The child was old enough to be standing on the seat but not old
enough to realize that licking public transportation windows was
gross.

Alabama turned toward her own window to watch the world
chug by below her. The elevated trains in Chicago were so much better than the trains in any other city. Alabama loathed underground
trains, like the ones in New York, which made her feel claustrophobic and smelled like pee. The trains in Chicago sometimes smelled

like pee, but at least there was fresh air every now and then to get the smell out.

Alabama's new doctor would like Chicago, she decided just then. She would like that the trains didn't smell like pee, and she would like that there was a lake nearby, a nice clean lake, unlike the water in some cities, which Alabama suspected to be filled with flesh-eating bacteria and toxic runoff.

Alabama's new doctor was named Gwendolyn, which just didn't sit right with Alabama. Alabama didn't have anything against the name Gwendolyn in particular, but in this case, it simply didn't match the person. If you asked Alabama, her doctor was more of a Tiffany, which Alabama considered to be one of the classiest names to exist.

Gwendolyn was Benno's girlfriend, although in Alabama's personal opinion, Gwendolyn could do much better than a glacier hike tour guide who seemed unfamiliar with a razor. Gwendolyn could have dated anybody—an actor or an athlete or a senator. (Alabama didn't know if Iceland even had senators, as the Icelandic people seemed much too agreeable for politics.) Anyway, the point was that Benno was a five, maybe a six when he shaved, whereas Gwendolyn was a ten, easy.

Benno was the one who had made Alabama go see Gwendolyn in the first place. By then, Alabama's balayage had been dismally overgrown, so she had agreed to go on the condition that she could get her hair done afterward. (She would have gone on her own already if she'd had a car, but she hadn't, as hers was probably in some warehouse somewhere all taped up as evidence.)

Alabama's gaze zoomed in from the street below the tracks to her own reflection in the train window. She had stopped coloring her hair almost eight months ago now—one, because it was expensive, and two, she sort of liked the brown. It made her feel like a different person, but in a good way.

Alabama leaned back in her seat. In the end, Alabama was glad Benno had made her see the doctor. Benno was an unrelenting nag, worse even than Henry, but overall, she was glad for a lot of the things he had done. He was the one who had gotten her the new ID and passport and phone. She had appreciated the phone in particular, as it had allowed her to stay up to date on everything happening back home.

Gwendolyn was very interested in the phone—Instagram in particular. She was more interested in hearing about that than she was about the things Alabama's old doctor had talked about. Alabama's old doctor had been *obsessed* with talking about Alabama's mom, who was not all that interesting when you really thought about it. The most interesting thing her mother had ever done was the one time she had gotten spectacularly drunk at a party and kissed one of the busboys. (Alabama was the only one who had seen it happen. It had felt like the first time Alabama had ever really seen her mom.)

Gwendolyn cared about Alabama's mom an appropriate amount, which was to say, not all that much. They had breezed right on past Alabama's childhood and gone straight to Alabama's much more interesting adulthood. Unlike Alabama's old doctor, Gwendolyn understood social media. She seemed to be under the impression that Instagram in particular held some big secret as to what Alabama had done. Alabama supposed this wasn't technically wrong, although with hindsight, Alabama could see that everything was so much bigger than that.

Gwendolyn didn't *technically* know that Alabama was in Chicago right now, as Alabama had only said she was thinking about a trip. Gwendolyn had seemed surprised by this, but she hadn't badgered Alabama to tell her where or when or for how long. That was the thing Alabama liked about Gwendolyn, maybe even more than she liked Gwendolyn's Balenciaga bucket bag (and Alabama adored a designer bucket bag). Gwendolyn didn't *pry* the way Alabama's old doctor had.

Probably the most prying Gwendolyn had done was in the beginning, when she had wanted Alabama to explain how she had gotten there. "Like, how I got on earth?" Alabama had said, and Gwendolyn had chuckled, even though Alabama thought doctors were not supposed to chuckle at their patients.

But Alabama supposed she understood it, Gwendolyn's need to know how Alabama had wound up in her office. It was, after all, an unusual story. A heroic story too—perhaps not the heroic story Alabama had been planning, but still, Alabama had puffed up and up as she had told it, realizing how brave she had been.

When Alabama had first gone into the water that night, it had been so cold, she had been too frozen to move. It was as though her brain had shut off. But then something had snapped, and on impulse alone, her body had sprung to life. With a strength she had never before experienced, she had thrown her arms forward, kicked her legs. Her forehead had been bleeding. Frigid water had belted her continuously in the face. And yet, miraculously, she had made it out of the sinking car and all the way to shore, where she had heaved in greedy gulps of air.

She couldn't actually remember her run from the bridge to the GoIceland office, which had been unthinkably long. She could barely even remember Benno answering the door, although if she thought about it hard enough, she could recall some individual details of his expression—the arch of his eyebrows, the way his lips had parted just so. Mostly what she remembered was the color of his face—sheet white, like he had seen the walking dead. Then again, she had been closer to dead in that moment than she had been to anything else.

What had come next flitted in and out of her memory in fits and spurts. Benno had led her into the office, where he had produced a blanket and tended to the cut on her head. Tom had arrived at some point, although she couldn't remember when. She had been shivering and nearly delirious, but she had still somehow gotten the story out.

The details had come easily, much more easily than lies sometimes did. She was fleeing an abusive husband, she had told them. She needed to disappear without a trace. Maybe Benno and Tom had detected genuine hurt in her voice, and that was why they'd believed her. Maybe Alabama was just very good at telling lies people wanted to believe. The trick to a good lie, Alabama had learned, was to sprinkle in just enough true things for it to sound like the truth. She had told Benno and Tom about Henry's tomato garden and budgeting habits right before she'd told them how he had a tendency to clock her under the chin.

Overhead, a robotic voice called out through the train's speakers, alerting the mostly empty car to their next stop. Outside, tall buildings had sprung up in place of blue sky, their windows now even with the trains on the elevated track. She could see inside some of them, catching glimpses of offices she imagined to be filled with stern-looking women and men in stiff suits. The train was entering Chicago's Loop, the business district.

Gwendolyn had prescribed Alabama pills, just like her old doctor had. Unlike her very stupid old doctor, however, Gwendolyn had actually explained what the pills did. Apparently, "antipsychotic" was just a name, not a diagnosis. "Of course you're not a psychopath," Gwendolyn had said, horrified that Alabama had even for one single second thought that. "You know how you train your body to run?" Gwendolyn had asked her. "Think of the antipsychotics like training your mind to think."

The pills had been fine in the beginning. Tolerable. Alabama had given them a real shot, anyway, for Gwendolyn's sake. Alabama's only complaint was this one annoying side effect, which was really so minor she hadn't thought it was necessary to even bring up. If Alabama had chosen to talk about it, though, she would have called it *little blips,* tiny episodes she couldn't explain. She would be wiping a crampon or boiling some water, and the strangest sensation would overcome her, like she was waking up even though she hadn't been asleep.

As the train started to slow, the robotic voice called out again. Alabama waited for it to stop before standing up. She stepped onto the platform behind the woman and her little boy, who was hell-bent on swinging from his mom's arm like it was a rope. The woman seemed annoyed by this.

It was a perfect day—a little chilly on the breezy platform, but comfortable on the sidewalk below. The steel steps led Alabama to a corner that held one of Alabama's favorite little restaurants, a place that served tofu bowls and detox shakes. Whenever Celeste and Alabama came to the city, they stopped for a salad, which they would eat from recyclable cardboard boxes while they talked and talked and talked.

The day Alabama had decided to come back to Chicago, she had thought about those salads, of all the crazy things. Robin Sinclair had just announced her trip to the city, some confusing business thing with Hollie that Alabama didn't understand. And yet Alabama had understood enough for her blood to start boiling the way it had stopped doing for a while. She had wondered whether the pair of them—Hollie and Robin—would stop at Alabama's salad shop. She had imagined Hollie traipsing around Alabama's entire city with one of Alabama's detox shakes.

And then the final straw, when Celeste had mentioned getting lunch with Hollie. Celeste, *Alabama's* best friend. Alabama had booked her plane ticket that very same day.

She had been off her pills for a while at that point, although she had declined to tell Gwendolyn that. She had stopped the day her account had reached a million followers on Instagram. A million! What a feat.

She hadn't posted since her big disappearance. In fact, she had done nothing with her account except clean up the occasional mean comment. And still, despite the lack of new content, people had flocked to her profile. They had loved the tragedy, just as

Alabama had anticipated. It was almost funny, how predictable people could be.

When she had stopped the pills, Alabama had been watching her follower count tick upward for weeks. But then, when it had finally happened—a million!—Alabama had felt nothing. Nothing. Not a single lousy thing. It was the pills, she had realized. The pills had changed something in her fundamentally.

She hadn't told Gwendolyn when she had stopped, and she certainly hadn't told Benno, who would have done the whole *We just want to help you* shtick. He did want to help her, probably, but what did he know about her? About anything?

She didn't tell Benno or Tom about Chicago either. Benno had dropped her off at Gwendolyn's office the way he usually did for an appointment, only this time she had walked straight on past it and caught a taxi to the airport. She suspected he was extremely unhappy about this, now that he knew what she had done, and she did feel bad that she hadn't said goodbye. Maybe she would go back one day and apologize.

Or maybe not.

As Alabama made her way down the sidewalk, she noticed all the things around her that had previously been background noise. A drug store on the corner. A flower box by the curb. The homeless man with a cardboard sign, his clothes all the same shade of gray. She dropped a few quarters into the man's cup, and he dipped his head in thanks.

Millennium Park was exactly how she remembered it. For a while, she sat on a ledge beside strangers watching their kids play in the fountain. Alabama watched too, watched how they danced and twirled and shouted. At one point, Alabama took off her shoes and padded around the wet concrete with them, except she got out of the way before the fountain blasted her with water.

When it was time, Alabama put her shoes back on and checked her phone again. Robin Sinclair was not an influencer, but she acted like one. She had started documenting their trip through Chicago since their plane had touched down. It was slightly nauseating to Alabama how *she,* of all people, was in Hollie's inner circle, but Alabama was healthily not allowing herself to dwell on it too much.

Alabama started toward the sidewalk, which bustled with people moving every which way, rushing and meandering and huffing and smiling. She thought about all these people and felt a little rush of excitement that none of them, not a single person, knew what Alabama had in her purse.

She came to a busy corner, where people waited at a crosswalk that hadn't yet turned. Alabama stopped, standing with the crowd but also separate from them in one very important way. She reached into her bag and touched the knife, running one finger along the sharp edge. It had been her first stop after landing in Chicago. She had gone to a department store and perused the various departments like any old person, poking around the towels, studying the bedding. The cashier hadn't batted an eye when Alabama had bought the knife set. She had probably looked at Alabama and expected she would use the knives for normal knife purposes—chopping veggies, slicing cheese. Not everyone had an imagination like Alabama had.

Alabama had been slightly disappointed that the woman hadn't recognized Alabama, even though Alabama was admittedly thicker than she had been, and her hair was darker too. The cashier would be stunned when she saw the news later. Alabama imagined her telling reporters about the encounter, how her plump little face would grow all serious and gray.

The tricky thing about a mysterious death, Alabama had come to learn, was all the unanswered questions. Sure, the questions were, in some instances, what made a story a legend. But legends were made in lots of ways in lots of situations, not all of them involving some big mystery. Would anyone care about the Black Dahlia, for example, if they hadn't known exactly how she had died?

Alabama recognized the risks of what she was doing. It was possible that Hollie wouldn't take the bait. Hell, it was possible Hollie really had changed, although Alabama didn't think so. In Alabama's experience, most people, when you really got down to it, stayed exactly the same.

And the real Hollie, the one Hollie tried to keep hidden, had reached for the bread knife that night in the kitchen. That Hollie had, for however briefly, been ready to kill.

Imagine thinking you could hide that from people. Imagine thinking you could just walk around someone else's city, thinking no one would ever know who you really were. It was offensive, actually, to Alabama and to everyone else who had ever thought Hollie was perfect. Alabama's blood bubbled at the thought.

Alabama wondered what they would call her, Alabama, when it was all over, if they would give her a spunky little nickname like the Black Dahlia. Of course, Alabama's story would be different.

Alabama would not be killed, for one thing—just attacked. And unlike that poor Dahlia, they would know exactly who had done it. It would be so vicious and public and—Alabama felt another little jolt—such a *shock*. Alabama was alive! Risen like Jesus Himself! Only a monster would attack Jesus in broad daylight. Only a villain would stab Jesus with a knife. And Hollie would. She would see Alabama and grab the weapon. Alabama knew this because Hollie had done it once before.

All she needed was a little push.

ACKNOWLEDGMENTS

LIKE ALMOST ANYTHING, publishing a book is only possible with the right people supporting you. This book would not be here without my people, especially:

My agent, Sam Hiyate, for believing in my writing, even—and especially—the times I started to doubt it. Also, a special thanks to Michaela Stephen and Kaitlin Sooklal for your sharp yet kind observations.

My editor, Melissa Rechter, for seeing this book exactly as it was intended to be.

My copyeditor, David Heath, for making this book shine.

Nicole Lecht for designing the cover of my dreams.

All of the wonderful people at Crooked Lane, including Rebecca Nelson, Madeline Rathle, Dulce Botello, and Hannah Pierdolla.

Anyone who has ever read any of my writing, particularly Jaclyn Goldis, my writing partner, impromptu therapist, and friend. This book would not be what it is without you. Also, a huge thanks to Amy Nizzere, my OG reader and cheerleader. Thank you for sticking with me on this journey.

My friends Andrea Reynolds, Erika Harkins, and Hannah Hallgarth, for encouraging me all the years (and years and years) I've been talking about writing, and for generally tolerating my years (and years and years) of BS.

The other members of *The Perfect Ones* street team, Robyn Black, Rebecca Brumbaugh, Marcy Burke, Nancy Carey, Cristina Chavarriaga, Lorraine Clark, Laura Decker, Christianna Foster, Ali Hopkins, Beth Jones, Sarah Jordan, Mara Lucey, Abby Marella, Betsy Parker, Lisa Purpora, Suzanne Scott, Nicole Shank, Melissa Vinton, and Amanda Westrich, for your seemingly endless enthusiasm.

ACKNOWLEDGMENTS

ιy brother, Nathan Clarke, always the devil's advocate.

My sister and my person, Sam Richardson, for being the ulti-
e NicoleHackettBooks hype girl. Also Zach Richardson for
ɔmising to read this book even though I know you have absolutely
ɔ real interest in reading this book (lol).

My parents, Jerry and Jacque Clarke, for raising me to believe I
can do anything.

My children, Harrison and Harlow, my favorite reminders of
what really matters.

And, of course, my husband, Derrick. You know better than
anyone how much this book means to me. I hope you know you have
always meant more.